GOOD
BAD
GIRL

By Alice Feeney

Sometimes I Lie
I Know Who You Are
His & Hers
Rock Paper Scissors
Daisy Darker

GOOD BAD GIRL

ALICE FEENEY

PAN BOOKS

First published 2023 by Flatiron Books

First published in the UK 2023 by Macmillan

This paperback edition first published 2024 by Pan Books
an imprint of Pan Macmillan
The Smithson, 6 Briset Street, London EC1M 5NR
EU representative: Macmillan Publishers Ireland Ltd, 1st Floor,
The Liffey Trust Centre, 117–126 Sheriff Street Upper,
Dublin 1, D01 YC43
Associated companies throughout the world
www.panmacmillan.com

ISBN 978-1-5290-9028-4

1 3 5 7 9 8 6 4 2

A CIP catalogue record for this book is available from the British Library.

Designed by Donna Sinisgalli Noetzel
Chapter opening illustrations by Rhys Davies

Typeset by Palimpsest Book Production Ltd, Falkirk, Stirlingshire
Printed and bound by CPI Group (UK) Ltd, Croydon, CR0 4YY

MIX
Paper | Supporting
responsible forestry
FSC www.fsc.org FSC® C116313

Visit **www.panmacmillan.com** to read more about all our books
and to buy them. You will also find features, author interviews and
news of any author events, and you can sign up for e-newsletters
so that you're always first to hear about our new releases.

For daughters of mothers of daughters . . .

GOOD
BAD
GIRL

The End

Mother's Day

People say there's nothing like a mother's love. Take that away, you'll find there's nothing like a daughter's hate. I told myself things would be different when I became a mum. I was determined not to make the same mistakes as my mother, and I believed that my child would always be loved. That's what I promised my daughter the day she was born.

But I have. Made mistakes. Bad ones.

And I have broken my promise more than once.

I feel drunk from tiredness. My mind is a mess and my thoughts feel slow, jumbled, clouded by the fog of exhaustion. But she needs things and she needs me to get them for her. Doing, finding, being what she needs became my occupation the day she was born. A job I thought I wanted and now can't quit. Being a mother is a curious mix of love, hate, and guilt. I worry I am the only person who has ever felt this way, and despise myself for thinking unthinkable thoughts.

I wish my daughter would disappear.

I push the buggy along the high street, hoping to get inside the supermarket before the rain comes, when an elderly woman blocks my path.

"Isn't she adorable," she says, staring at the sleeping child before beaming back at me.

I hesitate, searching my befuddled brain for the correct response. "Yes."

"How old?"

"Six months."

"She's beautiful."

She's a nightmare.

"Thank you," I say. I tell my face to smile but it doesn't listen.

Please don't wake her.

That is all I ever think. Because if someone or something wakes her she will start to cry again. And if she cries again, I will cry again. Or do something worse.

Inside the supermarket I hurry to get the things I need: baby formula, nappies, coffee. Then I see a familiar face—an old colleague—and for a moment I forget how tired I am all day, every day. I listen to the childless friend who has become a stranger talk about their life, which sounds significantly more interesting than mine. I live alone and I miss having conversations with adults. We chat for a while. I mostly listen, as I don't have much to say—every day is exactly the same as the day before for me now. And while I listen, I forget that I no longer have any dreams or ambitions or a life of my own. My daughter became my world, my purpose, my everything the day she was born.

I sometimes wish she hadn't been.

I know I must never share these thoughts or speak them out loud. Instead I pretend to be okay, pretend to be happy, pretend to know what I am doing. I'm good at pretending but it is exhausting. Like everything else in my life. Like her.

The conversation lasts less than three minutes.

My back is turned less than two.

One minute later my world ends.

The buggy is empty.

Time stops. The supermarket is suddenly silent, as though someone has turned down the volume. Muted a life that was always too loud. I never thought I would wish to hear her crying, long to see that tiny scrunched-up face, endlessly screaming and red with inexplicable rage. The only sound now is the thud of my heartbeat in my ears, and I feel wide-awake for the first time in days.

I stare at the empty stroller, wondering if I left the baby at home. I was so tired yesterday I put my phone in the fridge by accident. Maybe I forgot to put the baby in the buggy before I left the house today? But then I remember the elderly woman on the street, she saw the baby. The friend who is now a stranger saw the baby too. I saw the baby, five minutes ago. Maybe ten. When *did* I last see her? The panic rises and I spin around, looking up and down the supermarket aisle. She's gone. The baby is too young to crawl. She didn't climb out by herself.

Someone has taken her.

The words whisper themselves inside my head. I feel sick and I start to cry.

I look up and down the aisle again. The other shoppers are going about their business, behaving as though nothing has happened. It's been seconds since I noticed she was gone but it feels like minutes. Am I dreaming? I've had this nightmare before. I sometimes wished she wasn't born but I didn't mean it. I never meant it. I love her more than I knew it was possible to love.

I'm shaking and I'm crying and my tears blur my vision.

I wished my daughter would disappear and now someone has taken the baby.

I whisper her name.

Then I scream it.

People stop and stare. I feel as though I can't breathe.

Life is suddenly loud again. I start to run, desperately looking for any sign of the child or the person who has taken her. I see a woman carrying a baby and I feel rage, then relief, then humiliation when I realize it isn't her. I apologize and keep running, keep searching, keep screaming her name even though she is too little to know how to answer. People are staring at me and I don't care. I have to find her, I need her, I love her. She is mine and I am hers. I would do anything for her. I will never think bad thoughts about her again.

But she is gone.

My chest hurts as though my heart is actually breaking.

And I am crying. And I am falling to the floor. And people are trying to help me.

But nobody can help me.

The child, my world, my everything has been taken.

I wished my daughter would disappear and now the baby is gone.

I already fear I will never see her again and it is all my fault.

Because I know who has stolen her.

And I know why.

Frankie

Another Mother's Day

She was her mother's daughter. People often said that, and Frankie agrees as she stares at the framed photo of her little girl who has been gone too long. They share the same green eyes, same smile, same wild curly hair. She slips the silver frame into her bag and takes one last look around the prison library. Today is her final day as head librarian at HMP Crossroads, not that anyone else knows that. Yet.

Mother's Day has never been easy, and nothing Frankie does to distract herself from her grief works anymore. There is no greater pain than losing a child and it's hard to forget someone you so badly want to remember. Her daughter was a teenager when she disappeared, but that doesn't make it any easier than losing a younger child. And it doesn't help that she can't tell anyone what really happened, not that talking about it would bring her daughter back. Better to keep busy. Hard work has always been the best cure for heartbreak.

She switches off the outdated computer and picks up her mug. It was a gift a few years ago—handmade and hand-painted—with a wonky handle and Frankie's name on the front. Her *other* name. The one that is redundant now. Mum. It's the only mug she likes to drink from, at work and at home, so she takes it everywhere. She never leaves it *here*. Frankie doesn't like other people touching her special things. She walks the fourteen steps from her desk to the library door, then turns off the lights and stands in the darkness for a moment, no longer trusting herself or her senses. Her tired eyes sometimes see shapes inside shadows these days, things that her mind insists aren't really there. So she turns the lights back on, listens to the hum of silence, and waits for her breathing to slow down.

Frankie wasn't always afraid of the dark.

She turns the lights on and off three times, but everything is the same as before. The same as it always was. People spend too long adjusting to the light instead of the dark, it's why they are so unprepared when bad things happen to them. Frankie counts down from ten before locking the library door for the last time. She has thirteen keys attached to the belt of her uniform to choose from, but can select the correct key for every lock without looking. The cut and shape and feel of the cool metal in her hands bring comfort. She likes to push individual keys into the tips of her fingers until they hurt and leave a mark. Feeling something—even pain—is better than feeling nothing at all.

There are twenty-two steps from the prison library to the stairs. She likes to count them. Silently, of course. Counting things has always helped Frankie to keep calm. She reaches another door, finds another key, then steps through into the stairwell before locking the previous door behind her.

There are forty steps down, then five to the outside door.

The big key this time.

Fifty-eight steps across the courtyard, sticking to the path, avoiding the grass.

The big key again.

Eighteen steps to reception. Twelve to her locker, where she retrieves her phone and sharp objects. It took Frankie a while to get used to being searched on her way into work, and having to leave her personal belongings behind each day. But she learned to adapt. She knows that doesn't make her special; the ability to cope with change is as essential as water or air. The same rules apply to all things and all people. Everything in life that is now normal was once unfamiliar.

She checks her phone but there are no new messages or missed calls. She sets an alarm to remind herself to set another alarm later. Frankie likes setting alarms on her phone for everything, it's the only time it makes a sound. There are thirty-two steps to the outside gate. She always walks more quickly for this part of the journey but does not know why. Fast, determined steps, as though she is trying to outpace herself. Or run away. She whispers the number of steps left like a numerical mantra. Or a prayer.

Thirty-two. Thirty-one. Thirty. Twenty-nine.

It's as though all the numbers in her head need to find a way out of her. Buzzing like bees until they escape her lips and fly away.

Nineteen. Eighteen. Seventeen. Sixteen.

Frankie knows the guard at the final checkpoint well enough to say hello. He's asked her to go for a drink with him, twice. Frankie said no. She prefers to drink alone and *people* cannot be trusted. Not trusting people was her mother's number one rule and it is one she inherited. Frankie doesn't know why men find her attractive, maybe it's her prison uniform. A uniform that is nothing more than a stereotype, a fantasy, a disguise. We all play daily dress-up games, choosing which character to be when selecting something from our wardrobe. Deciding who we want others to see us as, hiding behind our clothes. The world is full of people who are good at being bad, and people who are bad at being good. She has always thought of herself as a good bad girl. Someone who made the best of the bad life she was born into, and tried to do something good with it. But when Frankie looks in the mirror these days, all she sees is a plain-looking woman in her thirties. A woman with dark circles beneath her eyes and a mess of dark curls that have always refused to be tamed. A woman who resembles someone she used to know.

A ghost.

The guard steps out of the little security hut that borders the *inside* and *outside*. He smiles and she feels herself shrink. His name badge says Tom but he looks like a Tim.

Thirteen steps. Or was that twelve?

Everyone calls it a hut, but it's made of thick reinforced concrete walls, with barbed wire on the roof, and it is staffed with armed guards 24-7. Tom is a little older than Frankie. He's tall, but his broad shoulders are always a little hunched, as though he is embarrassed by his own height.

Ten steps. Nine.

Frankie stares down at her feet to avoid his gaze—she does not like people looking at her—and notices that her shoelace has come untied. It can wait; there is no time to stop.

Five steps. Four.

Tom looks down at her, but only because he is six feet tall and she is five foot nothing.

Three.

She is close enough now to smell the tea on his breath.

Two.

Frankie pushes one of her keys into her fingertip until it hurts.

One.

She reminds herself to breathe as the guard starts to unlock the outer gate. It is camouflaged by the inescapable, tall, thick concrete ring fence that surrounds the prison. Frankie tries not to stare at the bloody white feathers that decorate the barbed wire on top. Tom smiles again and she tries to smile back, but her face won't let her. She is relieved that he doesn't try to start a conversation.

Frankie can't remember how to have them, and she needs to carry on counting the seventy-three steps from the gate to her van.

Life has taught her that other people should be kept at a distance. *People* can't be trusted. People can't be counted on, so she counts other things instead. Counting things that are real makes the walls of her world feel more solid. And Frankie likes walls, even the ones that surround the prison. She builds imaginary ones just like them around herself all the time, to keep *people* out.

Frankie locks the doors as soon as she is in her ancient blue and white Volkswagen camper van. She puts her special mug on the passenger seat and wishes the person who made it was still here. Losing her daughter is the worst thing that has ever happened to Frankie. Worse than all the other worst things that happened before it.

Frankie whispers the words that sometimes make her feel better:

You're okay. You're okay. You're okay.

We live in a world where it is too easy to lie.

She checks her Mickey Mouse watch—the same watch she had as a child—and sees that she needs to hurry or she'll be late. It's hard to drive away from the prison for the last time. Her job is the only thing that has kept Frankie sane recently, but she's about to lose that too. They'll never let her return to the library at HMP Crossroads when they find out what she's capable of: the terrible things she has done, and the horrible thing she is about to do. The future can seem too uncertain when your past catches up with your present.

Frankie needs something to calm her down. Turning on the radio seems like a good idea, but the voices coming out of it are all talking about Mother's Day, so she switches it off. She searches inside her handbag and finds a packet of Rolos. There are ten chocolates in total, which is good because ten is a good number. It is the Pythagorean symbol of perfection; humans have ten fingers and ten toes, there were Ten Commandments and the number ten symbolizes the completion of a cycle. It must be a sign because Frankie has come full circle. She counts each Rolo as she eats them but saves the last one for her daughter, carefully wrapping it in the gold foil, never quite willing to give up all hope. One is a lonely number. The Pythagoreans did not consider it to be a number at all, because number means plurality and one is singular. The number one reminds Frankie of how alone she is in the world.

She can feel herself starting to spiral to the darker corners of her mind, so she takes a can of Mr. Sheen from the glove compartment, squirts some of the polish onto the steering wheel, and massages it into the leather with a cloth. Frankie breathes deeply; she finds the smell of cleaning products calming. She is afraid of dirt almost as much as she fears the dark, but with good reason. When life throws enough dirt at you some always sticks. She puts the polish back and checks the other three things inside the glove compartment:

An old ten-pound note from 1999.

A newspaper clipping.

A silver ladybug ring.

She slips the ring onto her finger and notices that her mind is finally quiet and calm. She has stopped counting. Frankie knows what she needs to do and no longer cares about the consequences. The only good thing about losing everything is the freedom that comes with having nothing left to lose.

Patience

My Sunday morning shift begins with the elevator doors closing and trapping me inside. The whole thing shudders before grumbling to life, and the Victorian contraption reluctantly carries me to the top floor, groaning all the way. I stare at my reflection in the tarnished mirror and an eighteen-year-old girl glares back. Sometimes I don't know who I am anymore. I know my name, it's written on my badge: Patience. I know where I live: London. I know where I work: here, sadly. I know what I like to eat, to drink, to read . . . but I don't know *me*. I can't remember who the real me is.

The girl in the mirror is wearing thick-rimmed nonprescription glasses. She doesn't need them, but she thinks they make her look less pretty. According to others, her green eyes are her best feature. That's why she tries to hide them. She wishes it were easier to disguise her worst feature: the distinctive freckles on her nose. Her long, wild, curly hair has been tamed into a plait, which rests on one shoulder of her black-and-white uniform like an unloved pet.

A uniform that still looks too big for her, even though it was the smallest size they had.

The girl I used to be is gone.

The girl in the mirror is all that is left of me.

It isn't because I wanted to fit in, I just didn't want to stand out.

The old elevator chimes to signal my arrival on the top floor. I adjust my star-covered backpack—it's heavy but I daren't put it down—and heave the metal gate to one side before pushing the cleaning trolley out into the dimly lit corridor. I push some of the elevator buttons with the door held open—which is normally all it takes for it to stop working—buying myself a little time. The floorboards creak and the trolley wheels squeak as though conspiring to give me away, but there is nobody up here to see me. Everyone else is busy elsewhere, distracted. I still check twice in both directions before letting myself into room thirteen. Doing something wrong is sometimes the right thing to do. Everyone knows that, even if they pretend not to.

The bedroom is dark, but I know my way around. Room thirteen is a large double room with an en suite bathroom. Recently redecorated, because they had to do something to hide what the last occupant left on the walls. The first thing I do—once I've locked the door behind me and parked the trolley—is unfasten the shuttered doors on the far side of the room. I fling them open, letting in the light the space has been starved of and revealing a small balcony. The white curtains billow out like ghosts and the sounds of the city let themselves inside before the air gets a chance. A chaotic symphony of traffic and life rises up to greet me in a glorious crescendo, drowning out all the unpleasant thoughts inside my head.

I step out onto the tiny tiled balcony and peer down at the busy London street below. People rush by in both directions, talking on their phones or staring at their screens, hurrying past each other. They behave as though they are important people going to important places to talk about important things. But from up here they all look so small. So insignificant. If someone were to fall, or jump, or be pushed over this balcony, I'm almost certain they would die. I wonder if other people think about death as often as I do. It's an occupational hazard for me.

I close my eyes, just for a moment, enjoying the warmth of the sun on my face. With my eyes closed, I can pretend to be anywhere. And I do, pretend. There is no better place to hide than inside your own dreams. For a few seconds, the city seems strangely still and quiet, as though waiting for what is about to happen. The perfect moment of solitude lasts less than a minute, and it is the closest I'll get to a break during my twelve-hour shift.

I step back inside the bedroom, catch an unwelcome glimpse of myself in the mirror above the dressing table, and see that girl again. The one masquerading as me.

I look like a maid but that is not what I am.

The building looks like a hotel but that is not what it is.

This is where people come to die.

It still surprises me that people pay good money to stay in bad places like this.

I have been working at the Windsor Care Home in London for almost a year. Its name makes the place sound royal, but it isn't fit for a queen. It's barely fit for purpose. There aren't enough staff, and the care home manager is a monster disguised as a well-dressed, fiftysomething woman. Her name is Joy. Which is ironic really, because I have never met anyone more miserable.

The fees for the elderly residents who live in this beautifully restored Victorian building are astronomical, but I get paid significantly less than the minimum wage to work here. Which I do twelve hours a day, six days a week, in exchange for cash. The former "palace," as it is described in the brochure, is a four-story town house with eighteen rooms. Residents—or their relatives—need to be well-off to get a room here. But the money can't mask the stench of loneliness, death, and despair. God's waiting room might look luxurious but it feels like a prison with wallpaper and patterned carpets. I freeze when I spot the shape of someone hiding beneath the bedsheets in room thirteen.

"It's *me*," I say, carefully lowering my heavy backpack to the floor.

An elderly woman sits up in the bed. She is wearing pajamas covered in pink flamingos. "Why didn't you say so?" she says, clapping her hands together. "Oh, Ladybug, I am *so* happy to see you!"

Her hair is a mess of white curls with a few purple heated rollers left in, and her heavily lined face is a picture of glee. Her Scottish accent always makes me smile, and her words trip over themselves in their hurry to leave her mouth, the way people speak when they don't often have someone to talk to.

"Where have you been?" she asks. "When you didn't come yesterday, I was worried you might have quit! *Joy* came to see me instead. She said I'd have to eat in the dining room with *the others* because of staff shortages. The woman is an ignoramus and only fluent in bunkum. She tried to starve me out of my room but I survived on custard creams and Werther's Originals. I thought it might be *her* again, so I was pretending to be dead. Did you think I was?"

"No and sorry, I had a day off yesterday. Has nobody been in to check on you today?"

She shakes her head and I shake my own as though headshaking is contagious. Sadly it doesn't surprise me that none of my colleagues have come to check on someone who would have probably just told them to go away.

"You might have to start going downstairs again sometimes," I say. "You used to at least have your meals down there, even if you refused to eat with the others."

"Would you want to eat in a dining room with the walking

dead? It's like feeding time at the zoo. Besides, I had May for company back then so it wasn't all bad."

May was Edith's neighbor in room twelve. They ate their meals together and played Cluedo in the conservatory, away from *the others*. They were like two peas in a pod and could often be found giggling like schoolgirls. But then—quite out of the blue—I came to work one day and May's room was empty. The bed had been stripped, her things were gone, and so was she. "I know how sad you still are about May dying—"

"That's a bucket full of hooey. I'm angry, not sad. May didn't die, she was murdered. She knew something was rotten about this place, so they got rid of her."

"We've talked about this before—"

"That's all anyone wants to do these days: talk. Nobody remembers how to listen."

"I hear you, promise. It was lovely that you found a friend here and that you two had so much in common." May and Edith were both former detectives and would spend hours in each other's rooms watching old episodes of *Murder, She Wrote*. "And it's very sad that May is gone," I say.

"Was murdered," Edith mumbles, but I choose to ignore her.

"You could try getting to know some of the other residents? Make some new friends?"

"What for? I have you."

"I can't be here every day, and you can't survive on whatever food is hidden beneath your bed. I think leaving your room once in a while would be good for you, and *the others* aren't all bad."

"*The others* are all old, or ill, or incontinent, or insane. I am none of those things and I do not belong in this place. I haven't met a single person here who is still fully hinged, including the staff—no offense. Besides, I found ways to amuse myself while you were gone. How does my hair look?" she asks.

I smile. "Great, but I think you're supposed to take all of the rollers out."

"Why? They make me look *interesting* and at least ten years younger."

"All I know is that's what other people do."

"You should never worry about what other people do or don't do. I never have."

Edith Elliot is eighty years old. She has an almost full set of marbles but one year ago, without her knowledge or consent, her daughter moved her into the Windsor Care Home. Edith was tricked into signing some paperwork which resulted in her losing her home and independence. Her daughter then left Edith here one day without even saying goodbye. Joy—the world's most miserable manager— gave Edith the tour and explained that this was now her home. Edith hasn't left the building since and now refuses to leave her room.

"How was your day off?" she asks. "Did you do anything nice?"

"No," I reply, trying to make the bed with Edith still in it.

"Did you make any new papercuts?" she asks, turning to look at a small framed piece of art on the wall. It was a Christmas present from me. I have been cutting paper since I was a child, but these days I do it with a knife. A very sharp one. I cut and I slash and I slice until I have made something out of nothing. I make paper people, animals, birds, trees, the sky, the sea, entire towns made from my imagination, and it makes me feel less lonely. The red-and-black papercut on the wall is of ladybugs. Edith has insisted on calling me Ladybug since the first time we met—she seems to think it is my name—and I have given up correcting her.

"I didn't have time to make any new papercuts yesterday," I say.

"You must *make* time for the things you love most. You'd be a dunderhead not to; you're a talented artist."

She doesn't understand how tired I am after working here. Sometimes I don't have anything left in me for anything else. "I'll try."

"Do or do not. There is no try," says Edith. "Do you know who said that?"

"Shakespeare?" I guess, plumping up her pillows.

"Yoda," Edith replies with a grin. I didn't have her pegged as a *Star Wars* fan. The woman is full of surprises.

"Here, I want you to have this." She reaches over to the bedside table and picks up a little wooden box I don't remember seeing there before. She opens it, revealing a silver ring shaped like a ladybug.

"Thank you, but I can't—" I start to say.

"Please," Edith insists. She holds the ring out in front of me, her hands bent out of shape like gnarled twisted twigs. "I can't wear rings anymore—my fingers are too thin, anything I try to wear falls off—but this ring used to mean a lot to me, and I want you to have it."

"Accepting gifts from residents is against the rules—"

"Poppycock and fiddlesticks to *the rules*. Would you really deny an old woman her dying wish?"

"You're not dying."

"We're all dying from the day we are born, it is only a matter of time. Ladybugs are a symbol of new beginnings, love, and luck. I hope this little ladybug might bring you all three."

Luck has never liked me but I take the ring and slip it onto my finger. It fits perfectly. "Thank you. I'll give it back when you're feeling better," I say. The ring looks old and I wonder how Edith came to own it, and why she is so obsessed with ladybugs. She recites the same nursery rhyme whenever I leave her room:

Ladybug, Ladybug, fly away home.
Your house is on fire and your children are gone.
All except one, and her name is Anne.
And she hid under the—

A sound in the corner of the room interrupts my memories. My mind is always too full of unfinished thoughts.

We both turn to stare at the star-covered backpack on the floor. It is moving, all by itself.

"Did you bring him today?" Edith whispers.

I nod. I did something bad, but it was a good thing to do. Good and bad aren't as different as some people seem to think. Mother's Day is as difficult for Edith as it is for me—I doubt she'll get any visitors—and I wanted to cheer her up.

Edith's first day as a resident at the Windsor Care Home was also my first day here as an employee. It could have been a coincidence, if coincidences were real, which they are not. We met in this room a year ago, where I found her sobbing in an armchair. There are endless rules and regulations at the Windsor Care Home. One of them is no pets. Not content with tricking Edith into coming here, her daughter took Edith's beloved dog and dumped him at an animal rescue center. So I found him, spent all of my savings, and adopted the dog. I secretly bring him to see Edith whenever I can, then take him home with me again at the end of my shift. Nobody else knows that I do this. I'd lose my job if anyone found out, but seeing them reunited makes the risk worthwhile.

Dickens is an eight-year-old border terrier and my only other friend. I love him almost as much as I have grown to love his owner. I unzip my backpack and he runs out, leaps onto the bed, and licks Edith's face, wagging his little tail so fast his whole body wiggles with it. Dickens has got very good at being still and silent when he's in the backpack—he spends most of his time sleeping these days—which makes smuggling him in that much easier. He's also a little bit deaf—though I sometimes wonder if it is a case of selective hearing—but the rest of him is in full working order. There is something quite magical about the bond between a dog and their human. Seeing the two of them together makes me so happy.

"Look, I've got a new toy for you," Edith says to Dickens, throwing a black-and-white cuddly bear for him to fetch. "It was a gift sent in the post from my daughter, for Mother's Day. What am *I* going to do with a teddy bear at my age?" Dickens fetches and returns the bear. "But at least you can get some enjoyment out of it," she says, throwing the toy for him to fetch again, which he does, gripping it in his teeth and giving it a shake for good measure.

I take the toy from Dickens. "Why don't we put this away for now? We don't want anyone downstairs to hear him running about." I place the teddy bear on the dressing table. "And before I forget, I managed to get everything you wanted."

Once a week, Edith gives me her bank card to buy her a *Radio Times* magazine, a book, a packet of custard creams, a large bar of Dairy Milk, three cans of ready-mixed Pimm's and lemonade, and two lottery scratch cards. We always scratch one card each, but the most we've ever won was a pound. I take all the items from my bag and put them on the bed.

"You should hide this somewhere safe," I say, trying to give the bank card back. "Valuable things have a habit of going missing around here." Residents are not allowed to leave the care home alone, it's against the rules, but Edith does still have some money tucked away that her family didn't manage to get their hands on, and I don't mind getting her things she wants from the outside world.

"Keep the card for now, there are a few more items I need you to get for me. I've made a list," she says, ripping a page from her favorite notebook. She keeps it by her bed at all times and calls it her "List of Regrets and Good Ideas." She writes her regrets at the front and her good ideas at the back. The only spare pages are toward the end.

"It looks like a lovely day out there. I wish I could take Dickens for a walk instead of being locked away in here," she says.

"You're not locked away. You could at least leave your room. This isn't a prison."

"Isn't it?" she asks. "Prisons come in all shapes and sizes, and sometimes we build our own without realizing. But you'll be pleased to learn I am planning an escape!"

I sit down on the edge of the bed. I spend all day every day on my feet and they permanently ache. "That doesn't sound like a good idea."

"It isn't a good idea, it's a great one. I've got myself a lawyer who is going to help me."

"What? How?"

"The letter I asked you to post for me last week was to a law firm. I found them in the back of the *Radio Times*, and their slogan is 'No win, no fee,' so they must be good. They think they can help get my house back. I reckon my daughter must have rented it out and I can't stand the thought of strangers living in my home. If the 'no win, no fee' chaps can reverse the power of attorney, then Dickens could live with me again, and maybe you could come and work for us? Care for me at home?"

"That sounds nice," I say, unsure whether to believe anything Edith just said. The lawyers sound dodgy and—like a lot of the residents—her memories sometimes get muddled. The only way I have seen any of them leave the Windsor Care Home is in a hearse.

"Excellent! Then we have a plan. And here is the list of those extra few things I need you to get for me with my card. If you don't mind?"

"I don't," I say and stand up, aware that I can't stay much longer.

"And why don't you withdraw a little cash for yourself? I'd like to repay you in some small way if you'll let me."

"I've told you before, I'm happy to help. I don't want your money, but I do need to start work or I'll never get all the rooms done. I'll come see you both at the end of my shift. Remember to keep quiet. It's against the rules, so don't let anyone see or hear Dickens—"

"I know, I know. You don't need to worry about us," Edith

says, stroking the dog. "We'll be good. I always stick to the rules, unless I don't agree with them, then I break them all. But thank you, again. For everything. I'd be dead already without you." Something about the way she says it makes me shiver, and Edith looks sadder than normal when she sees that I am leaving.

I feel a bit unsettled as I exit room thirteen but I'm not sure why. Sometimes my mind plots against me in secret, like a meddling mother who always thinks they know best. I have grown very fond of Edith, and I feel bad for lying to her about so many things. But I doubt she'll ever find out. And I'm certain she'll never escape from this place.

I've lied to Edith Elliot about almost everything since the day we met.

Frankie

Frankie slots the key into the ignition of the van. It is a relief when it splutters to life on the first attempt. It doesn't always. She thinks this is a sign that she is doing the right thing, but still feels an overwhelming sense of sadness as she drives away from the prison for the last time.

Frankie Fletcher has been the head librarian at HMP Crossroads for almost ten years. The so-called library was just an empty storage room when she started, with a sad stack of dusty old novels in the corner. She has always loved books, so that was never going to do. Her first ever job was working in a beautiful little bookshop by the sea in St. Ives. She was sixteen, couldn't believe she was getting paid to do something she loved so much, and has been working with books in one way or another ever since. Before working at HMP Crossroads, she worked as a librarian in a small town called Blackdown. When budget cuts forced the council to close the library, Frankie worried she'd never find another job—especially one which fitted around being a single mum—but then she spotted an advert for a prison librarian. Given that she had plenty of experience but no real qualifications, it was the only position she could get an interview for. She took the job because she needed to and stayed because she wanted to.

Books matter more to her than who is reading them or where they are being read.

A good book can be a light in the darkness.

A good book can cure loneliness, change minds, or even change the world.

A good book is nothing less than magic.

Books sheltered her from the reality of an unhappy childhood, letting her hide between the pages of a story whenever real life got too loud. In an adulthood that proved to be no less problematic, books provided her with work, money, and purpose. Books kept a roof over her head and books put food on her table. She owes whatever happiness she has in the real world to fiction.

Which is one of the many reasons why Frankie believes that everyone should have access to books. The memories of her time working at the prison play on a loop inside her mind as she drives. When she accepted the role as head librarian at the city's only women's prison, she did so with a mix of anxiety and optimism. Her fear of the unknown was almost neutralized by the idea of teaching others how stories could save them. She spent her first few days keeping to herself, everything about the prison was intimidating and it wasn't pretty. The slate gray brick buildings had once been home to a mental asylum, and the Victorian exterior was bleak and uninviting. Even the sounds of the place scared her. There were hourly bells, the banging of doors, the slamming of gates, the jangle of keys, and the occasional scream. Counting was the only thing that kept Frankie calm. The regular herd of footsteps and chatter below the library window, when inmates were moved from one part of the prison to another, reminded her of a school. One where all the girls were bad.

She missed the quiet and calm of the local library where she used to work. And the books. So she sat at her lonely desk, fired up the old computer, and started writing to anyone she could think of who might be willing or able to help. She wrote to publishers, sometimes to authors direct if she could find their contact details and was feeling brave. Every letter was the same—asking if anyone might have some books they could donate.

When she had more books than she knew what to do with, she persuaded the prison workshop manager to build her some bookcases. Frankie knew that other people thought she was pretty back then. At thirty-eight she can still turn heads now, and men have always seemed only too happy to help her. It's as though they can sense that she needs rescuing—albeit from herself—and for once she took advantage of that fact. One week later, the library walls were lined with beautiful bespoke pine shelves, handcrafted by the workshop manager and his all-female team of trainee carpenters.

She tells herself it was all worth it but doesn't always believe that. Life seems better at punishing bad deeds than it is at rewarding good ones. Frankie knows she's helped a lot of women in the prison over the years—she even taught some inmates to read. It felt good to help other people to help themselves, but the job was draining and often thankless. She won't miss any of her colleagues, but she will miss some of the prisoners. Like a young girl called Liberty who volunteers in the library. She's the same age as Frankie's daughter and reminds Frankie of her a little bit. Made her miss her little girl even more than she already did.

There was too much red tape when she started the job—still is—and too small a budget to redecorate. So Frankie baked brownies for the head caretaker, who gave her some spare paint in return. She used it to transform the dark space she had been given into a bright and airy sanctuary for the inmates. And for herself. Nobody would believe her if she confessed that a prison library felt more like home than home these days. It's hard to feel at home in a haunted house. Even one that floats. Frankie has lived on a narrow boat on the River Thames for most of her life.

The journey from South to West London takes even longer than it should, due to an unscheduled stop. But Frankie needs to visit someone she hasn't seen for a long time—someone she feels she really ought to say goodbye to before she does what she is planning to do. Her footsteps feel heavy with dread as she makes her way toward the entrance; counting them doesn't help. She's here because she thinks she should be, not because she wants to be. It is Mother's Day after all.

Frankie notices that all of the other visitors appear to have brought flowers, and tries to ignore the familiar feelings of guilt as she sits down.

"Hello, Mum," she whispers.

There is no reply. There never is. Her mother was a woman whose grudges had grudges.

When the other visitors have moved far enough away that they won't overhear, Frankie tries again.

"I know it has been a while since I last came to see you. Sorry about that."

Frankie stares down at her shoes, sees that her shoelace is still untied and worries she must look a mess. Her mum could always make her feelings known without speaking them out loud. With just a look. Normally one of disappointment. Frankie can feel all her past hurt and resentment bubbling to the surface; she should probably leave before saying something she might regret. A mother's least favorite child always knows that's what they are. And when a least favorite child is an only child it leaves a scar.

"I always tried to make you proud, but it was never enough, was it?" Frankie whispers, looking over her shoulder to make sure nobody can hear.

Sometimes silence is an answer in itself.

Frankie persists, determined to say what she came here to say.

"But maybe you were right to think so little of me. I did something terrible, Mum. Something I can't tell anyone else about. And now I have to do something even worse. I don't know if I can go through with it. I don't know what's right anymore. I feel so broken and lost and alone and I—"

Frankie starts to cry and reaches for a hankie hidden in her sleeve. She doesn't know why she came here today. She may as well talk to a wall.

"Anyway, I can't stay long. I just wanted to say hello. And goodbye."

She stands up and looks around the cemetery. When she is sure that nobody is looking, she takes a bunch of white roses from a nearby grave and puts them on the one she has been sitting in front of. The one she sometimes comes here to talk to. She kisses her fingertips then touches the name engraved on the white marble headstone. The one-way conversations aren't so different from the ones they shared when her mother was alive and in the care home. Her mum hated that place so much that a wooden box six feet under probably came as a relief.

"Happy Mother's Day," Frankie whispers, before saying goodbye for the last time.

Edith

The knock on the door of room thirteen makes Edith jump. She has never been fond of visitors. It was the same when she lived in her own house, not just here at the Windsor Care Home. Edith has always been very wary of *people*. Dogs are considerably more loyal and trustworthy. She holds Dickens and covers his mouth to stop him from barking.

"Who is it?" she asks.

"It's me," says a familiar voice on the other side of the door.

Edith hesitates. Regrets asking the question. Wishes she had kept quiet.

She misses her daughter but no longer recognizes the woman she has turned into.

"Please open the door, Mum. We need to talk."

Edith slowly climbs out of the bed, her bones creaking in protest. It feels like she is about to lose her balance—like it always does these days when she stands up too quickly—but there is no time to lose. She holds on tight to Dickens and carries him to the bathroom, noticing how old her hands look. Her freckled skin has a bluish tinge and appears almost translucent. The woman she glimpses in the bathroom mirror doesn't just look old, she looks elderly. Frail. Smaller than the person she used to be and thought she still was. Age sneaks up on us all like an unwelcome thief.

"You stay in there and keep quiet," she whispers, gently putting the dog down on the tiled floor and shutting him inside the bathroom.

Edith hobbles over to the bed, ignoring the pain in her hip, and tries to brush away any dog hairs on the sheets and on her flamingo print pajamas. Removing any and all evidence of the dog as fast as she is able. Her daughter had Dickens taken away from her once already, she's not going to lose him a second time.

"Are you okay? You know you shouldn't lock this door," says the patronizing voice on the other side of it.

Edith turns the key, twists the handle and—with a little effort—pulls the door open. "I shouldn't be here at all, but here we are," she says.

The prodigal daughter stands in the doorway, eyes down, shoulders slumped like the sad and scared little girl she used to be. Except now she's in her fifties.

"Can I come in?" she asks.

"If you must."

Edith looks her up and down. Her daughter looks older than she remembers, but then it has been several months since they were in the same room, maybe even a year. Time is hard to tell these days. Edith wrinkles her nose at her choice of dress; too short, too *red*—it was never a good color on her—but she knows better than to criticize. Out loud. It's clear that her advice is no longer listened to or wanted. Edith's appraising eyes finally land at her daughter's feet. She cannot understand why a grown woman would choose to wear trainers during the day, as though she has just been for a run or can't afford proper shoes.

She stares at the flowers her surprise visitor is carrying—already wilting and looking past their best, on discount no doubt—then studies her daughter's face. It looks a bit like hers used to. She notices that her daughter's hair is parted at the side instead of in the middle—which has never suited her—and is in need of a trim. She takes it all in and wonders what happened to the child she used to know and try to love. Edith should never have left Scotland. Moving to London and raising a child in the city is one of her biggest regrets. Children in Scotland respect their parents; she should have stayed there. It's as though this fiftysomething woman, this version of her daughter she barely recognizes, gobbled up the good one. Her good little girl grew up to be bad.

Edith can't help noticing the details people try to hide about themselves. It's one of the unwanted perks of being a detective for thirty years. Retired now, of course. And Edith was only a *store* detective, but it's almost the same as being a real one. Besides, in lots of ways her job was harder. She had to prevent crimes before they happened, not just solve them. And she was good at it. The best. Regional employee of the month on numerous occasions.

"To what do I owe the honor?" Edith asks, folding her arms and wishing she had bothered to get dressed today. The cotton pajamas feel like insufficient armor.

"It's Mother's Day."

"Is it? I didn't know," Edith lies.

"I sent a card. And a gift."

"The cuddly toy? Was that from you?"

"Don't be like that, Mum. Please. We both know I didn't have a choice."

"Did someone force you to send me a stuffed bear?"

"You know what I mean."

"People always have choices, they just pretend not to in order to feel better about making bad ones."

And so it begins. Her daughter sighs, the same way she used

to when she was being difficult as a teenager. "There's a bit of a problem with the care home fees."

"What kind of problem?" Edith asks.

"I can't pay them."

"Then don't. I can go back to *my* home, where I belong."

"I've sold what I can to make ends meet but—"

"What have you sold? *My* things? You better not have sold *my* house."

"I've only sold the things you don't need, to pay for things that you do."

"If you think you can hornswoggle me again—"

"Nobody is trying to trick you, Mum. Least of all me. I wouldn't dare. The care home manager has been very understanding until now but you might lose your place here if I can't find a solution. And if you don't like it here—"

"Don't like it? I hate it. You may as well have put me in prison and left me there to rot."

"Well then you won't like the alternatives because this is one of the better options. I thought I could keep paying the fees by seeing extra clients, but I'm quite far behind now and—"

"So let me live at home again. It's *my* house," Edith interrupts.

"You know you can't. You fell over and nobody knew for days, remember? And you kept forgetting to take your heart medication—"

"Poppycock. There's nothing wrong with my heart."

"Because you don't have one."

"Pardon?"

"Maybe you know better than all the doctors who said you need to take the pills. After all, you know better than everyone."

"Don't speak to me as though I'm a child."

"It's hard not to when you keep behaving like one. What about the time when you left the gas stove on? Nearly blew up the whole street. And let's not forget the time when—"

"Then let me live with you. In the pink house." Edith's voice trembles and she hates herself for being so weak, so vulnerable, so needy. She's never needed anyone her whole life. It's as though their roles have been reversed. She used to make all the difficult decisions for them both, but now her daughter has become the parent in the relationship and Edith doesn't like it. Not one little bit. Nobody does what she wants them to these days. Nobody listens. Clio shakes her head and Edith knows what that means. She shouldn't have had to beg her own child to do the right the thing, shouldn't have had to ask at all. She wishes she hadn't.

"You're looking a little red and bloated, dear. Are you feeling quite all right?" Edith asks.

"I'm fine, thank you—"

"It's probably the menopause. Your grandmother puffed up like a balloon and lost her looks too when it happened to her. I was lucky, it must have skipped a generation."

Her daughter sighs and shakes her head. "I found this in a box of your things."

"What is it? I'm surprised you didn't sell it like everything else."

"I thought you might like to have it here," her daughter says, taking something heavy-looking from her faux leather bag. Even her accessories pretend to be something they are not. Edith doesn't recognize the object in her hand at first. But then the metal statue of a magnifying glass triggers a flood of memories, none of them good. The words *Happy Retirement!* are engraved on the chunky bronze plinth it is welded to.

"Why did you bring this?" Edith asks with a face full of disdain. She begrudgingly takes the statue, stares at it, then puts it on the dressing table as far away from her as she can. "Are you *trying* to hurt me?"

"No! Of course not."

"Then why remind me of things I want to forget? And why can't I live with you?"

"We tried that. You living with me, remember? It didn't work," the woman who *looks* like her daughter says. She wonders where her real daughter went. The one who did what she was told and didn't answer back.

Edith feels dizzy. "Stop asking me if I remember things. Being old doesn't mean I am senile. I. Do. Not. Belong. In. A. Home."

Her daughter stares at her. One moment she looks like a little girl again, the next she looks like this *woman*. A *stranger*. "Do you have a vase somewhere?" the woman asks. "Something I can put these flowers in?" She looks around the room, then heads toward the bathroom where Dickens is hidden.

"There's nothing in there," Edith says, raising her voice more than she intended to.

The woman puts the flowers on the bed instead. "I'm sorry, Mum."

"No, you're not. And after everything I did for you."

"Ha! That's a good one."

"What is that supposed to mean?" Edith asks.

"'How are you, Clio? How's work? How are you feeling? Tell me what you've been up to.' That's the sort of thing most mothers might ask their children when they haven't seen them for a while. You have zero interest in me, or my life. All you've done for years is criticize me and keep me at arm's length. Like a stranger. But now you want to live with me?"

"I don't know what I did to deserve such an ungrateful, spiteful, selfish child."

"Yes, you do."

Clio

Clio hurries back down the stairs wishing she hadn't come at all. Her mother has always excelled at knowing how to push all of her buttons. Clio is a size twelve, same as always, and does *not* look bloated. She pauses to check her reflection in her compact mirror just to be sure, not that she gives a damn what her mother thinks. At least the exchange helped to make the decision, now Clio just needs to find the care home manager. She avoids the lounge. It's filled to its chintzy brim with residents and their relatives making the obligatory Mother's Day visit, and watching other people playing happy families tends to make her feel sad. She wants to get this over and done with and get back home—where nobody can hurt her—as soon as possible.

Clio prefers not to leave her house too often since the pandemic. Aside from popping to the health food store or her yoga class three times a week there is rarely any need. She rather enjoyed lockdown and finds being in close proximity to other people unpleasant and unnecessary these days. She preferred it when staying at home was what everyone did, so that when she went out she could still be alone.

The care home manager's office door is closed, as always. Clio knocks but doesn't wait for a response before walking in, and finds Joy sitting behind her desk eating chocolate chip cookies. The office is small and smells of supermarket tea and cheap perfume. There are some meaningless framed certificates on the wall—qualifications as pointless as the woman claiming to have them—along with a filing cabinet and a large safe. On Joy's desk is an open magazine, a plate of cookies, and an exotic-looking plant which appears half dead. If the woman can't keep a cactus alive it does not bode well for the people in her care.

Clio guesses that Joy Bonetta is probably in her early fifties, just like her. Unlike her, Joy looks her age and then some. She dresses like the stereotype of a middle-aged woman, wearing a knitted twinset that is at least one size too small, a long floral skirt—with an elasticized waistband, no doubt—and a pearl necklace which rests in a lackluster fashion on her ample bosom. Her short hair is styled in a series of tight ringlets in a halo of ugly around her head.

Clio finds the woman repugnant, but forces her face to smile.

"Can I help you?" Joy asks with her mouth still full of cookie. A few crumbs escape and land on her chins.

Clio struggles to hold her smile in place, then takes the seat opposite without being invited. "I do hope so. I'm Edith Elliot's daughter." Joy stares at her blankly. "We spoke on the phone earlier this week." The woman's vacant expression still doesn't change. "About my mother, in room thirteen?" This time Clio's words hit the target.

"Ahh," says Joy. "I do remember. And I'm afraid my answer is still the same."

Clio's smile falters. "There must be some kind of arrangement we can—"

"I'm sorry. Truly, I am. But this is a business and I'm afraid that if residents—or their relatives—can no longer afford the fees, alternative accommodation needs to be found. I said the same thing to your—"

"Surely you could wait a couple of weeks?"

"Contrary to popular belief, good things rarely come to those who wait. I have a waiting list longer than a monkey's arms. Places in residential care homes are few and far between in the city, and I'm afraid the demand for good ones far outweighs the supply."

"I wouldn't call this a good one."

Joy raises an overplucked eyebrow. "As I mentioned on the phone, if you want to remove your mother before the end of her tenancy agreement, there is an additional charge of eight thousand pounds plus tax to facilitate an early departure."

"That's more than the monthly fees. If I had that kind of money I'd just pay. I mean, if she *died* you wouldn't charge me extra for an 'early departure' would you?"

Joy leans across the desk, so close that Clio has to resist the urge to offer the woman a breath mint. "That would be a tragedy, of course, but if room thirteen were to become vacant because the current occupant *died*, the only additional expense—all of which are clearly listed and explained in our terms and conditions—would be for a deep clean of the room. We care very much about our residents and their loved ones, and I understand the financial burden can be impossible. I am here to help in *any* way that I can."

Clio stares at the woman. "*Any* way?"

There is a knock on the door before Joy gets the chance to answer. "Come in!" she shrills.

The door opens and an elderly man with a walking stick stands glowering. He's wearing a shirt and tie beneath his cardigan, and has a full head of curly white hair.

"Yes? What is it?" Joy barks in his direction.

"I want to make a complaint," he says.

"You've already made three today, Mr. Henderson. As discussed, that's your daily limit."

"If there weren't so many things to complain about I wouldn't have to. That woman is here, the one asking questions, wanting to know the names of residents and what rooms they are in. She's up to no good, if you ask me."

"I didn't. I never do."

"And afternoon tea is late. And the elevator is broken, *again*. And you said you'd stop people stealing my things—"

Joy holds up a hand, as though stopping traffic. It certainly stops the old man complaining, for now. She heaves herself up from the desk and waddles toward him. "Afternoon tea will be served shortly, Mr. Henderson. Nobody has stolen anything. Last time you lost your wallet it was in your pocket, remember? Everyone who works at the Windsor Care Home is carefully vetted. I promise you that you and your things are perfectly safe."

"What about the elevator? I can't climb the stairs with my hip."

"The repair man is on his way again, and the elevator will be fixed by the end of the day." She ushers him out of the room and closes the door before turning back to Clio.

"Maybe think about it," Joy says.

"About what?"

"It is always a difficult path to navigate when a loved one reaches the end. Have you spoken to the rest of the family?"

"About *what*?" Clio asks again.

Joy bristles. "If you can't afford this month's fees, and your mother remains in good health, please ensure you make the necessary arrangements for alternative accommodation for her."

"And if I don't? Then what? It isn't as though you're going to chuck an elderly woman out on the street."

"We can only look after residents who pay for their care. This is not a charity."

"I'm starting to wonder *what* this is."

"Do let me know what you decide about room thirteen."

Clio snaps. "I will end you if anything happens to my mother."

She stands to leave, flings open the office door, and walks right into the old man still loitering outside it. He was clearly eavesdropping and heard every word.

Patience

I only have one more bedroom to visit on the top floor of the care home before I can get back to Edith and Dickens. As a trainee carer with no qualifications, it is my job to clean up after the residents as well as care for them. I make their beds, clean their rooms, wash their clothes. When necessary—if they need help, which many of them do—I wash *them* too. I dress them, brush their hair and false teeth, cut their toenails, feed them, talk to them. I help them go to the toilet, which can be tricky if they are unsteady on their feet, or can't remember where the toilet is. Every resident is different and each one requires a different level of care. At eighteen I'm the youngest person on the team, and I basically do all the jobs nobody else wants to do. It's a hard way to make a lousy living, but it's also the only job I could get, and keeping it hasn't been easy.

I check the time on my phone and see that I have a text message:

Hi Patience, we need to talk. How about I come over later—

I delete it without reading the rest or replying. Any message starting with "we need to talk" rarely ends well. I'm pleased to see the top floor of the home looks empty again; there have been too many visitors here today. The place is full of them on days like Mother's Day. They come crawling out of the woodwork once or twice a year, sniffing out their inheritance. I think as little of them as I know most of them think of me. I'm just the invisible help, taking care of the people they don't want to, or don't know how to.

I slip the phone back in the pocket of my polyester uniform, then push the trolley that is piled high with cleaning products and fresh linen to the next bedroom door. The trolley seems as reluctant to go inside the final room as I am, its wonky wheels squeaking in protest on the patterned carpet. The door is locked—even though it shouldn't be—so I use the master key to let myself in.

Room fourteen should be just as beautiful as room thirteen—they are decorated exactly the same way, with identical furniture and matching far-reaching views of the city—but room fourteen is currently occupied by a man who should be dead. Mr. Henderson hates the world but refuses to leave it. Every time life conspires to kill him, he survives. War, a pandemic, and an unfortunate incident with a double-decker bus all failed to do the trick. Our exchange when I arrived downstairs for my shift today is still playing on a loop inside my head. It began with his usual greeting.

"You again? Nobody likes you."

"I guess that's why I get paid the small bucks," I said with a smile, trying—as always—to remain cheerful. "Good morning, Mr. Henderson."

"Piss off, you little runt. Stay out of my room and don't touch my stuff."

"I wish I could and didn't have to."

"Less of your lip, you little shit. Your generation are all the same. Bugger off back where you came from, you ugly little bastard."

He calls me *that* word a lot: bastard. And whenever he does

I think it might be true: I am a fatherless child. But he uses that word when speaking to most of the staff, so his insults are rarely personal, just rude. Rich people have the poorest manners. I bite my tongue and remind myself that Mr. Henderson is just a sad old man. If he does have any friends or relatives they never visit. I think some people are lonely for a reason. Most people tend to think that the elderly are all kind and cuddly, the generic geriatric is a friendly cardigan-wearing grandparent, with an endless supply of tea and wisdom. But from what I have seen working here, bad young people grow up to be bad old people. Hate doesn't fade with age.

I heave open the sash windows in room fourteen, keen to let in as much fresh air as possible, so it can mingle with the stale variety in Mr. Henderson's bedroom. Then I pop in my earphones and choose a suitable soundtrack before pulling on my heavy-duty black rubber gloves. I start in the windowless bathroom, tugging the cord to shed some light on what I already know will be unpleasant viewing. This part of the job used to make me feel sick, but it's human nature to adapt, adjust, evolve. It's how we survive. Armed with industrial disinfectant, I observe the scene and assess the damage. There are damp towels all over the floor, toothpaste and beard trimmings in the sink, and shit stains in the unflushed toilet bowl. In any other room, I would pick up the toilet brush and open the bleach. But after what Mr. Henderson said to me downstairs earlier, I use his toothbrush to clean away the unpleasantness he has left behind. It's a fancy toothbrush. Electric. Expensive. It does the job nicely and I flush the toilet to rinse it clean.

When the bathroom is finished I return to the bedroom. I strip the sheets from the bed first, relieved that there are no unpleasant stains today. Sometimes Mr. Henderson likes to leave surprises for me to find. Sometimes I imagine pushing him down the stairs. Last week—as well as the standard insults and hitting me on the arm with his walking stick—he accused me of stealing things from his room and I almost lost my lousy job because of it. So I swapped his dentures with a set that had belonged to a resident who died. It was days before anyone could figure out why they didn't fit. But that's not the same as stealing. *This* is stealing.

Once the bed is made, I have a little nosey through the drawers in the dressing table. I find a chocolate bar, unwrap it, and take a bite. Then I check the wardrobe, wondering why one man who never leaves the building needs so many fancy-looking shirts and ties—dressing like a gentleman doesn't mean someone is one. In one jacket I find a silver money clip containing a hundred pounds in ten-pound notes. I slip most of the cash in my pocket and notice that the money clip is engraved: *Grandad*. The idea of someone so unpleasant having a family when I have nobody makes me want to cry. I hear his words inside my head again: "Bugger off back where you came from, you ugly little bastard."

People who throw stones don't seem to understand that they sometimes bounce back.

"He's just a different generation," miserable Joy said when I dared to complain the last time he hit me with his walking stick. As though age is an excuse for hate and abuse. I showed her the bruises on my arm but she didn't care. Joy knows I'm trapped here for financial and other reasons. She is the variety of manager who always manages to make everything worse. I *hate* her—all of the staff do—and she uses my situation like a boot to walk all over me.

I think I know why today's collection of insults upset me more than usual.

I can't go "back where I came from" because I don't know *where* that is.

But I do know *who* I want to be, and *where* I want to go, and that's worth something. As soon as I have saved up enough money, I'm getting out of here.

I select a new track from the playlist on my phone and turn up the volume, then I continue my secret scavenger hunt. I find three miniature bottles of scotch in the bedside cabinet, so I drink one and confiscate the rest. Alcohol is against the rules.

Then I find the letters.

There must be fifty of them, written by hand on thick white paper. They are love letters, filled with affection, devotion, and tenderness, all addressed to Mr. Henderson's wife. The most recent one was written yesterday.

She died five years ago.

> *I miss you being by my side at night. I miss holding your hand, hearing your laugh.*

This is a version of the old man I have never known.

> *I saw a robin on the hedge today and it made me think of you.*

I feel the heavy pain of his grief and loss with every word.

> *I do not know how to be me without you.*

I read several of the letters before putting them back. Trying to equate the person who wrote them with the person downstairs is incomprehensible. I was wrong about the man I thought I knew, just like he is wrong about me. There is always a reason why people behave the way that they do. Sometimes bad people are just sad people in disguise.

There is a small glass display frame hidden away at the back of the bedside cabinet. I've become fascinated by what people choose to bring here, the things they want close by at the end. A life's worth of possessions reduced to a single box of keepsakes in an unfamiliar room. I take the frame out for a closer look at two medals inside. One is gold and shaped like a star, the other is a silver cross and the inscription suggests that they are from the second world war. The things this man must have done for his country do not excuse his behavior now, but they do make me regret my own. I accidently drop the frame and the glass shatters.

It takes far longer to clean up the mess than it should, tiny bits of glass seem to be everywhere. When finished, I squeeze the medal and the small broken frame into the pocket of my tunic, hoping there might be a way to repair it. Then I start putting the rest of Mr. Henderson's things back where I found them. I have never been good at being bad.

The music in my ears stops just as I'm starting to put back the cash I took from Mr. Henderson's jacket.

But then I hear something else.

There is someone in the room.

They have been watching me.

"What do you think you are doing?" asks Joy. I turn around slowly, my hands hovering in midair as though I am scared of being shot. Joy is standing in the doorway looking too pleased with herself. She is a small-minded woman who is overly fond of wearing cotton-candy-colored twinsets; I see that today's is blue. Her ringlets remind me of pigs' tails, and her beady eyes look darker than usual. They are currently focused on the money I am holding. The money I was about to put back.

"This isn't what it looks like," I say in a small voice that sounds like an imitation of my own.

"Of course not. Never is. Mr. Henderson said you were stealing things from his room so I thought I'd come and check for myself. Looks like he was right. Empty your pockets onto the bed."

"I can explain—"

"Empty your pockets."

I do as she asks—what choice do I have—putting the ten-pound notes and the miniature scotches on top of the clean white sheets.

"Is that everything?" Joy asks, tilting her head to one side when I don't answer. "Please don't make me search you myself."

The thought makes me shudder. I reach inside my pocket again and pull out some other things that do not belong to me. Everything except Mr. Henderson's war medal and Edith's bank card. Joy's beady eyes are already bulging, don't want her to start shitting kittens.

"Is it just room fourteen you've been stealing from?" she asks, her turkey neck starting to turn red with the stress and glee of it all. She calls all of the residents by their room numbers.

"I didn't—"

She tuts and holds up a hand. "Don't bother lying. I would call the police myself, but seeing as you working here isn't completely official that makes things complicated. And now I have another gap in the roster to fill. You're fired, obviously, and don't bother asking me for a reference."

I start to panic. Work is hard to come by without any ID, or a bank account, or a real name. "Please, I can explain." Her face is a stop sign but I carry on anyway. "I can't lose this job."

"And I can't employ a thief."

"I'm not a—"

"Get your things and get out. Leave your keys and your badge in my office, and you can return the uniform once you've washed it. I don't have time to listen to your lies. Thanks to you I have even more work to do."

She points at the door.

My bag is still in Edith's room.

So is Dickens.

I can't leave without him but Joy has followed me to the landing. She is leaning against the rickety top floor banister, watching me as I walk toward the stairs. It doesn't seem as though I have many options, and there is no time to decide what to do. Right and wrong are so hard to tell apart sometimes.

"And don't bother trying to get another job in a care home in this city. I'm going to make sure *everyone* knows not to employ a girl called Patience."

"Go ahead," I say, and mean it.

Patience is the answer to so many of life's questions.

Patience is what I've needed to learn in order to survive.

Patience is what it says on my name badge, but it is not my real name.

Edith

Edith isn't sure how long it has been since her daughter left the Windsor Care Home. Long enough for her to think that she isn't coming back. Not that she cares. Except that she thought her daughter said she would pop in again before leaving. Maybe Edith misheard. Or maybe she misunderstood. It doesn't matter. She's used to sitting here for hours on her own with nobody to talk to and nothing to do, and has learned to be patient because it is her only option. She sits on the bed, stroking Dickens for comfort, re-living the latest argument with her daughter and wondering how and when and why it all went so wrong.

It's a question she knows the answer to but wishes that she didn't.

Her life wasn't always like this. When Edith was a store detective people showed her the respect she deserved. Her job gave her a purpose and put a roof over their heads. She was a good mum—even if her daughter doesn't think so. Edith would never have won a mother of the year award, and she might have made a few mistakes—who hasn't—but she did her best. At her age, she knows that doing your best really is all anyone can do. Being a parent is rarely about making popular decisions. She did what she needed to do to take care of them both.

Someone knocks on the door and Edith panics—she didn't lock it. Her worries soon translate into hope. She thinks maybe her daughter has returned after all, come back to apologize and take her away from this awful place. Take her *home*. Edith picks up Dickens and hides him in the bathroom again, he looks suitably unimpressed with the arrangement. Someone knocks a second time, and it's lucky the old dog is a bit deaf these days or he'd bark. Edith hurries to get back in her bed. She brushes away the dog hairs once more and smooths down the sheets. She's ready but still feels an overwhelming sense of unease when she sees the door handle start to turn.

Edith didn't say to come in.

She pulls the duvet right up under her chin, considers pretending to be asleep, then decides to keep one eye open as the door squeaks, the floorboards creak, and someone walks into her room.

"Oh," she says. "It's you."

Frankie

When Frankie arrives at her final destination, she feels a bit bro-ken. She keeps replaying recent events and her reactions to them, feeling as though every decision she makes is wrong. It is as though she has driven to a different world when she stares out of the win-dow. One where she already knows she doesn't fit. The Notting Hill mews Frankie parks in front of looks more like a film set than somewhere real people might live. This corner of the city has been landscaped with wealth and success, not like the stretch of the River Thames where she lives. Each of the pretty town houses is immaculately painted in a different pastel shade. There are well-tended hanging baskets filled with colorful flowers, and potted plants on the cobbled pedestrian street. Every house has an expen-sive looking security system.

Frankie turns off the engine and sits in the van for a while, waiting for time to catch up with her. The alarm on her phone hasn't gone off yet, so she knows she is early. She notices the pa-per cut on her index finger. One of the library books did it to her earlier. It's amazing how a wound so small can refuse to heal and inflict so much discomfort. The cut hadn't hurt until she saw it again, and it makes her wonder whether all pain is real or merely imagined.

She climbs into the back of the van to get changed, pulling off her prison uniform and replacing it with a black dress she has been saving for this occasion. Then she gets back into the driver's seat and checks her reflection in the rearview mirror. Sad green eyes stare back. The dark circles that appeared beneath them when she lost her daughter have never left. Frankie has changed her hair color and style often over the years, but her curly bob looks as tired as she feels today. Her hair is determined to turn gray at the roots—despite her relatively young age—and her skin is so pale she looks like a ghost. She feels like a ghost, sleepwalking through life, waiting for the final chapter.

Frankie's hands are clammy and she can't stop them from shaking as she pulls on a pair of red leather gloves. It's ironic really, most people who have met her—a quiet, shy, prison librarian—probably couldn't imagine her committing a crime. It's amazing what a person can be driven to do when they are out of options. On paper, Frankie is a good person. Sometimes good people do bad things, sometimes they have to. But Frankie wishes that it hadn't come to this. Sadly it is human nature to squander love and stockpile hate. She counts from lonely one up to perfect ten then opens the van door.

Frankie counts her steps from the van to the front of the pretty pink town house too, knowing that there should be exactly thirty-four. This isn't the first time she has visited this place, but it will be the first—and last—time she goes inside. Every single step seems to sharpen the pain of her memories as she crosses the cobbled street. Her mind is a whirlwind of all the things that have been taken from her. Things that Frankie fears she will never get back. Someone has to pay for what Frankie has lost, and that someone is inside the pink house. She notices the lock on the front door—one which would be ridiculously easy to pick—and realizes she could have let herself in anytime if she had chosen to. But she wants to be invited.

The alarm on her phone still hasn't sounded. She is early, and thinks perhaps she should wait. Having put this off for as long as she has, surely a couple of minutes won't make much difference. Maybe it's best to get it over with. She raises her fist to knock but then stares at the shiny, polished house number: thirteen. She hesitates again, while words about numbers hiss inside her head: *Thirteen: prime number, compound number, unlucky number, persons present at the Last Supper, teenager, the number of men she has . . .*

She interrupts her thoughts before they derail her completely. Thirteen is a numerical paradox: lucky and unlucky at the same time. Perhaps it is another sign that she is doing the right thing. *Or* is the universe trying to warn her that what she is about to do is wrong? Two wrongs don't make a right, but they can make the world seem more even. Less off balance.

Frankie's alarm on her mobile phone pings and, at the exact same time, the door to the pink house opens.

"I'm Clio. You must be Frankie," says a well-groomed middle-aged woman wearing a red dress and matching trainers. She offers her hand and a warm smile, neither of which Frankie feels sure how to take. "There's a secret little camera above the door, see?" the woman adds, pointing at a small round black object that most people would never notice. "I saw you waiting. You looked a bit scared to knock so I thought I'd just come and say hello. Everyone gets a little nervous the first time, so please try not to worry. Come on inside." The woman is so friendly it makes Frankie feel sick. She is aggressively kind. The variety of person people only like because they feel they really ought to. The woman frowns and it spoils her face. "You are Frankie, aren't you?"

Frankie stares at her as though she is speaking a foreign language. She hadn't known about the camera above the door. She can't help wondering whether it was able to see her parked outside so many other times before today. She hesitates, scared now that this woman might already know who Frankie is and why she is here. She tries to reply, but the words get caught in her throat. It feels as though she is choking on all the things she cannot say. The woman seems to understand, as though this was the response she was expecting. She turns to enter, gesturing with a manicured hand for Frankie to follow.

Which she will.

But not before thinking about the thirty-four steps it would take to return to the van. Maybe it isn't too late to turn around, walk away, and never come back.

Frankie looks down at her Mickey Mouse watch and sees that it has stopped. If she needed another sign—there have been plenty—then this is it. Even time has run away from her. She silently counts to three—the best number there is—before following the woman inside the pink house.

Patience

"Don't get too attached to anyone in God's waiting room."

Joy told me that on my first day at the Windsor Care Home and I should have listened.

Nothing that has happened since she fired me feels real. I have done things I didn't think I was capable of, bad things, things I can't change. The journey back to Covent Garden is a blur at best. I tripped over a homeless girl outside the tube station. I didn't see her sitting there, and I worry that I've become so exposed to wrong-doing and injustice I don't even notice it anymore. The homeless girl is somebody's daughter too. We looked the same age. I gave her a ten-pound note from my pocket—knowing that she needed it more than I do—and she was so grateful I wished I had given her more. Bad things happen to teenagers who run away to London. I'm one of the lucky ones. Life in the big city tends to be a lot smaller than the dreams people have of it. People forget that nightmares are dreams too.

I turn the corner and it starts to rain, a fine mist coating my skin. The road is soon wet with a pretty pattern of blurred reflections from the streetlights and brightly lit shops. Covent Garden is filled with tourists—it always is—and it feels as though they are all staring at me. Whenever I look up, none of them are. I shiver, partly from the cold, partly because of something else— guilt probably—and walk a little faster across the cobbled piazza. Things are too noisy inside my head for me to get my thoughts straight. When doing something wrong is the right thing to do, does that make it okay?

My world was so quiet before moving to central London, sometimes the city still feels too loud. The attic flat where I have been staying for almost a year is hidden away high above a small art gallery. You wouldn't even know it was there unless you knew to look, and most people are too busy looking down at their phones to look up these days. Desperately scrolling for opinions that mirror their own. The attic window is small and round, like a porthole in the sky, peeking out from the roof of the building like a secret eye. The attic itself is barely big enough for a single bed, but someone like me could still never earn enough to live in it. Even flats the size of a shoebox cost more than I could afford. I don't pay rent, but I do pay for the privilege of living here in other ways.

Kennedy's Gallery has been in Covent Garden for over a hundred years, and looks more like an architect's afterthought than part of any original plan. It's a slim brick-built Victorian town house, four stories high, and sandwiched between two much grander, bigger buildings. It almost looks as though the space it occupies used to be an alleyway. Perhaps it was. Places can become more than they were, given the opportunity, just like people. The gallery has been handed down from one generation of middle-class, art-loving men to the next. Until now. The latest, Jude Kennedy—my landlord— has failed to produce an heir to the gallery throne, and the future of the business keeps him awake at night. I know, because that's often when he comes to visit me.

Jude is a well-polished individual in his forties, with tanned skin and floppy hair. He's always smartly dressed in clothes designed to be worn by a younger man. Like so many seemingly successful people he has more charm than talent, but life has been kind to him. And in return, he has been kind to me. Or at least kind enough to let me live in the attic above his gallery.

There are only three formal conditions to our arrangement:

1. *I cannot make any noise during the day.*
2. *I am not allowed to have visitors.*
3. *Once a month I have to give him something I don't want to.*

I'm quite certain that everyone who meets Jude thinks of him as a confident and charismatic success story, a man who inherited a business which has provided him with happiness and wealth. But we all wear masks, and I know Mr. Kennedy well enough to have seen the man behind his. If he were a book, his cover would be far more clever and beautiful than the words written inside. Like so many people who appear to be living the dream, it isn't *his* dream that he is living.

I feel physically lighter when I see that the gallery lights have been dimmed; it normally means he has gone home for the day. I turn down the small alley that leads to the rear of the gallery, where the bins are kept, and unlock the back door. It reveals the familiar dark narrow staircase, which twists and turns and creaks all the way to the attic at the very top of the building. I know which steps groan the loudest—the ones to avoid treading on when I don't want to be heard down below—and I know that there are one hundred and twenty-three steps in total. It irritates me that my brain insists on counting them. Bad habits can be contagious. I open the attic door as quietly as possible—just in case anyone *is* still in the gallery downstairs—then creep inside, locking the world out behind me.

Although I am a mere five foot three, there is only one corner of the attic where I can stand up straight. Thanks to the proximity of the sloping ceiling, I've got used to ducking down at all times to avoid hitting my head. Sometimes we all have to become smaller versions of ourselves to fit the story life writes for us. There is a single bed pushed up against the back wall, a bookcase made from two old wine crates, a tiny desk, and a small shelf which serves as a kitchen. (It holds a microwave and kettle.) There is a cupboard-sized "bathroom" with a toilet and miniature sink—the only source of water—and a night-light in the corner of the room, which projects a galaxy of stars on the ceiling from sunset to sunrise. I am afraid of the dark, always have been.

The walls are covered in papercuts.

I have been making them for five years or so. I started when I was thirteen by creating and cutting my own greeting cards. But the designs grew in size, as did my imagination. I have always felt shy about my work; sometimes I think I only create things for myself. But I do dream of being a real artist one day. Life without dreams is just a slow kind of death according to Edith.

There is an old drawer beneath the bed. I used to have one like it when I was a child—a secret place for storing secret things. I use this one to store my paper, pens, glue, and knives. They are only of use to me when the blades are perfectly sharp so I have a lot of them. The drawer is also where I keep my Japanese tea tin. It is a thing of beauty—black and gold with pretty and intricate scenes of people and trees and birds—and it once belonged to my mother. But I do not use it for storing tea. Neither did she. I keep my dreams hidden inside the tea tin instead. I open the lid and try to squeeze all the cash from my pockets inside it. Technically I stole the money from Joy's office. But I was owed a week's wages, plus compensation for all the emotional distress the woman caused me, so I didn't feel any guilt. At least not about that. I need the money to get out of here and I almost have enough.

I realize that I haven't eaten again all day, so grab my only bowl and fill it with chocolate cereal. Then I crouch down to avoid the low beams in the ceiling and sit in my favorite place: the attic window. From the street it looks like a tiny round porthole, the kind you might find on a ship. But up here, up close, it's much larger than people might guess, it is almost as big as me. The design reminds me of a clock and whenever I sit here, on my makeshift window seat made from wooden crates and secondhand cushions, I feel as though my time is my own again. During the day, the window bathes the entire attic in the most beautiful light. At night it's my window on the world, where I can sit hidden in the darkness, looking out over the rooftops watching the theater of life on the streets down below.

The circular window frame pivots open. I could climb right out onto the roof if I wanted to—it's one of the many safety issues which prevents Mr. Kennedy renting the space to a paying tenant. But it's a useful feature when I need to store things that are best kept cold. I do not own a fridge. I open the window and reach for the carton of milk I've been keeping on the ledge. As I pour what is left of it over my cereal, I can hear Big Ben chiming in the distance. I notice Edith's silver ladybug ring when I pick up my spoon. I feel so guilty about what has happened to her.

I almost choke on my cereal when someone knocks on the attic door. I know it's *him*. He must have avoided all of the creakiest steps so that I wouldn't hear him coming up the stairs. I stay perfectly still so that he won't hear me. I can't deal with this now.

He knocks again. "Patience, are you there?" I don't answer. Don't move. "If you ignore me tonight, I'll just come back tomorrow."

A minute passes and feels more like an hour.

I don't make a sound until I hear Mr. Kennedy go back down the stairs, all one hundred and twenty-three of them. Then I peer out of the attic window and watch him walk away down the street toward Soho. The rain is falling hard now, washing everything outside clean. Angry droplets of water splash against the window before crying down the glass like tears. I cry too. I sit and I cry and I stare out of the clock-shaped window, wishing I could turn back time. He can come back tomorrow if he likes—I'll be gone by then—I just need him to stay away tonight. Now that the coast is clear beyond doubt, I grab my coat and prepare to head back out. It is frightening to know what I am capable of when pushed too far, but I still need to finish what I started.

Frankie

Frankie follows the woman into the pink house. All of the doors in the hallway are closed except for one. She feels disappointed that she won't get to see more of the place, having waited so long to be inside. Clio Kennedy appears to have a good life and a beautiful home.

"Thank you for seeing me on a Sunday," Frankie says.

"I can take your coat and bag if you'd like?" Clio offers as they pass a wooden stand.

"No." Frankie grips tighter on to her handbag, as though afraid the woman might steal it. "Thank you," she adds, not wishing to sound rude.

They step into what looks like a rather bare and boring lounge. But that isn't what it is. It is a room for questions that have no correct answers. The walls are all painted gray except for one, which is decorated with an expensive-looking wallpaper covered in birds. It makes Frankie want to fly away. It doesn't look like a typical counseling office, but then Clio doesn't look like a typical therapist. She sits down on a plush turquoise armchair on wheels, and gestures for Frankie to sit on the canary yellow couch opposite.

Frankie perches awkwardly on the edge of her seat. There is a surprising amount of light in the dark room, a large metal clock above the fireplace—which is already busy counting down their allotted sixty minutes—and a little desk in the corner with a laptop, small vase of fresh flowers, and an old-fashioned rotary phone. Frankie can't help staring at it all. She can't quite believe that they are finally together in the same room. Face-to-face for the first time. She hopes that the after-hours appointment will mean they are less likely to be disturbed.

"It's good to meet you, Frankie."

The woman's words already sound like lies. Hearing her say her name out loud causes something to twist inside Frankie's chest, and she wonders whether it is possible to literally break a person's heart. It isn't just the woman making her feel so uncomfortable, it is the room itself. Frankie wishes she had seen it before their appointment because it isn't how she imagined, but there were no pictures online. Everything is so *nice*, too nice; it is making it harder to do what she came here to do. She knows she needs to count to calm down, but it isn't easy in an unfamiliar place.

Four walls, three windows, two chairs, one woman in the pink house.

Frankie finds it difficult to look directly at her, as though she is the sun.

She has seen therapists and counselors and psychiatrists before, a whole cast of them over the years, but none of them were like this woman. Clio's face is almost as familiar as her own, despite the fact that they have never met. Frankie has always felt like a work in progress, but Clio looks like a woman whose life has gone according to plan. Her hair is aggressively styled into an obedient bob with a side parting, and her makeup is subtle, but expertly applied. The red dress looks more classy than flirtatious, flattering her petite frame, and the matching red trainers make her seem fun. She looks younger than her fiftysomething years, but her face doesn't match her youthful body. The dress and trendy trainers are an insufficient disguise. Her age is hiding in the lines around her eyes and the shadows beneath them. Frankie's eyes widen when she sees an unexpected blemish: what looks like a tiny spot of ketchup, or blood, on the woman's chin. Perfect people who live in perfect houses are rarely as perfect as they seem.

Frankie looks for more imperfections but finds none. She notices that the woman's trainers look brand new, as though they have never been worn outside, and wonders if she keeps them in a box. Frankie stares down at her own shoes: one of her laces is still undone and her sensible black brogues are worn at the heel and in need of a good polish. Some Mr. Sheen would have helped. She tucks her feet as far away from herself as possible, as though ashamed of them. She had considered making more of an effort, but it all seemed so pointless. Why should she pretend to be someone or something she isn't? But you only get one chance to make a good first or last impression. Compared to the woman in the pink house, Frankie looks like she got dressed in a charity shop in the dark.

It doesn't matter. A bad impression is more memorable than a good one.

Frankie can feel the woman's eyes creeping all over her. It makes her itch. She is being studied, which makes her want to run and hide.

"I want you to feel comfortable," says Clio, causing Frankie to feel the opposite. "Counseling is nothing to be ashamed of, but I know it can be difficult, opening up to a stranger. I've been doing this for a long time, and I promise that talking to someone about whatever is troubling you can help. I'm here to listen to whatever you want to say. Why don't you start with what brought you here today?"

Revenge. Grief. A broken heart.

Frankie doesn't say any of the words in her head out loud. She rarely does, even when she is alone. Her chest feels tight, as though she might have forgotten how to breathe. She stares at the woman, then down at her gloved hands and feels the pain from the paper cut on her finger. How can something so small hurt so much? There are no cuts on Clio's hands, instead she has neat red nails to match the dress, the trainers, the lipstick.

The oversized metal clock on the wall seems to get louder, as though mocking Frankie and all the thoughts buzzing around inside her head.

Ticktock. *Go home.* Ticktock. *Get out.* Ticktock. *Leave now.*

"Take your time," Clio says, as though she thinks she can read Frankie's mind.

She can't. She wouldn't have invited her in if she could.

Time is something Frankie struggles to tell these days. Time can be borrowed, wasted, or stolen. Time can bend or break, it can hurt or heal. Time can rewrite history. But time is too precious to be taken. *People* get taken from our lives and sometimes they never come back. Frankie has *taken her time* for far too long.

She stares at the clock again as it counts away the seconds and minutes too fast. She needs to count things of her own to drown it out, but there is so little to focus on in the room.

Four walls, three windows, two chairs, one woman in the pink house.

Frankie shakes her head, as though trying to dislodge some suitable words. The ones that escape surprise her.

"I'm here because of my daughter," she manages to say.

It is the truth and a lie at the same time. Clio's eyes stare at her with a mix of curiosity and kindness that seem genuine, willing her to continue, completely oblivious that Frankie has lost everything because of what Clio did.

"Do you want to talk about your daughter?" she asks.

No, I want to talk about the weather.

Frankie sees a flash of something in the woman's eyes and worries that she has spoken out loud. But it is like a flickering flame and once the breeze of her words has died down, Clio resumes her penetrating stare.

Frankie can't tell Clio that her only child ran away from home a year ago.

Frankie won't tell her why.

She isn't going to look for something she'll never find anymore.

"I don't know if I can do this," Frankie whispers, trying to blink her tears away.

Clio offers her a tissue from a pretty silver box, but she doesn't take one. Can't. Won't. The only things she came here for are answers and an ending. A tiny frown forms on Clio's face, ruining its perfection.

"Are you all right?" Clio asks, leaning forward a little, as if genuinely wanting to know.

As though she cares.

"No," says Frankie with a little shake of her head, still avoiding eye contact. It is an honest answer and she starts to count one last time.

Four walls, three windows, two chairs, one woman in the pink house.

Frankie glances at the clock again. Her appointment is nearly over, her hour is almost up. It is now or maybe never.

"My name is Frankie Fletcher. You don't know me, but I'm here because—"

The sound of a mobile phone rudely interrupts the speech that Frankie has spent weeks rehearsing. The ringtone is ridiculous, as though mocking her.

"I'm *so* sorry," Clio says. She reaches inside an invisible pocket in her dress, takes out the phone, frowns but then taps the screen. "I thought it was on silent. It's very unprofessional of me and I apologize. Do go on."

Frankie stares open-mouthed. Things are not going according to plan.

Four walls, three windows, two chairs, one woman in the pink house.

The awkwardness of the scenario feels infinite and obscene. Frankie begins her preprepared speech again, as though she can only remember her lines if she starts from the beginning.

"My name is Frankie Fletcher. You don't know me, but I'm here because—"

The mobile phone starts to ring in the woman's hand, but silently this time.

Clio squints at the vibrating phone and stabs the screen with one of her red nails. "Sorry, again. Please continue."

Frankie can feel herself starting to sweat, even though the temperature in the perfect room, in the perfect pink house is, of course, perfect. She shakes her head in disbelief, takes a deep breath, then tries once more.

"My name is Frankie—"

The old rotary phone on Clio's desk starts to ring then. The landline is high-pitched and relentless.

"I'm so sorry, I really am. I can only imagine there must be some kind of family emergency," Clio says, rolling her chair over to the desk and picking up the phone.

Family.

The word feels like a slap.

Clio's face drains of color as she listens to whoever is speaking. "I understand. I'm going to call you from a different number in less than a minute," she says, putting the phone down and turning to Frankie. "I just need a moment. It is an emergency and I have to take the call, but I'll be right back, so stay there." She leaves the room without another word, closing the door behind her.

Frankie looks around in disbelief, wondering what she is supposed to do now. Then she stands and starts pacing as though she is locked in a cell. In some ways she is: we all build our own prisons, constructed from bricks of fear and invisible bars. She counts her steps from one side of the room to the other, but stops when she hears a police siren in the distance. It suddenly occurs to her that she does not know who the woman was speaking to on the phone. What if the woman in the pink house already knows who Frankie is? What if she has secretly called the police? The siren outside is getting louder. The alarm bells ringing in her head are joined by the alarm on her phone going off, informing her that her appointment is over. The clock on the wall chimes in agreement.

Frankie starts to panic, but then she spots something and time slows down until it feels as though it has stopped. She didn't notice the piece of art on the wall next to the window when she first walked in—why would she with so many other distractions and things on her mind—and she couldn't see it from where she was sitting before, it wasn't directly in her eyeline. But now that she does finally see it, Frankie stands perfectly still and stares at the small, framed papercut. The intricate design has layers of black paper trees over a turquoise background, and the trees have eyes. Lots of them. In the corner she sees a hand-drawn ladybug. Frankie recognizes the style of the artwork immediately, and the familiar delicate shape of the cuts in the card. It is beautiful and unique and she knows who made it. What she doesn't understand, is how a piece of art by her missing daughter ended up on a wall belonging to the woman in the pink house.

Clio

Clio stands in the hallway of her beautiful Notting Hill town house. She listens to a voice on the other end of her phone, but feels unable to process the words she hears. The first few were easy enough to comprehend:

"Hello, I'm calling from the Windsor Care Home. It's about your mother . . ."

After that, it is as though the woman is speaking a foreign language. Her words sound familiar, but Clio struggles to translate them. They are too hard, too heavy, too final. Too frightening. Clio needs to sit down. She perches on the bottom step of the staircase, just like she did as a child. She feels like one now.

"Are you sure?" Clio asks. It seems like a strange question, given the circumstances.

"I'm so sorry to be calling with such upsetting news," says the voice. Clio wonders how often the stranger on the phone has to make calls like this one. Weekly? Daily? She guesses that delivering bad news is surely part of the job in a care home for the elderly.

They probably have a prepared script. The line has been silent for an awkward amount of time, so Clio tries and fails to compose herself. The person she wants to call is the one person she can't. Whatever words she ought to say in response won't come out, and Clio doesn't know what to do or how to feel.

"I'm on my way," she says eventually, not moving.

"You don't have to—"

"It's fine," Clio insists.

She hangs up while still sitting on the stairs, her phone in her hands, her thoughts elsewhere. Then she remembers the woman sitting in the consultation room, what was her name? She said it often enough as though it was supposed to mean something. Clio wishes she had said no to seeing a new client on a Sunday now, but the woman sounded so desperate on the phone. And Clio needs the money. Houses like this and habits like hers are not cheap.

Clio writes notes about each client after every session, and keeps them in numbered case files in a large pink filing cabinet in her office. She can't remember the woman's name, but the new client is Case File 999. It feels like it might have been a warning now. Or a sign. But Clio doesn't believe in those. She does believe in being professional at all times, and abandoning Case File 999 during their first session together is far from ideal. Hopefully any damage can be swiftly repaired.

Clio stands and smooths down her dress, wishing it were so easy to remove the other unwanted creases and folds from her life. The choices we make when we are young can haunt us forever. If she could go back, warn her younger self not to make the mistakes that cost her everything, of course she would. Clio doesn't believe people who say they have no regrets, they are the kind of clients no amount of therapy can help. She checks her reflection in the hallway mirror, adjusts her face, and tries to look like the version of her who knows how to help people. She sees a spot of something red on her chin and wipes it away, disappointed with herself for not noticing it earlier. She feels like a fraud; her own life is far more of a mess than any of her clients' lives. Like all medicine, giving advice to others is easier than taking your own.

All she has to do is apologize to the new client, explain what has happened, and ask the woman to come back another time. Both appointments will be complimentary, that ought to do the trick. Something for nothing can dilute most forms of disappointment. But nothing in life is ever free, not really. Clio thinks most people would be far happier if they accepted that fact. She takes a breath, paints a smile on her face, and opens the door.

Clio is about to say how sorry she is, but the consulting room is empty.

She would have seen if Case File 999 had left the house—the woman would have had to walk straight past her in the hallway to get to the front door. That isn't the only thing that has changed. A piece of art is missing from one of the walls and an old ten-pound note has been stuck in its place. After thirty years of working as a counselor Clio thought she had seen and heard it all. Apparently she was wrong. The thin white curtains billow slightly, blown by the breeze like two lazy ghosts, and Clio sees that the sash window is wide open.

Case File 999 has climbed out of it and taken the framed papercut with her.

Frankie

Frankie's narrow boat, *The Black Sheep*, has been moored to this quiet corner of the River Thames for ten years. It was her favorite place in the world until it wasn't. Even when she and her daughter had to move location—which they often did—the boat was always home. The Thames is the longest river in England, winding its way through nine different counties—as well as the city of London—and traveling on the water is a good way to get from one part of the country to another undetected.

Frankie can't stop thinking about the woman in the pink house. She went there to tell the truth, not to find it, but truth is like water and always leaks out eventually. Everything is different now. She has a reason to hope, an incentive to carry on. There might still be a way to get her little girl back. One person's truth is rarely exactly the same as someone else's. Truth tends to stretch and bend out of shape to best fit its owner. People remember things differently and our memories can make liars of us all. But the woman in the pink house is definitely a liar, Frankie knows that much is true.

One of the biggest benefits of living on a narrow boat—and there are many—was that whenever danger felt close enough to find them, all they had to do was turn the key and sail away. It's easy to be invisible if you can make yourself disappear. The boat might only be capable of traveling at six miles an hour, but it had proved itself to be the perfect getaway vehicle on more than one occasion. Besides, mathematicians agreed that six was the smallest perfect number. The word *six* means "flow" in Chinese, and people all over the world think it is lucky. The only reason Frankie hasn't sailed away already this time, is because then her daughter wouldn't know where to find her.

Frankie was only eighteen when her little girl was born, around the same age her daughter is now. She was a beautiful baby but she did cry a lot back then. Frankie was determined to love the child the way she wished she had been loved, but those first few months of being a single mum, while still a child herself, were the most difficult of her life. The overwhelming responsibility, the permanent exhaustion, the fear: it isn't something you can ever really explain to someone who hasn't gone through it.

Things were tough financially too, but Frankie always found ways to make ends meet. She grew vegetables in pots and grow-bags on the deck, and had a pet chicken called Eggitha Christie who gave them more fresh eggs than they could eat. They didn't have much in terms of material things, but they didn't want for anything either. They had each other and that was enough. For a while at least. Life has a funny way of giving you joy then taking it back.

The red and black narrow boat was called *The Black Sheep* when Frankie inherited it, and she saw no reason to change the name. We all need someone or something familiar to cling to when we come unmoored, drifting can be dangerous. The boat is a bit of a Tardis: much bigger than it looks from the outside. It takes thirty-two steps to walk from one end to the other. There are eight little round portholes, each offering a different view of the riverbank and the weeping willow trees that sway outside. Despite being a narrow boat, it is still large enough to have two bedrooms— one at each end—a compact bathroom, and a generous living area in the middle of the boat, consisting of a small galley kitchen and a snug with a wood-burning stove.

Frankie opens the stove door wearing a novelty oven glove shaped like a fox, and puts another log inside. A large fly buzzes around the boat, distracting her from her thoughts, so she grabs a nearby can of Mr. Sheen—which is good for more than just polishing—sprays the fly, and watches it fall to the floor. The silence that follows seems just as loud. Frankie doesn't know what to do now that things didn't go according to plan. She stops putting off the inevitable and walks the fifteen steps from the snug to her daughter's bedroom. She knows she'll have to switch the light on and off three times, so does it quickly. The first time is fine. The next time the room lights up, despite being so fast, Frankie imagines seeing a girl crying on the bed. The third time the room is empty again.

You're okay. You're okay. You're okay, Frankie whispers to herself. If she says the words often enough she hopes they might sound true.

Her daughter's bedroom is exactly the way it was before she ran away. There is artwork on the walls, clothes on the chair, a cuddly toy on top of the pillow. The lid of the old upright piano is open, which is strange; Frankie thought she'd closed it. The cold, and maybe something else, ushers her out of the room and her fifteen steps back to the snug feel like a speedy retreat. She folds herself into the little armchair next to the wood-burning stove, and stares at the flames as they dance and flicker, casting a moving pattern of shadows around the boat. This is her favorite corner of *The Black Sheep*: her own little reading nook. There is an old oak bookcase draped in fairy lights, its shelves crammed full with her favorite novels and a collection of scented candles. She lights the one that claims to help people relax. In case that doesn't work—it never has before—Frankie removes the cork from an already opened bottle next to her chair and pours some red wine into her Mum mug. She used to drink wine like this when her daughter was still here, pretending it was tea. She notices the small cut on her finger again as she raises the mug to her lips. A paper cut is a tree's revenge, so she puts another log in the stove.

Paper has played a big role in her life: she works with books, all of the stories Frankie has read and loved during her lifetime were printed on paper, and her daughter enjoyed nothing more than cutting beautiful pictures out of it. She looks at the framed papercut leaning against the wall, the one she stole from the pink house earlier, and it is like staring at a ghost. Her daughter made that papercut. Frankie is sure of it and for the first time in a long time she feels something resembling hope.

There is no signature on the artwork—just what looks like a hand-drawn ladybug in the bottom right-hand corner—but there is a name printed on a shiny gold sticker on the back of the frame: *Kennedy's Gallery, Covent Garden*. The name and the place are familiar, it is somewhere Frankie visited many years ago. The gallery would be closed now, but she plans to go there as soon as it opens in the morning. The wind has picked up outside, enough to make the river a little choppy and the narrow boat creak and sway from side to side. Sometimes—when there's a storm—the pictures swing on the walls. Frankie starts to pour herself another glass of wine before realizing the bottle is empty. It's no bother, she has another one like it. Her tolerance of alcohol has always been higher than her tolerance of people. She doesn't drink for pleasure, she drinks for pain. And oblivion. But before she can find the corkscrew, she hears the sound of the piano. Just two keys at first. Played so quietly, she almost doesn't register them at all.

Frankie is alone on the boat, she is sure of that. She always locks the door as soon as she steps on board—locking doors is a hard habit to break when you work in a prison. She wonders if her imagination or tiredness are playing tricks on her, but then she hears the two notes a second time.

Her mind tries to calm itself by counting as she creeps toward her daughter's room.

Five steps from the snug to the kitchen.

The boat is still rocking from side to side, and she hears the piano again.

Four steps to the tiny passageway.

A piano has eighty-eight keys. Fifty-two white keys. Thirty-six black keys.

Three steps to the end of the boat.

There is definitely a storm on the way. Maybe she imagined the sound.

Two steps to her daughter's bedroom.

She hears the piano once more. Louder this time.

One step to the bedroom door.

It is open.

Frankie thought she had closed it.

It's too dark to see inside the room, so she stands perfectly still in the doorway, listening to the imperfect silence as the sound of river water laps against the hull. She *must* have imagined it. Her daughter used to play the piano and Frankie has scared herself into hearing the ghosts of her own memories.

She turns and starts to walk away, keen to get back to that unopened bottle.

The sound of the piano starts again.

Loud but not clear.

There is no discernible melody, just noise, like someone hitting all of the piano keys at once. The sound gets louder as Frankie turns back toward the bedroom, her trembling fingers reaching for the light switch.

Clio

Clio resents having to leave the house again, twice in one day is two times too many. But given the phone call she received it would seem strange, suspicious even, if she didn't return to the Windsor Care Home. She is happiest in her own home, where she feels in control, queen of her own—albeit lonely—castle. Not that she'd ever share that information with anyone. The person she presents to the world no longer has much in common with the person she has become.

When they finally arrive she pays the taxi driver—the exact amount, no tip—and heads back inside the care home. The cab ride here was painfully slow, thanks to London's all-day rush hour and the cabbie's tedious attempts at small talk. It gave Clio too much time to think unwelcome thoughts. As she walks into the building, every step she takes feels heavy, as though she can't remember how to walk forward. Or as if something deep inside her is warning her to keep out, turn back, stay away.

Inside, the place is almost too quiet and calm. Not at all what she was expecting. There is nobody in the hallway or the lounge, just the sound of muffled voices down the corridor and out of sight. Clio doesn't waste her time looking for the care home manager, or any member of staff, instead she quietly heads up to the top floor, taking the steps two at a time. She's almost certain the elevator will be out of use, it normally is. Clio is keen to get back to her mother's room and preferably alone. After all, that *is* what you're supposed to do when you lose something—retrace your steps.

There have been so many false alarms from the care home before today. Too many. Clio remembers them all:

"Your mother seems confused."

Nothing new there.

"Your mother is refusing to eat."

She refused to eat when Clio tried to cook for her too.

Your mother had a fall.

Probably doing something she shouldn't have been doing.

Clio has been a therapist for too long not to recognize classic cries for attention. That's often all they were. But *this* feels different.

"I'm so sorry, she's gone. We did everything that we could."

Clio used to visit once a week when her mother first moved into the Windsor Care Home. Until she made a friend named May, a few months in, Edith refused to come downstairs like the other residents. Clio would sit in her mother's bedroom for an hour every Tuesday, but Edith wouldn't speak to her and made it clear that she didn't want to see her daughter anymore. So Clio stopped visiting. When her mother kept refusing to speak on the phone, Clio stopped calling. It wasn't the first time they had deliberately lost touch. Their relationship has had more downs than ups, and there have been multiple occasions over the years when they haven't spoken to each other for months. Ever since Clio was a teenager, things between them have been delicate and difficult.

Edith wanted to live with Clio in the pink house, not move into a care home. But living under the same roof wasn't a good idea: the house is too small (a lie), the stairs are too steep and narrow (the truth), it is where Clio works and she doesn't have time to keep checking up on/caring for her mother (a lie and the truth). Clio just didn't want to (the whole truth). Her home is also her office—she sees clients most days—she doesn't have the time, patience, or energy to take care of her elderly mother on top of all that. Or her flea-ridden dog. A residential care home was the only option, but Edith used the situation to paint her daughter as a villain to anyone who would listen.

They hadn't seen or spoken to each other for months again until today. And now this.

Clio navigates her way through the maze of corridors and guilt until she finds herself outside room thirteen. She gently pushes the unlocked door open, and feels a strange sense of relief when she sees that the room—and bed—are empty. Unsure of how long she has to do this before someone else comes along, Clio starts looking for clues. Anything that someone who didn't know what to look for might have missed. There is a pot of her mother's favorite moisturizer on the dressing table, the same brand she has been using for thirty years. Not all of the memories it stirs are unwelcome—she had a happy childhood until she didn't—and Clio slips the cream into her pocket.

She bends down to look under the bed. Her mother's old pink leather suitcase is missing, and all Clio finds are some half-eaten packets of custard creams, a *Radio Times* magazine, a single slipper, two paperbacks, and a Scrabble board. She has no idea where her mother has been getting these things from. By all accounts Edith never left her room, let alone the care home. She checks inside the bedside cabinet and is surprised to find some letters. The first is from a lawyer, and Clio's hands start to tremble as she reads it. We don't always know what we're looking for until we find it.

At first Clio can't quite process what the words mean.

Based on the evidence you have provided, we would be happy to assist you in reversing the power of attorney.

She turns the page and carries on reading.

As you know, we have a no win, no fee policy. Rest assured we are confident that we can get your home back and evict any existing tenants.

She checks the date on the letter before reading on, and sees it was sent this week.

And we have changed your will as instructed. A copy is in the post.

Clio drops the letter. This is something her mother failed to mention earlier. She opens the other envelopes that were in the bedside table, until she finds one with a thick wad of papers inside. She feels sick as soon as she starts to read them.

It is true. Her mother has somehow changed her will, and Clio feels a mix of hurt and rage. She skim-reads the rest of the document until she finds the important bit. Everything her mother still had—a small but significant amount of shares and savings—was supposed to be divided between two people and Clio was meant to be one of them. Now there is only one name in the will and it isn't hers.

She takes one last look around room thirteen but sees nothing of value or interest except for a curious-looking notebook beside the bed. The front cover says "List of Regrets and Good Ideas." Clio recognizes her mother's handwriting. She turns to the first page.

LIST OF REGRETS
1. My daughter

Clio slams the notebook closed and puts it in her handbag along with the lawyer's letters. If she can prove her mother is unhinged— which shouldn't be too difficult—there might be a way to invalidate the new will. Satisfied that she hasn't missed any clues, and that there is nothing in the room to suggest or explain where her mother is now, she leaves the room. Clio hurries back down the carpeted stairs, but everything is still surprisingly quiet when she reaches the ground floor. It's been hours since her mother went missing, and they clearly haven't found her yet. The only person in the normally busy hallway is a smartly dressed young woman in her late twenties. She has shoulder-length blond hair with a single pink highlight on one side, and is wearing a tweed trouser suit over a *Star Wars* T-shirt. Clio needs to talk to *someone* about what has happened, and guesses this girl might be the night manager. She's far too young for the job, but it can't be easy finding staff to work in a place like this.

"Excuse me, are you in charge?" Clio asks.

The young woman half smiles. "Yes, I suppose I am."

"Was it you who called about my mother?"

"No. I don't think so."

The effort it takes to remain polite is exhausting—the staff here have always been incompetent—but good manners tend to result in better results than bad ones, so Clio persists. "Well, do you know who did?"

"I can't say that I do but—"

"You do work here, don't you?"

"I am working but I don't work here," says the young woman, speaking in riddles and tucking the silly strand of pink hair behind her heavily pierced ears. She studies Clio in a way that Clio normally studies others and it is unnerving. Clio waits for her to say more but she doesn't. Sometimes the gaps between a person's words are more interesting than the words themselves.

"Sorry, I don't understand," Clio says eventually.

"I'm a detective," the woman replies, as though that should be a sufficient explanation.

Clio flushes with embarrassment and something else but soon

recovers. "Then you *do* know about my mother. She's the one who has gone missing. I presume that's why you're here?"

The detective shakes her head. "I'm not here about a missing person. I'm here about a murder."

Patience

I walk faster than normal across the cobbled street in Covent Garden. It feels as though I need to put as much distance as possible between myself and what I already know I am going to be accused of. But there is something else I need to take care of first. *Someone* else. If I can stick to the plan until tomorrow then maybe everything will be okay. I pop to the corner shop to get supplies, then head toward St. Paul's church.

Not to confess. I need to collect what I have hidden there.

Covent Garden used to be covered in fields a couple of hundred years ago. Those fields were turned into an enormous fruit and vegetable market, which has since turned into shops and buildings which have become a tourist hot spot near London's best theaters. There are very few actual gardens in Covent Garden these days, except for the magical one behind St. Paul's church. It's my favorite place to hide when real life gets too loud.

It's known as the actors' church, because of its location I suppose, in the heart of London's Theatreland. I think I could have been a good actor: I've had plenty of experience. Most people play the roles life casts them in without even knowing that's what they're doing.

The benches in the pretty secret garden outside the church are all engraved with meaningful messages. I pass my favorite which says: *Promise you won't forget me. If I thought you would, I'd never leave.* I think there are two kinds of people in the world: the ones who wish never to be forgotten, and the others who hope not to be noticed in the first place. I seem to be both, depending on my mood.

It feels colder inside the church than it did outside. My footsteps echo on the ancient stone floor and the place has an eerie feel to it. I spot the old pink leather suitcase exactly where I left it and feel a rush of relief.

"Did you remember to buy custard creams?" asks Edith, holding the suitcase in one hand and a dog lead in the other. Dickens wags his tail when he sees me.

"Yes, and the tea, a pint of milk, and a bottle of chardonnay. I'm sorry it took so long. I had to be sure the coast was clear and that it was safe to take you home."

"Oh, I'm so excited! I haven't had a glass of wine for months *and* I'm finally going home!" Edith replies. I don't bother to correct her that it's *my* home we're going to. She is still wearing my hoodie over her own clothes and it's not a terrible disguise.

"I got you a treat too," I tell Dickens and he wags his tail again. He's been eyeing up the bowls of cat food in the church, left here for hungry strays. I've always found it strange how some people care more about lost animals than they do about lost humans.

Edith smiles. "Thank you for helping me escape, Ladybug."

"You're welcome," I reply. It isn't as though I had much of a choice. "I just hope we don't get into too much trouble."

"If you don't go looking for trouble it won't find you. Stop fretting. Everything will be all right in the end. If it isn't, then it isn't the end yet."

Frankie

There is an intruder in Frankie's home. She didn't imagine the sound of the piano's keys, but the overwhelming terror she felt before has been replaced with extreme irritation. Frankie does not like cats. Especially black ones who come onto her boat uninvited, let themselves inside her daughter's bedroom, and jump all over the piano. Not to mention them being bad luck, which is something she has already had more than enough of.

"This boat is called *The Black Sheep*, not *The Black Cat*," she says, picking up the creature, holding it at arm's length, and carrying it outside. The cat stares at her with big green eyes when she sets it down on the riverbank, then runs away, disappearing into the shadows.

It takes a while to clean her daughter's bedroom. Frankie hoovers and dusts and polishes with Mr. Sheen until she is satisfied that there are no traces of the uninvited guest. She wants the room to be *exactly* as it was—a bit of a mess but impeccably clean—just in case. She's shocked when she checks her Mickey Mouse watch and sees how late it is. The watch is one of the only things Frankie still has from when she was a little girl—it was her mother's—and she wonders if it might be time to get a new one, and to stop holding on to a past she can't change.

Frankie was determined to create a better childhood for her own daughter. She tried to make sure her little girl knew she was loved, and created a home where she would always be safe and welcome. She was homeschooled and Frankie kept close tabs on who she spent time with. They moved around a lot, but her daughter was good at making new friends to replace old ones. The River Thames was home more often than not, but they'd spent time living on Grand Union and Regent's Canal too. Frankie knew that leaving a place sometimes made her daughter feel sad, but it was important not to get complacent, or too fond of one location, in case they needed to move again. There had been no need to run away for years until her daughter did. Now Frankie is even more careful than she was before.

There are hardly any personal items belonging to Frankie on the boat, only small things she could easily grab if she needed to leave in a hurry. Like a precious photo album containing pictures of her daughter growing up. There are no letters, no bills, no paperwork. Frankie double-checks that the front door is locked, then switches off all of the lights, before heading to her bedroom at the other end of the boat. She lies down on the bed in the darkness and relives the last time she saw her little girl, replaying what they said to each other, just like she always does before she goes to sleep.

"You promised to tell me who my father was when I turned eighteen."

"I can't," Frankie whispered then and now.

So her daughter left, to try to find him herself.

It was a story that was never going to have a happy ending.

Frankie did what she did to protect her daughter from the truth. She didn't have a choice but it cost her everything. The worst parts of our history have a bad habit of repeating themselves. And then today—despite all of her planning—everything went wrong.

Probably because Frankie was so upset before her appointment at the pink house.

How was she supposed to know that popping into the care home to pay someone a quick visit would end the way did?

Clio

"A murder?" Clio says.

"Yes," the detective replies. "I'm afraid you've stumbled into a crime scene so I'm going to need to find someone to interview you—"

"Who?"

"A junior detective. We have to interview everyone at the—"

"No, I mean who has been murdered?"

"I really can't say until we've spoken to the next of kin."

"But I received a phone call earlier, about my mother. They said she was missing . . ."

"It's not your mother."

"How do you know?"

Clio feels the detective studying her and the experience is unsettling. She is relieved when some police officers interrupt them and begin cordoning off the care home with tape. The detective untucks a strand of pink hair that was behind her pierced ear, then folds her skinny arms across her flat chest. Clients often do a similar thing, it's a classic sign of anxiety, a way to create a physical barrier when feeling overwhelmed. The young woman is clearly out of her depth. "My own beloved grandmother passed away in a place *just* like this. And before her time, if you ask me," she says.

It seems like an odd thing to say and Clio hadn't. She wrinkles her nose without meaning to. "I didn't catch your name."

"My bad, I didn't introduce myself. DCI Charlotte Chapman," the detective says holding out a hand. Clio notices that her finger-nails are painted different colors, and can't help thinking that the woman is too young, and too inappropriately dressed, to be a detective. "What do *you* think would make someone kill a care home manager? In your *professional* opinion?" DCI Chapman asks.

Clio looks shocked. "I thought you needed to inform the next of kin."

"I do."

"Then why are—"

"You're a psychiatrist, aren't you?"

Clio wrinkles her nose again. "I'm a therapist. How do you know who I am?"

"It's my job to know who people are, what they do, what they are capable of doing. I get the impression that the care home manager wasn't a popular woman."

Clio shrugs. "I wouldn't know."

The detective takes out a notebook, licks her finger, and flips through a few pages. She doesn't seem at all anxious or out of depth now. "Forgive me: You are Clio Kennedy, aren't you? The red dress and matching red trainers made me think that you were." Clio frowns. "You were seen and heard arguing with the care home manager earlier today. Joy Bonetta threatened to evict your mother because you can no longer afford the fees. Is that correct?"

"Seen by *who*?" Clio asks, but then remembers the crusty old man loitering outside Joy's office door earlier.

"Interesting question, but not the right one. Do you always take the stairs here, even though your mother's room is on the top floor?"

Clio feels her cheeks flush. "Exercise isn't a crime, is it?"

"Depends who you ask. Murder, on the other hand, most definitely is. It seems a little strange to me that you didn't take the elevator just now."

"It seems a little strange to me that you are wasting my time instead of doing your job."

The detective half smiles again. "You threatened the care home manager earlier today, and were heard saying . . ." she checks her notes once more. "Let's see, 'I will end you if anything happens to my mother.' Does that ring a bell? Now your mother is missing and Joy is dead. It's not my first murder case, but it is the first time I've arrived at the scene and found a dead woman in an elevator with a sign around her neck. Whoever did this wanted the world to know that Joy, like the elevator, was out of order."

"Should you really be telling me all of this?" Clio asks.

"Only if I want to see your reaction to what I am saying. Did you know someone else visited the care home pretending to be you this afternoon and signed the visitor book with your name?" Clio stares at her but doesn't answer. "It is a tad suspicious finding you at the scene of the crime, snooping about the place."

"I'm not *snooping*. As you said, my mother is *missing*."

"Well, that is something we can at least agree on. And yet here you are, in the one place she isn't. It's early days of course, but the way I see this case at the moment, there are three suspects, two murders, and one victim. You, Clio Kennedy, are currently suspect number one."

Patience

"This isn't *home*," Edith says as I usher her down the dark alley at the side of the art gallery.

"No," I reply. "But it's somewhere I think we'll be safe for tonight. This is where Dickens has been living with me these past few months." Edith looks suitably unimpressed. She doesn't look like herself at all wearing my hoodie, and there is an edge to her I've not witnessed before.

"This street looks familiar—where are we?" she asks.

"Covent Garden."

"I know that," she snaps, although I'm not convinced she did. "This small world of ours has shrunk into a small town." I'm not sure what she means, but then she softens into the version of Edith I know. "Well, if this is what you think is best. I trust you."

I almost wish she didn't.

Dickens runs up ahead, climbing the familiar one hundred and twenty-three steps. Edith needs to take them a little more slowly, so we stop for several breaks along the way. She uses the handrail to heave herself up, determined to reach the top. I take almost all of her bags as well as the old suitcase, and hold her other hand to make sure she doesn't topple over.

"Almost there," I say.

"I do hope so," she replies, a little out of breath as I unlock the attic door.

"Oh my," Edith gasps as she steps inside. "It's like being inside an art gallery. A wonderful one," she says, staring at all my papercuts, which cover every inch of the walls. "Ladybug, you should be very proud. You really are an artist."

I feel myself blush. It seems strange to let someone see my work before I am ready to share it with people. It's hard to describe the feeling I get when someone says they like what I have created—there is nothing quite like it. Sometimes it feels like magic, making something out of nothing with just some paper and a knife. I think we all start off as blank canvasses before the world paints us with thoughts and feelings we pretend are our own. And I like that. It means we are capable of change. Each piece of work is a labor of love and hate and pain and joy, and there is a little piece of me in all of them. I never sign my name, but since Edith started calling me Ladybug, I've been drawing one in the bottom corner of each papercut. Just to know they are mine.

Dickens heads straight for his dog bed, turns in a circle three times, then lies down and closes his eyes. I'm glad he knows to make himself at home and hope Edith will do the same.

"You can get changed back into your own clothes now if you want?" I say to her.

"I think that's a good idea. I look like a hooligan or someone who chooses to be unemployed, wearing this thing, no offense. I've never liked *hoodies* but I confess they are rather comfortable. Can I have a little privacy while I change, dear?"

"Of course," I say. Edith and her old suitcase disappear inside my excuse for a bathroom. She reappears a short time later wearing a polka-dot dress and cotton cardigan. She laughs when she sees that I keep the milk out on the window ledge.

"Do you want a cup of tea?" I ask.

"Why on earth would we drink tea when we have wine?"

I laugh too, and the sound it makes is strange, unfamiliar. I help her slide the suitcase under the bed—there is nowhere else to put it—then concentrate on opening the bottle of chardonnay. My heart sinks.

"I don't have any wineglasses," I say.

"You must have something we can use."

It feels wrong to be celebrating after what happened earlier, but I pour some wine into a tumbler for Edith and drink mine from my mug. Doing so reminds me of my mother.

"Do you think we'll get away with it?" Edith asks.

I choke on my wine. "Get away with what?"

She laughs. "Running away!"

"Oh, that. Time will tell."

"I hope not but I suppose it might. Time can only keep our secrets for so long."

The sound of footsteps coming up the stairs startles me, as it always does. Edith looks equally scared when she sees my expression. I try to appear and remain calm—as though there is nothing to worry about—then I hold my finger to my lips and she nods in understanding. I flick off the lights that can be seen from beneath the door and we sit in the dark in silence. The moonlight from the window shines a natural spotlight on the door, and the night-light illuminates our anxious faces with moving stars.

Someone knocks once. Then again.

We can see their shadow beneath the frame.

"Hello?" says a man's voice. "Is anyone in there?" I don't answer. "I've got a large pepperoni, some garlic bread, and two chocolate brownies. The address just said the attic above the art gallery. Is anyone home?"

"Yes," I say, opening the door just enough to take the pizza I had forgotten ordering. "We're home."

Clio

"I'm leaving now," Clio says to the detective. "You've kept me hanging around for ages and I've got better things to do."

"Like look for your mother? I quite agree. Don't worry, we know where you live if we need to speak to you again," DCI Chapman replies. Everything about her—the blond hair with a strand of pink, her stick insect figure, her attitude, her age, her wrinkle-free, beautiful skin—irritates Clio to her core.

"Is there a reason why you are being so rude to me?" Clio asks, not really wanting to know the answer.

"Probably, you're the expert. Isn't everything linked to mommy issues these days? Please don't take it personally, I'm told I'm rude to everyone." The detective turns and leaves the room before Clio has a chance to reply.

A police officer leads Clio toward the back of the care home, away from the main entrance which is now a hive of activity. She glances over her shoulder to see the hallway filled with people wearing forensic suits. Once outside, she walks along the street until she is far enough away from the care home, the cordon, the police cars, and DCI Chapman to not be seen. Then she takes some deep breaths and tries to calm herself. She managed to keep it together until this moment—it's amazing what our bodies are capable of when it comes to self-preservation— but now she is trembling all over. Her legs feel too shaky to walk on, as though she might fall if she tries, so she leans against a wall to get her balance. If people knew she had been questioned by the police, about a *murder*, she doesn't think she could live it down. She could lose everything she's worked so hard to hold on to. Clio hasn't smoked for over twenty years but she'd kill for a cigarette right now. She could kill *him* too. She is tired of always being the one to deal with things and figure everything out on her own, so she tries to call *him* again. His phone seems to be permanently switched off and she wonders what lies he'll tell this time: working late, dinner with a client, forgot his charger. Or perhaps he'll surprise her with a new excuse. It seems doubtful, having known him for all these years. Predictably he doesn't answer, so for now she has no choice but to hail a taxi and go home.

Back in the pink house she locks the doors, then pulls all the blinds and curtains. After that she turns off the lights and heads up to bed. She checks to see if there are any emails from clients wanting to book sessions. There aren't. Instead, her inbox is clogged full of emails about Mother's Day. It makes Clio want to unsubscribe from every company that sent them and she deletes them all. Sometimes she wishes she could unsubscribe from her life and sign up for a new one. She tries to sleep, when she can't she tries to meditate, but the thoughts about her mother and what happened today are too loud.

Clio replays today's events over and over, trying to imagine a different outcome, aware that her own doubts betray her true feelings. People only question whether they did the right thing when they fear what they did was wrong.

How did it come to this? The memories flash in her mind like snapshots. Some of the ones that haunt her the hardest are from her early childhood, when it was just the two of them: her and her mother. The worst are from a couple of decades ago. The woman Edith was then is almost completely unrecognizable from the small, frail, elderly woman she saw in the care home today. Thoughts of her mother make Clio feel a mixture of anger, hurt, and guilt, just like always, but she has other things to worry about. Like not being able to afford to pay the mortgage this month. Life seems determined to replace one problem with another; there is always something to worry about.

She will call the bank in the morning, see if they can wait a little while longer.

Then she'll call the lawyer who has changed her mother's will.

Clio doesn't know how to solve the problem of DCI Chapman.

She calls *him* again, not caring about the late hour. With each unanswered ring another little piece of her dwindling patience expires. Clio doesn't leave a message. She stares at the ceiling in the darkened room, longing for sleep but unable to switch off her thoughts. She wonders what she would say to herself if she were one of her clients.

"When did the problems in your relationship with your mother begin?"

That's the question she would ask but it is a difficult one to answer. It's hard to pinpoint the moment when her relationship with her mother unraveled, there were so many. There was the time Clio announced she didn't want to be Catholic anymore. She stopped believing in God around the same time she stopped believing in Santa Claus, and her churchgoing mother didn't speak to her for weeks. What is a child supposed to do when they don't believe in the same things as their parents? There was the time Clio ran away as a teenager, her mother never really forgave her for what happened then. And then there was that terrible Mother's Day that destroyed whatever was left of their relationship. No wonder they had become strangers who just happened to be related.

She scrolls through a list of words in her mind before finding the right one.

Estranged. That's the word people use nowadays.

Clio looks it up on her phone, unsure why, as though the meaning of the word might explain why it happened:

estranged no longer close or affectionate to someone; alienated

The etymology of the word offers little comfort: taken from the French word *estrange*, which traces back to the Latin word:

extraneare to treat as a stranger
extraneous not belonging to the family

Clio used to have a family. She made her own when the one she was born into rejected her. She used to have people to love and be loved by, but not anymore. She glances around the beautiful bedroom and is proud of how far she has come from the horrible little bungalow where she grew up. The pink house really is a thing of beauty, a little big for one person perhaps, but Clio is never really alone. Her guilt and her grief are always with her. Like unwelcome tenants. She wanted her life to be about more than this or, perhaps, what she really wanted was less. It's funny, the versions of ourselves we show to the world and the ones we leave at home. Clio has been so many different people, to so many different people, that she sometimes struggles to remember how to be herself. Which is even sadder now that all of those people she was trying to please are gone.

The truth, which often hurts more than a lie, is that Clio's mother didn't love her. Didn't like her. Didn't want to know her. Abandoning a child doesn't always mean leaving them. The weight of rejection is still heavy even after all these years, but she's grown stronger as she has grown older, strong enough to rise above it.

Her mother didn't love her because she wasn't the daughter she wanted her to be.

That's the truth.

She picks up her phone and dials again. This time she does leave a message.

"We need to talk. Things haven't exactly gone according to plan. If this ends badly for me you ought to know it will end badly for you too."

Patience

I pour what is left of the wine into Edith's tumbler and my mug. I didn't think I could eat a thing after what happened earlier, but I've managed to devour half a pizza.

"Can I interest you in the final slice?" I ask Edith, holding out the box. Dickens sniffs the air and wags his tail. "Not *you*."

"No, thank you, Ladybug. It was a real treat though, I haven't had a takeaway for years!"

"Are you sure it's okay for you to drink another glass?"

"Unless you are expecting me to drive a car somewhere or operate heavy machinery. I did work on a building site once upon a time."

I smile. "No heavy machinery, not tonight anyway. Did *you* enjoy all the jobs you had?"

"My dear, most people work to earn money, simple as that. I didn't really enjoy working in a supermarket, just like I'm guessing you don't enjoy working in a care home. It was my job to catch desperate people doing desperate things and I felt sorry for all of them. There were plenty of times I wished I hadn't seen what I saw, or done what I did. But I was desperate too. I needed a job and that was all I could get after my daughter was born. I sometimes wish I had been a *real* detective—I was always pretty good at solving mysteries. I suppose we're all detectives in the story of our own lives. All searching for clues about why we are here, piecing together the fragments of our existence, trying to solve what and how and who we are compared with who we should be."

I think on her words for a while. The evening has been far more enjoyable than I expected. I've heard a lot of Edith's stories before— she does tend to repeat herself sometimes—but there were plenty of tales I didn't know. Edith has lived such an interesting life compared to me. She had all kinds of jobs before she became a mother and a store detective. She was a postwoman, theater usher, she once drove an ice cream van, and she worked as an air hostess for years before her daughter was born. It sounds as though that was her favorite job out of all of them.

"One of my adventures abroad resulted in Clio," she tells me. "I loved her father. We enjoyed secret rendezvous, gallivanting in Paris, Venice, Rome . . . I hoped we'd get married. Unfortunately he was already married to someone else, which I didn't know until after I got pregnant." She was a single mum, just like my mum. But I imagine that must have been even more difficult fifty years ago. I've never left England, but Edith has traveled so far and met so many interesting people. It seems unfair that she is alone at the end. Maybe she always was. Maybe we all are.

My phone buzzes on the bedside table but I choose to ignore it.

Edith stares at my mobile, then at me. "I know I'm old and a little out of touch, but isn't it customary to answer those things when they make a noise?"

"Not if it's someone you don't want to talk to." I pick up the phone, read the start of yet another message from Mr. Kennedy, and put it down again.

"Man trouble?" Edith asks.

"Ha! Something like that." Sometimes lies can save someone, not just hurt them. "Can I ask you something?"

Edith takes another sip of her chardonnay. "You can ask me anything, doesn't mean I have to answer."

"It's fine if you don't want to. Maybe it's because it is Mother's Day and I miss my mum, but I wondered what happened with you and your daughter. I know she put you in a home, and I know she took Dickens away from you—which is unforgivable—but she obviously cares. She was there for you today . . ." Edith looks away. I know she doesn't want to talk about this but there are things I think I need to know. "How did things get so . . . horrible between you?"

Edith sighs and puts down her glass. "We are not the sum of our children, they are an impossible equation which we must learn to love rather than try to solve. But love isn't always enough." I frown. "You'll understand one day when you have children of your own. I was young when I had my daughter and very much alone. I grew up in a small coastal village in Scotland and unmarried girls who got pregnant were not welcome. Rather than embarrass my own mother—who cared so much about what other people thought she forgot to have any opinions of her own—I moved to London. It was the best and worst thing to do in the circumstances but it meant I had no support: no family, and the people I thought were friends soon disappeared when I wasn't as much fun as I used to be. I worked and saved until the day before Clio was born. Then I worked even harder to keep a roof over our heads and food on the table. It wasn't perfect but I did my best."

"Did you love her?"

"Of course. I still do. You look surprised by that. There are infinite varieties of love. We've both made mistakes over the years but that doesn't mean I don't care about her anymore. She's lonely but alone by choice. I confess I've always found it a little strange that she chose a career involving helping others when she has never been able to help herself." She shakes her head and tuts. "I'm just too old and too tired of her blaming me for things that happened a long time ago. My daughter is the villain in my life, I am the villain in hers. We both believe our stories are true."

I stare at her, observing the faraway look on her face. It's as though she has disappeared inside a memory. A very sad one. "I'm still not sure I understand."

"Neither do I if I'm honest. I loved my daughter, still do, but sometimes love gets lost and no matter how hard you try you can't find it again. When you've lived as long as I have you learn that our memories can make liars of us all. No two people will remember a moment exactly the same way, and sometimes people don't agree on the facts of what did or didn't happen. I read once that there are two sides to every story and that means someone is always lying, but I don't think that's true. Truth bends. Sometimes it becomes unrecognizable. I didn't need to be the hero in her story, but I grew tired of her treating me like the villain."

I don't know what to say to that. Edith stares at my face as though reading my mind and asks a question I don't know how to answer.

"Tell me about your mother," Edith says, and I want to but I can't. She seems to sense my discomfort. "Do you miss her?" she asks.

Always.

"Sometimes," I say.

She nods. "You are not your story. How you got to this point in your life doesn't have to define the rest of it. You're still young enough to be whoever you want to be, but if you are lucky enough to be loved by someone you love too, don't ever let it go. That sort of thing doesn't happen too often, sometimes it doesn't happen at all. Write your own story and make it a good one."

I hear Big Ben start to chime midnight out above the rooftops in the distance.

"Maybe we should think about getting some sleep?" I say.

"Good thinking. I'm knackered, you must be too."

"You can have the bed and I'll be fine on the floor."

"Don't be a nincompoop. We'll share it."

"It's a single bed . . ."

"We'll go top-to-toe."

It isn't long before we are both tucked in at opposite ends of the bed, with Dickens making himself comfortable on top of the covers between us. I think Edith is asleep already, but then she whispers something which makes me want to cry.

"When someone you love becomes someone you can't, it is the very worst kind of heartbreak. Goodnight, Ladybug."

Frankie

Frankie's alarm goes off before sunrise, but as usual she is already awake. She normally likes Mondays—the start of a new week has always felt like a clean slate—but she has a bad feeling about today. It's as dark in her room as it is outside and she can still see the moon from her bedroom window. It's cold on the boat in the mornings, so she puts on two pairs of socks and wraps her robe around her. Then she shuffles toward the kitchen, hoping that a hot drink will warm and wake her up.

It's impossible not to be aware of the weather on a narrow boat, you can sometimes experience every season in a day. When it rains—like it is doing now—the sound on the roof is deafening. The boat feels at one with the river and the sky and it is good to feel connected to something. It reminds her of how small she is, how vulnerable, how insignificant. Just one storm could be the end of her *or* it might just pass her by. Sometimes trouble finds us no matter how hard we try to hide.

The kettle is also noisy and very old, but Frankie has never seen the point of replacing things that are not broken. She thinks she hears something on the deck but it's pitch-black outside the kitchen window, and all she can see is her own reflection. Old boats sometimes groan and creak just like old houses. Frankie finds her Mum mug and sees that there is a still a dribble of wine in it, she forgot to wash it before going to bed. She rinses it under the tap now, rolling up her sleeves to avoid getting them wet, and notices the tiny tattoo on her wrist. Frankie never wears short sleeves, even in summer, because she likes to keep it hidden.

The tattoo says *Shh* in an italic font.

She had it done years ago, to remind herself of the importance of secrets and the importance of keeping them. Everyone wants to excavate their problems these days. They all want to talk about what is bothering them rather than doing something to fix it. Talk talk talk. Share share share. Other people like to collect gossip. They feed on it, gobbling it down, too greedy to know when to stop, so that they get fat on the stale sugar of other people's lives. Frankie finds other people and the things they talk about exhausting. She's glad she lives alone. The thought is accompanied by a rush of guilt about her daughter. Then she thinks about yesterday—what she saw, what she did—and she knows she needs to keep busy, take her mind off everything that has happened and what might happen next.

She drops a tea bag in her mug.

Then she hears an unfamiliar sound out on the deck, again.

She didn't imagine it.

The rain has stopped. The sun has started to rise, enough to light the river outside and reveal a cloud of mist rising from it. Frankie wonders if the black cat has returned but then there is a knock on the door. Cats don't do that. It's five a.m. Nobody should be knocking on her door at this time in the morning. Nobody should be knocking on her door at all, because nobody knows where she lives.

Unless her daughter has come home.

Frankie runs to the door, frantically slides the bolt, removes the chain, and yanks the door open. It's a young woman, but it isn't her daughter. The stranger has shoulder-length blond hair with a single pink highlight on one side, and she is wearing a gray trouser suit with a T-shirt underneath. Frankie stares at her, then at the T-shirt which has an image of an old movie poster: *The NeverEnding Story*.

"Can I help you?" Frankie asks, with an edge to her voice she meant to hide.

"I do hope so," the woman replies. Her enthusiastic tone and lopsided smile both seem out of place. "*The Black Sheep*, what a great name for a boat. I've always wanted to see inside a narrow boat, can't imagine living on one, any chance I could come in?"

Frankie wonders if the woman is crazy. "No."

"Sorry, silly me. I always forget to introduce myself." She produces some ID from her pocket and Frankie stares at the word *police*. "My name is Charlotte Chapman. I'm a detective and I wondered if we could have a chat? I apologize for the early hour, but I saw that your light was on and that you were up. I confess it wasn't easy to find you—"

"Is this about my daughter?" Frankie has been dreading this moment. She's had recurring nightmares about the police coming to tell her something unimaginable has happened to her little girl.

DCI Chapman shakes her head. "It's about an incident at the Windsor Care Home. Do you know it?"

"No." Frankie starts to shut the door.

"You were there yesterday."

"You've made a mistake."

"I don't think so. There are no cameras in the care home—or I'd have put this case and myself to bed by now—but there is one in the car park at the back." She takes out her phone, taps it a few times, and shows Frankie an image. "This blue and white camper van, parked outside the care home yesterday, has the same registration as the one parked over there on the street. The van is registered here and belongs to someone named Frankie Fletcher. That is you, isn't it? It certainly looks like you, getting out of the van and walking toward the care home on this footage."

Frankie wishes she didn't live in a time where there were cameras everywhere. She hides her panic well. "That is my van but I wasn't visiting the care home. I just used the car park to pop to the shops—it's sometimes impossible to find a space big enough."

"Shh," says the detective and Frankie frowns. "The tattoo on your wrist, haven't seen one like that before." Frankie rolls down the sleeve of her robe to cover it. "What shops did you visit?"

"Sorry?"

"You said you parked there to visit the shops."

"The supermarket just down the road from the home. I was out of milk."

The detective smiles, taps her phone again. "Speaking of milk, old people drink a lot of tea don't they? I can't stand the stuff myself, tastes like pond water, but this is teatime at the care home a few months ago. As you can see from the decorations, it was Christmas. There were lots of visitors—more than usual because of the holidays—and this is a picture of one of the residents. The staff called her Aunty May. Sweet old thing but easily confused— convinced she used to be the queen of England, kept asking *everyone* if they had seen her corgis—but here she is smiling for the camera when her granddaughter visited." She zooms in on the picture. "And that's you in the background. Do you see yourself? Very much *inside* the care home. Where you were seen again yesterday, around the time of the incident. You were the one person in this photo that none of the care home staff could identify. Maybe you got lost on your way to the shops on both occasions?" Frankie doesn't answer. "Not to worry. I have one final question: Do you know Clio Kennedy?"

Frankie stares at her for a long time without speaking, then shrugs. "I don't think so."

"That's a shame. She said she was with you at her home in Notting Hill around the time the incident took place. She would have been a good alibi for you, if only you knew her." The detective smiles again. "I know I look young—good genes—but I've been doing this a long time now. Too long. The reason why a person lies is almost always more interesting than the lie itself. So why are you lying to me?"

Frankie makes herself stand a little taller. "I haven't lied to you. I visited the care home a few months ago to visit an old friend. I'd lost something precious and thought she might know where I could find it. There's nothing illegal about visiting someone last time I checked. That's how I knew about the car park and how handy it was for the shops. I don't know anything about who died."

"Now *that's* interesting. I said there had been an incident at the care home. I didn't say someone had died. This is a crime with three suspects, two murders, and one victim. And you, Frankie Fletcher, are suspect number two."

The End

Mother's Day, twenty years earlier

"I know this is difficult, but when did you last *see* the baby? Was she definitely in the buggy in the supermarket?" the police officer asks, looking down on me in more ways than one. His crooked teeth are too big for his mouth, he has a bulbous nose and excessive facial hair. The man resembles an overfed walrus.

"Yes, she was in the buggy. My friend saw her too. I've told you this already."

He scribbles something in his notebook and I so badly want to read it. I'm convinced he isn't really writing anything at all, just making marks on the page. Killing time. *Wasting* time. He is using a fountain pen, the kind I was taught to write with in school, and I wonder if it sometimes leaks inside his pocket. I hope that it does.

"And how long were you talking to your friend?" he asks.

"I can't remember."

"Can you try?"

"No more than five minutes."

"She said it might have been ten."

I stare at him. I'm sure it wasn't that long but everything is a blur. "Maybe."

"So she was missing *maybe* ten minutes before you noticed?" he asks, every one of his words thick with judgment. His eyes say what his mouth doesn't: *Bad mother.* It's what everyone will think if they don't already. The weight of his unblinking stare is too heavy, so I look away. "The timing could be crucial to us finding the baby," he says slowly, as though I am stupid. I think some men are born patronizing.

"Ten minutes. At most," I say, and his face contorts into something even more unpleasant than before.

"You didn't look at her or check on her for ten minutes?" His tone and my shame gang up on me and gag my mouth so I cannot speak. I nod instead. Lost for words, for hope. Ten minutes is a blink of time when you are looking after someone all day every day forever and ever, amen. I blinked and the baby was gone. Why doesn't this man understand? Why doesn't he believe me? Why doesn't he *do* something?

"Do you remember what the baby was wearing?" he asks.

She has a name. Can you remember that?

"Of course I do," I say, finding my voice again, and wishing the small crowd of people that have gathered around us in the supermarket would go away. They don't *mean well*, they're not *concerned citizens*, they're just nosy *busybodies* with nothing better to do, enjoying the free show of someone else's heartbreak. People love a good tragedy so long as it is not their own. "It was a pink cotton sleepsuit."

"You're sure about the color?" he asks.

Maybe it was white?

"Of course I am. I'm also sure that you should be out there looking for her, not wasting time talking to me. Someone has taken her, why aren't you doing something?"

"You seem very certain that the baby has been abducted—"

"Well she didn't vanish into thin air!"

I wished my daughter would disappear and now someone has taken the baby.

"You need to stay calm. Getting hysterical won't help us, or the child."

Hysterical? I want to take the fountain pen from his fat fingers and stab him in both eyes with it. *That* would be hysterical, but also deeply satisfying.

"Is there someone you suspect? Someone you have had a grievance with? Someone who had a motive to take the baby?"

Yes. Yes. Yes.

I shake my head. "No."

Patience

I dream about people finding out all of my secrets, and it is a relief when the sound of my alarm wakes me from my nightmare. I reach for my phone to turn it off, keeping my eyes closed, my fingers tapping the screen until the attic is silent again.

Except that it isn't. Silent. I can hear someone breathing.

It isn't me. And it isn't Dickens—who always likes to sleep on my bed instead of in his own—there is someone else here.

My head hurts, the way it does when I drink too much. It takes a few seconds to remember the wine and what I did. The events of the day and night before start to uncurl and seep in, clouding the edges of my hangover and flooding my tired mind with memories, most of which I'd rather forget. If I were to tell someone my version of yesterday, I would paint myself as a hero who rescued a vulnerable person from a bad situation. But I worry other people will think I just kidnapped an elderly woman. I had my reasons, most of which were good. I sit up a little and see Edith's mess of gray curls on the pillow at the other end of the bed. She's still

asleep and the room is still dark except for my night-light projecting a galaxy of moving stars across the walls. Watching them
normally makes me feel calm, but I hear another unfamiliar noise.

I'm not imagining it. I can hear footsteps coming up the staircase toward the attic. They are not creeping or quiet. It is the
sound of someone who wants to be heard.

Mr. Kennedy did say he would come back when I refused to
open the door last night. Experience has taught me that he is a
man of his word, but I didn't think he meant returning at six a.m.
The gallery downstairs doesn't open until nine. It seems so obvious
now that I shouldn't have brought Edith here, but I thought we
had time to get up and get out before he came back.

If it is him then at least he can't let himself in, since I installed
the bolt and chain. My eyes dart to the door in search of reassur-
ance but find none. I don't understand, I *always* lock the door. I
must have forgotten after the pizza was delivered. Except that I'm
sure I remember checking everything was safe and secure before
I went to bed. Someone knocks, just the once, and Edith's eyes fly
open and find me. If her face is mirroring mine then I must look
terrified. I shake my head, lift my finger to my lips. I hear the
jangle of keys. Edith pulls the covers back, picks up Dickens, and
hurries to hide in the bathroom. Seconds later someone steps into
the attic and switches on the light. The bare bulb always makes me
think of interrogation scenes in movies.

"Well, isn't this a pretty picture? Looks like you had a party,"
Mr. Kennedy says, staring at the large pizza box and empty bottle
of wine. "Have you had a *boy* up here?" Dickens emits a low growl
and I cough to cover it.

Jude Kennedy likes to wear expensive suits and a permanent
frown. He looks good for a man in his forties. The designer clothes
suit him, as does his salt-and-pepper hair. He has an educated, vel-
vety voice that could charm or destroy you with a single sentence

depending on his mood. The look on his face now makes me want to disappear.

"I thought I was very clear about the rules when I let you stay here, but evidently I was wrong. No noise. *No* visitors. And after everything I've done for you," he says.

I remember the first time I met Jude Kennedy and wish that I never had.

I always knew that my mother had more than her fair share of secrets. She was a painfully private woman with no real friends. Her world seemed to revolve around me, which I loved her for and loathed her for at the same time. She didn't seem to want or need anyone or anything else, and she didn't seem to want me to want or need anyone else either. I was homeschooled. Whenever I started to feel settled in a place, or make friends, she would insist we move location. Again. It felt like we were constantly running away, sometimes in the middle of the night. Despite all of that, my childhood was a happy one, happier than most probably. But it always felt as though something was missing. I knew moving around so often wasn't normal. I was sure that it had something to do with my father, but she wouldn't tell me who he was. Refused to tell me anything at all about him but promised that she would when I turned eighteen. Then she broke her promise.

My mother kept her secrets in a small, ancient, black and gold Japanese tea tin. She hid it behind the loose skirting board in the kitchen. She said it was only to be opened in an emergency, but I opened it in anger after my eighteenth birthday and the contents were a surprise. There was a roll of cash bigger than I had ever seen and an envelope addressed to me. Inside the envelope I found a note:

If I ever don't come home, take this money and find somewhere safe to stay. I will find you when I can. Know that I love you more than I knew it was possible to love.

The only other thing in the tin was a business card for Kennedy's Gallery in Covent Garden, with Jude Kennedy's name in shiny gold letters on the front. Art is my first love and I certainly didn't inherit that passion from my mother—she has spent her life hiding inside books and other people's stories—but she had kept this man's card in the emergency tin, for *me* to find. *And* he owned an art gallery. Of course I thought he was my father.

I stole the money *and* the tea tin, packed a bag, ran away, took the train to London, and walked into Kennedy's Gallery with my head held high and my heart full of hope.

"Are you Jude Kennedy?" I asked.

"I am him. How can I help?"

I didn't hesitate despite all the clues that I was wrong. "I think you're my dad."

He laughed. Hard. Then stared at me. "Is this a joke?" I shook my head. "Who put you up to this? You had me for a minute. *I think you're my dad!* Is this an early April fool?"

It wasn't but I felt like one.

"Darling, I'm definitely *not* your father," he said.

"How do you know?"

"Well, I've never slept with a woman. So there's that . . ." I started crying like the little girl I still was back then. "Dear child, please don't cry. It tends to put people off coming into the gallery and business is not booming as it is. Are you all right? Maybe I can help?" he said.

And that's been the problem ever since.

He won't stop helping me.

He offered me a place to stay in the attic above the gallery. "Better than you ending up on the streets, I can do without that on my overburdened conscience." He even helped me to get a job at the Windsor Care Home. I was so grateful at first, for all of it. But sometimes people do kind things because they want you to feel in their debt. Because at some point they're going to ask you to give them something in return. And he did, and I have, and it has cost me more than I can afford to live with.

That's why he is here now.

He takes a closer look at one of my papercuts on the wall. "You owe me one of these to sell downstairs." He insists on choosing which one and never gives me a penny for them, it was the monthly "rent" we agreed on almost as soon as I'd unpacked my things. Then, in addition to that, he asked me to spy on someone at the Windsor Care Home. That was the real reason he helped me to get a job there. And that was why I befriended Edith at first, but then when I got to know her, I started to like her. I don't understand why he doesn't.

Last week he asked me to do something *unthinkable*.

And now he is here, wanting an update about her, not knowing that she is hiding in the bathroom.

"Any news about my mother? Is she dead yet?"

Edith

Edith recognizes the voice of her son in the attic.

"Any news about my mother? Is she dead yet?"

She covers her mouth with her hand to stifle the sounds that want to come out of it, and holds on to Dickens like a child clinging to a favorite toy. Her own son wishes she was dead. She could stop hiding in the bathroom and confront him, but she is too scared. Edith—who has spent a lifetime never being scared of anything or anyone—is afraid of everything and everyone after what happened yesterday. How could she not be?

It has been several years since Edith and her son were on speaking terms. Whenever they spoke they disagreed, so concluded it was best not to. The decision was mutual. Edith's reasons for not speaking to her son are quite different from her reasons for not speaking to her daughter. He was always a selfish blaggard—even as a child—but he grew up to become someone she doesn't know or want to. Someone she doesn't even recognize as her son. It's got nothing to do with him being gay—though she's sure that's what he thinks. Edith doesn't like her son because he is a thoroughly unpleasant human being and a nasty piece of work. She's ashamed of herself for raising such a despicable person. When people ask her if she has children, she reluctantly tells them she has a daughter. She doesn't mention Jude, hasn't for a long time. Edith often wishes she had never had children at all.

She hears the attic door close. It is quiet again, but she waits a few minutes before coming out.

"I can explain," Ladybug says, as soon as Edith opens the bathroom door. "Why don't you sit down?"

Edith doesn't move from the spot. She sees that her suitcase has been opened and the girl has been rummaging in her things. "How do you know my son?" Edith asks. The girl stares down at the floor, can't even look her in the eye. "The son I haven't spoken to for years. The son I've never told you about."

"I'm sorry you had to hear that. He helped me to get a job at the care home and since then I've been—"

"You've been what? Spying on me? Reporting back to *him*? Lying to me about everything? I thought we were friends, Ladybug. I thought I could trust you, but clearly I can't trust anyone."

"You *can* trust me."

Edith shakes her head. "I want to go home. *My* home. You said that's where you were taking me when we left the care home."

"You lied to me too," the girl says.

"About what?"

"Why did you never tell me that you had a son?"

"Because I don't. That man is a stranger to me," Edith replies. "And withholding the truth is not the same as lying. For years he only ever got in touch when he wanted something—money, usually—and I got tired of it. I don't talk about him because, well, I suppose not being loved by one child might just be bad luck. Both of my children growing up to hate their mother suggests that the problem might be me. I want you to take me home. Now. Like you promised. Then I don't want to see you again. Did he really ask you to—"

"We need to keep our voices down. The gallery is downstairs."

"So that's where I am, above Kennedy's Gallery! I *knew* this street looked familiar. Maybe I should call the police, tell them I've been kidnapped against my will."

"We both know that you haven't, but go ahead and call the police if you want to," the girl replies with a modicum of defiance Edith was not expecting. She doesn't sound like her Ladybug anymore.

"All this time, I thought you actually cared about me," Edith says, feeling like an old fool.

"I do care," the girl insists, staring at the open suitcase on the attic floor. "Did you take something out of here last night?"

"It's my suitcase, I can do what I like with it. Are you in cahoots with my son?"

"Of course not. I can explain everything—"

"Go on then. Has the cat got your tongue?"

The girl pulls a petulant face that is not becoming. "It's complicated and I don't think we have time for this now, but I hear you."

"Of course you can hear me. You have ears."

"When we first met and I found out that your dog had been taken away from you, I used my savings to get Dickens back. I've looked after him and done my best to help you ever since. Why would I do that if I didn't care? I would never hurt you or Dickens, never. You must know that. Do you believe me?"

Edith stares at the girl with a look of pure disappointment. "I believe you believe you."

"I'm sorry," she says. "I really am, but this place isn't safe for any of us now. I need to pack some things and get us out of here. Then we can talk properly. How does that sound?"

"While you pack, I want to take Dickens for a walk. Like I used to."

The girl stares at her. "Will you come back if I let you go?"

Let you go.

The words make it sound as though she is a prisoner, and Edith thinks maybe she is. Old age has made a captive out of her. She used to be so independent and free, but now she is dependent on others for everything. Edith doesn't have any cash and she gave the girl her bank card. She has behaved like an old fool but she isn't one.

"I need you to trust me," the girl says.

Edith nods. "I *do* trust you and of course I'll come back. I'm sorry we had a falling out."

The girl smiles and seems satisfied with her answer, even though it is a lie.

Edith cares very much about Ladybug but she has never fully trusted her.

How could she?

Edith has known who the girl really was since the first time they met.

Frankie

Frankie has to be extra careful from now on. She cannot get caught; she knows what happens to prison staff who commit crimes and go to jail. It won't matter that she was a librarian. If the police can prove what Frankie did and she ends up in prison it will be the end of her. She must find her daughter and then she needs to move away and start again. She's out of time and options.

Frankie has never been in Covent Garden this early in the morning before. She prefers it like this—quiet, without any crowds or noise, just the sound of her heels on the cobbled streets. She guesses it will take another thirty-three steps to reach her destination. It takes twenty-seven, so she wasn't far off. Sometimes the truth is closer than we think.

She stops and looks up at the beautiful, old, narrow building, taking a moment to appreciate its age and architecture, including the tiny attic perched on top. Kennedy's Gallery has "ESTAB-LISHED 1886" carved into the stone above its fancy-looking blue door, and Frankie imagines the same family working in this building for all those years, generation after generation, following in their ancestors' footsteps. Walking in so many shadows must make it hard to see your own path. Frankie takes a deep breath and knocks on the door. The gallery isn't open yet, but the lights are on and she can see someone inside.

When nobody answers, she knocks again. A little harder this time.

A well-dressed man with floppy hair squints in her direction.

"We're not open yet. Come back at nine," he shouts from a short distance, pointing at his expensive-looking watch. He speaks slowly, as though he thinks she might be a tourist, or dangerously stupid, or both.

Frankie stares back at him. The man is tall and tanned, with entitlement and fine lines drawn on his face. Midforties if she had to guess, which she doesn't, because she knows exactly who this man is. They've met before, even though she is certain that Jude Kennedy does not remember her. Sometimes being forgettable is a blessing. Twenty years ago she came here and asked for his help. He didn't help her back then. He just tried to sell her some lousy art and gave her his business card—which she kept—but she's going to make him help her now. Jude turns his back on her, so Frankie makes a fist and pounds on the door again. He spins around, rolls his eyes like a teenager, then marches toward the entrance, before pointing at the *Closed* sign. He has hands that have never known hard work.

Frankie holds up the framed papercut she took from the pink house. He stares down at it then up at her. The out-of-season suntan seems to visibly drain from his arrogant face. "I want to talk to you about this," she says through the glass door, seeing that she finally has his attention. "And I'm not leaving until I do."

"I've never seen it before," he replies, looking down on her in every possible way.

She flips the frame around. "Then why does it have the name of this gallery on the back?"

Jude looks past her at something in the distance. When Frankie glances over her shoulder, she sees a police officer walking down the street on the other side of Covent Garden. For a moment she thinks the detective who turned up at the narrow boat this morning is having her followed, but she's just being paranoid. The detective doesn't really know anything; if she did Frankie would have been arrested already. There is a tinkle of a bell, and when Frankie turns back, the door is open.

"You had better come in," Jude says, ushering her into the gallery. As soon as she is inside, he closes the door behind her again, using a series of complicated locks, bolts, and chains.

Frankie does not like being locked inside somewhere unless she has a key.

She takes in her surroundings. The gallery is bigger than its narrow exterior suggests, stretching away from the street. There is a surprisingly high ceiling and a mezzanine. The intricate spiral wooden staircase leading up to it looks as though it might have been carved from a single tree trunk. Almost every space on the gray walls is covered in artwork. There is something for everyone here, but the prices next to each piece mean that most people could only afford to look. Frankie is no art expert—that was her daughter's passion, not hers—but she thinks this place is beautiful. It would make a wonderful bookshop.

"I don't remember the piece of work you have there," Jude says, interrupting Frankie's thoughts. "But if I can help you, I will."

All of his words sound like lies.

"I want to know about the artist who made this," Frankie says, lifting her chin a little higher. People like him never respect people like her. "You must have records."

"I'm afraid some artists like to remain anonymous."

"This isn't a Banksy and I'm not an idiot. I've been working with criminals for years, and I know when someone is lying. You're not very good at it. Where did you get this papercut?"

He frowns at her then. "Do I know you?"

She hesitates, but only for a second. "My daughter made this piece of work," Frankie says, holding it up again until he can't avoid looking at it or her. "I'm sure of that. Certain. She's a teenager, practically still a child. So *where* and *how* did you get it?"

Jude's right eye starts to twitch: a nervous tic. A tell. "My memory is starting to refresh itself. While I can't remember the artist, I do think I remember who this piece of art belongs to now. The papercut you are holding isn't *yours*, is it? So where did *you* get it from?"

"Do you know where my daughter is?"

"I don't even know *who* your daughter is. Look, you are clearly very upset. It sounds as though you are looking for your child and if I can help you I will. What's her name?"

"Nellie Fletcher."

He shakes his head, looking almost relieved. "Then I'm sorry, but I can honestly say that I've never heard that name before."

Frankie searches his face and feels nothing but devastation as she concludes he is telling the truth. But then, just as she is about to leave, she sees another papercut on the desk behind him with a ladybug drawn in the corner.

Clio

Clio pays the taxi driver, then steps out into Covent Garden before watching the black cab drive away, wondering if she should have stayed in it. The shops and cafés are just starting to open, the sound of shutters and doors echoing around the street, but Kennedy's Gallery still has a *Closed* sign in the door window. No wonder the place hasn't made a profit for years. It bothers her that she has to knock, that he'll see who it is and will be able to decide whether or not to let her in. Clio used to have her own key.

She can see the shape of him inside the gallery, a shadowy smudge of a man sitting alone behind the desk at the back. Her hand makes a fist before it needs to because she doesn't have to knock after all. As if he can sense her presence, he looks up and sees her at almost exactly the same moment as she sees him. Time seems to stretch as they both stare at each other, their eyes saying what their lips will not. When words are left unsaid for too long their meaning can expire. He stands, slowly crosses the parquet floor, and lets her in. Jude Kennedy locks the door behind her, the

Closed sign still in place. They both know that this is a conversation best had in private.

It's the first time Clio has seen her younger brother for almost a year, but there is no hug. Not even a handshake. Even though he literally wouldn't exist were it not for her.

"I've been calling you," she says.

"I'm aware," he replies. "I thought we agreed to stop doing that."

Forty years fall away and she sees him as the child he used to be. Difficult. Stubborn. Selfish to his core. Seeing family can feel like time travel—and she'd rather not remember that out-of-date version of herself. As young children Clio and her brother were constantly competing for scraps of love and attention in a home that offered little of either. As teenagers they learned not to waste time looking for something that was not there. This place, the gallery, makes Clio think about her father. Not that she knew the man. She met him twice: the first time when she was ten years old, and once more when she was in her thirties. She figured she must have done something very wrong for him not to want anything to do with her, but she wasn't the problem. It was her mother their father wanted to stay away from. Unfortunately—for everyone concerned—he got her pregnant twice before figuring that out.

Clio felt so confident marching in here, but now she feels small and stupid and scared. But she won't let him bully her anymore. Not now. Not ever again.

"I take it you know?" Clio asks, looking him in the eye and waiting for him to extend her the same courtesy.

Jude looks at his expensive watch instead. "Know what?"

"About our mother?"

"Is she dead?"

"No! Missing."

"Is that all?"

Clio tries to resist the urge to punch him in his stupid smug face. "Don't you ever check your phone or listen to messages?" she asks.

"Not if I can help it and not if they're from you."

"This is serious. Someone has been murdered."

"Unless it's Mother I really don't care."

"What is wrong with you? I can't keep dealing with all of this on my own. She's your mother too."

His face seems to darken. "I know who and what she is. *I'm* the one who dealt with things when you were too busy, or too sad, or decided that you didn't want her to live with you after all. I'm the one who had to visit her and check up on her on all of the many occasions over the years when you turned your back. I'm the one who took care of—"

"You took care of yourself," Clio says.

"She needed help."

"Not the kind of help you gave her. You tricked her. Got her to sign things she would never have signed if she understood them. Arranged for her to move into a bloody awful care home, without her knowledge, or mine. Took everything she loved away from her, including her bloody dog, and then let her think I was responsible for all of it."

"You were. You asked her to move out."

"At least I let her move in when she needed someone the most. She would have been left to rot in her own house had it been up to you. She was falling over *all* the time, forgetting to take her heart pills, accidently leaving the gas stove on, almost blowing herself and the rest of the street up, and when we couldn't find a suitable place for her to live, you did nothing."

"You're just like Mum, do you know that? It's as though you've turned into her. Changing the narrative to whatever story suits your own conscience best. Turning a blind eye to anything that makes you look like a lousy daughter. I did what needed doing."

His words feel like a series of slaps, pinches, and punches, hard ones, but Clio still has a few punches of her own left to throw.

"Anything you did for her you did for the inheritance."

"Are you sure you're not projecting, dear sister of mine?" He shrugs. "It's only money."

Clio looks around the art gallery that was once beautiful. It was a shock when the father she only met twice left this place to her, her mother, and Jude—whom he only met *once*—in his will. All three of them have owned it since, though Clio and her mother are very much silent partners. It turned out that their grandfather owned the gallery before their father—a real family business for the family that never was. Despite all the opportunities and handouts her brother has received, he has only succeeded in running it into the ground. Clio wanted to sell the place from the start, she suspects they might have to now. Jude has never really cared about art or the people who make it. He only cares about two things: money and himself.

Clio turns to leave, but not without a parting shot. "Well, if 'it's only money' you won't be too upset to learn that our mother has changed her will, and applied to reverse the power of attorney that gave us control of her financial affairs. She's even instructed a lawyer to get her house back."

"What are you talking about?" he says, standing closer than Clio is comfortable with. Since they were teenagers he has always been taller, louder, stronger than her. He's also very good at knowing how to make her feel worse in order to make himself feel better.

"Our mother has outsmarted you," she tells him, unable to hide her glee. "Your plan to fool her into living in a care home, trick her out of her house, and siphon off a considerable chunk of her money to tide you and the business over didn't go unnoticed."

"You've been getting half the money—"

"Which I used to pay the fees for the terrible place you stuck her in."

"Well, you won't have to pay them much longer."

"What does *that* mean?" Clio asks but Jude doesn't answer. She takes the envelope out of her bag. "Here is a copy of Mum's new will. Still, as you say, it's only money."

"Money is never only money," he says, snatching the document from her hands.

"I know you've never been a fan of reading, so let me spare you the embarrassment of not being able to understand all the long words. Our mother is planning to leave almost everything she has left to a stranger."

He turns the pages until he reaches the relevant paragraph. "And I see she is leaving her third of *my* business to you."

"I don't care about the gallery. You're welcome to it, but I was counting on some cash."

"How on earth did a bedridden old woman change her will?"

"She's not bedridden, she just chooses not to leave her room. From the letters I've read, this dime-a-dozen lawyer visited the care home and the new will was witnessed by one of the other residents. A Mr. Henderson. We need to find Mum. There might still be a way to fix this, so that you don't have to lose the gallery—"

"So that *you* don't have to lose your precious pink house you mean? Don't act as though you don't need the money too."

"*I'm* the one who has been using my own money to top up the astronomical amount required to pay for her care. So, yes, things are a little tight."

"Join the club. All you ever do is complain about everything. You've done nothing to help run this place for over a decade, but you still think you're entitled to a third of it."

"Because I own a third of it!"

"And yet *I'm* the one who gave up my own dreams to follow in our father's footsteps and keep the family business alive—"

"The family business. You barely knew the man—"

"That wasn't *his* fault."

"Well, it wasn't mine either. And he left the gallery to *both* of us. It's mine, just as much as it is yours."

"Which is why you should have given me the loan when I asked for it."

"I told you, I don't have any more money."

"But you can afford to keep that ridiculous pink house? I don't know why you insist on staying in a home full of ghosts. It's far too big for a lonely old spinster."

Just like when they were children, Clio's brother has always known her weak spots. Where to aim a verbal punch to cause the most amount of hurt. She didn't always live alone.

"Are you going to help me or not?" she asks, feeling defeated.

"Seeing as you asked so politely, yes. If we can't find Mother dearest, then let's start by talking to the person she decided to leave everything to."

"If only I had thought of that. Problem is, I've never heard of Patience Liddell, which makes it a little tricky to find her. What's wrong? Why does your face look like you've had a stroke?"

Jude smiles, revealing capped teeth. "I know who Patience is, and more importantly, I know where she is."

Clio stares at him. "What? How? Where?"

He looks up toward the ceiling. "She lives in the attic upstairs."

Patience

I can hear raised voices downstairs in the gallery and I worry for a moment that Edith has gone in there to confront her son. I hurry to the round window and am relieved when I can see her walking on the cobbled street, heading out of Covent Garden and toward the river, Dickens trotting at her side. I miss living on the water. The sound of it lapping against the boat used to be the lullaby of my sleep. After everything that happened yesterday, I'm surprised I slept at all last night.

I worry about Edith being out there alone but she promised not to be gone long. It isn't as though she has anywhere else to go. Besides, I need a little time to get ready. Once I've taken her where I'm taking her, I won't be coming back here. I've packed most of my things, including almost all of my papercuts, but I'm leaving one behind. It's of a black fox I sometimes see from my window late at night. Black foxes are extremely rare and my mother always said they were unlucky. The papercut I call *Bad Luck* always makes me think of Jude Kennedy, so I'll leave it for him to find. A little bad luck to remember me by.

I pull out the drawer from beneath my bed and take the Japanese tea tin from its hiding place. Then I empty all the cash I have spent the last year saving onto the bed. Along with the petty cash I took from Joy's office after she fired me, I have almost five thousand pounds. By the end of today, once I take Edith where she needs to be, I'll have twice that amount. Enough to rent a little studio flat overlooking the river, and to fund my first year at art school if I'm lucky enough to get in once I apply. That's all I want: a safe place to live and to finish my education. I've worked hard. I deserve it. It's only natural to feel guilty because of what happened, but that wasn't my fault. At least that's what I keep telling myself.

I hear someone coming up the stairs toward the attic and am relieved that Edith and Dickens are back. She said she would only be ten minutes and we really should get going.

"Is this her?" says a woman's voice behind me. I drop the Japanese tea tin and spin around.

Mr. Kennedy is standing in the doorway with a woman I've seen before. She's wearing a black dress with black trainers today and is looking super unfriendly.

"This is her," Jude replies.

"*You're* Patience Liddell?" the woman asks.

"Are you deaf or just stupid? I already told you it's her," Jude snaps. "Where did *you* get all of that money?" he asks, staring at the cash on the bed.

"I've been saving up," I reply quietly, wishing I had left five minutes earlier.

"It must have taken a *long* time to save up that amount of cash on a care home assistant's salary. Are you sure it's yours? Perhaps it's our mother's?" Jude says. "I've just found out that you tricked her into changing her will."

I don't know what he's talking about. I stare at Jude, then at the woman, but her face is impossible to read. I know I should defend myself but I don't know how. I shake my head as though that might dislodge some suitable words, but none come out.

"Do you know where our mother is?" the woman asks and I don't know how to answer. "Patience is an interesting name," she adds, scanning every part of the attic with her sad looking eyes. "I wonder if it is your real one? I wonder whether anything you say is true?"

She snatches my purse from the bed and opens it.

I feel sick when I realize what the woman has seen.

"Well, this driver's license does indeed say "Patience Liddell" but I'm curious to know why you have our mother's bank card in your purse." She holds the plastic rectangle in the air. "My mother trusted you. *I* trusted you."

Jude frowns at her. "Have you two met?"

"Of course not," the woman snaps at him before turning back to me. "What I mean is, people like me have to trust people like you to do the right thing. With our loved ones. It's what we pay you for."

"You were right to trust me. So was Edith," I say.

"Then where is she?" the woman asks.

"Are you sure you don't know one another?" Jude asks again.

"*You're* the one who knew who this girl was and where she lived. Until now, I'd never heard of anyone called Patience and I'm running out of it," Clio snaps at him. Then she shouts at me, "Where is our mother?"

Jude speaks before I get the chance to answer. "I don't think the kid knows where the old bag is, but she's clearly been stealing cash from Mum's account—"

"Stop calling me a thief!" I say, finally finding my voice. "Edith asked me to buy things she needed and that's all I did."

"Then why do you still have her bank card?" Jude asks.

Clio stares at the ladybug ring on my finger. "And where did you get that?"

She seems to visibly deflate, like someone has pulled all of the stuffing out of her, but Jude is oblivious as a stone.

"None of this is my fault," I say. "The only reason I—"

"Don't say another word," the woman interrupts, with a look on her face that would silence a marching band. "I've heard enough lies."

Jude nods. "For once I agree with you. Maybe the police will have more luck—"

"I'm sure there's no need for that," the woman interrupts.

"I've already called them. They're on the way," he says.

She looks as shocked as I feel. "I thought we agreed *not* to call them yet?"

"Of course I've called the police, I don't know why we wouldn't. Our elderly and vulnerable mother is missing. This person who I tried to help—by giving her a safe place to stay *and* by helping her to get a job—has repaid my kindness by stealing what looks like thousands of pounds from our mother and tricking her into changing her will. Turns out she might have kidnapped her too! We can't *not* call the police. For all we know she might have killed her."

"How can you say that?" I want to shout the words but they come out as a whisper.

"You're clearly nothing but a liar, and a thief, and a very disturbed young woman—"

I don't wait to hear the rest of his speech; the world is too full of men who like the sound of their own voices. I grab my bag and as much of the cash as I can, then I push past them both. I'm out of the attic door and down the first flight of stairs before anyone can stop me. I'll change my name, start again, nobody will be able to find me. Maybe I'll go home, back to Mum, try to fix things. I run down the next flight of stairs, then another. I turn the final corner and just as I'm about to reach the outside door, I see two police officers at the bottom of the staircase blocking my path. A blond woman with a streak of pink hair appears behind them.

She smiles at me. "Hello, suspect number three."

Edith

Edith walks toward the river with Dickens, knowing that Ladybug is probably watching them from the attic window. The girl has underestimated her, and Edith fears she may have overestimated the girl. When certain she must be out of sight, she doubles back on herself and heads for St. Paul's, the church where the girl left her for a while yesterday. The place where Edith hid something she now needs to collect.

Edith is used to young people making judgments about her because of her advanced years. She thought Patience was different but Edith does understand. When she was a teenager, everyone over thirty looked the same age: old. And she is *eighty* now. Where did the years go? One of the benefits of getting older is that she is less concerned with what other people think of her. But she did want to be liked by Ladybug. Loved even, as foolish as that might have been. Maybe deep down we all want to be loved. Maybe we need to be.

"I fear I have been a fool," Edith says beneath her breath as they cross the road, and Dickens barks. "Don't pretend you weren't hoodwinked by her too. I thought dogs were supposed to be good judges of character." Dickens barks again. "Fine, you give her the benefit of the doubt if you want, but I used to be a detective." The dog tilts his head to look up at her. "I know I wasn't a *real* one, just a store detective, but the two occupations aren't so different." Dickens barks again. "What would you know? You're a dog. Do you remember May, my friend at the care home? *She* understood. But then she was a detective too. She was also all I had for company for a while, and she taught me that sometimes you have to pretend to be who people think you are to survive. I was good at being a detective, the best, according to the regional manager, but the work made me sad. Catching people who didn't deserve to be caught. Letting someone get away with doing something wrong is sometimes the right thing to do."

It starts to rain and Edith wishes she'd thought to bring an umbrella. She opens the gate to the church garden and Dickens follows her inside.

"Maybe we should give Ladybug one last chance? What do you think? What a terrible thing it is to be so old, and so very lonely, and to only know one kind person in the world."

Dickens barks again, as though he can read her thoughts.

"You're quite right. I might only know one kind *person* but I do know the best dog. Mustn't grumble, mustn't complain. Before a rainbow it must always rain. Come on, let's get inside the church until this shower passes. Things are gloomy now but I'm sure they'll brighten up."

Dickens wags his tail and Edith is convinced he understood every word. She has been having regular conversations with her dog for as long as she can remember. All dogs talk, but only to people who know how to listen. He sits down when they reach the church doors and Edith has to tug on his lead a little.

"Come on, I know you don't like religious buildings but there's nothing to be scared of," she says. Dickens shakes his head as though disagreeing with her, but he's probably just ridding the rain from his fur.

They sit in exactly the same church pew as yesterday, waiting for the person praying a few rows back to leave. Edith used to visit a church like this one every Sunday until she and God had a falling out. They haven't been on speaking terms for several years now. Edith's mother made her go to church every week. She hated it, then made her own children do the same, but only to get Clio into a good school. All the other schools where they lived were overfull and understaffed. So Edith made Clio and Jude dress up in their Sunday best and go to mass to try to make a good impression with the teachers and other parents at the Catholic school. To give them a better start in life than she'd had. A good education and better job prospects, so that they wouldn't have to work so hard and miss out on so much. Not that Clio appreciated that or anything else she ever tried to do for her. It isn't as though Edith wanted to get up early on a Sunday, having worked a six-day week. She stopped believing in God a long time ago. Faith and fear are too entwined to be seen as anything other than the same thing these days. But the feeling of sanctuary—whether real or imagined—is something she still finds so appealing. Throughout history, churches have been a safe place for people when they are afraid, or grieving, or need a place to hide. Just like Edith does now.

It's clear that Ladybug has been lying to her, about several things.

"Don't worry, Dickens. We just need to come up with a plan," Edith says, but she thinks the dog knows her too well because he stares up at her with big sad eyes. Her dog knows when she is happy, he knows when she is sad, and he knows when she is scared. Her dog knows her better than any person ever has. He whimpers quietly and Edith doesn't know how to comfort him because he is right to worry. "First of all, we need to get rid of this."

Edith reaches beneath the pew where they sat yesterday, until her fingers find the plastic bag hidden beneath it. When she is sure she is alone, she takes a peek inside. Edith never liked this thing. Why her former colleagues at the supermarket gave her a bronze statue of a magnifying glass as a retirement gift she'll never know. She appreciated the gesture, but she would rather have had the cash. The statue has been wiped clean, but there are bound to be traces of blood still on the thing. She doesn't need to be a real detective to know that. Edith knows the difference between when things need to be hidden, and when things need to be gotten rid of—it's something she's had to do before—and the murder weapon definitely needs to disappear.

Frankie

Frankie worries she is wasting her time sitting in the camper van outside Kennedy's Gallery, but her gut instinct is to stay. It was obvious that Jude Kennedy was lying about something—he seems like the variety of man who struggles with the concept of honesty—and she is now certain that the papercuts he was selling were made by her daughter. If he lied about knowing who she is, he might be lying about knowing where she is. Frankie still left when Jude asked her to, but has been watching the gallery ever since.

So far, she has counted twenty-eight people walking past: nineteen women, nine men. There have also been twelve black cabs, three people walking their dogs, and one ice cream van. Frankie sees a traffic warden approaching and curses beneath her breath. She's already had to drive around the block once to avoid getting a ticket. The street is chockablock full of double yellow lines making it impossible to park legally, but nowhere else has a clear view of the gallery. Which is still closed, even though its opening hours clearly state it shouldn't be.

Frankie takes her eyes off the gallery for a moment to stare up at the beautiful old church she is parked outside. The sign says it is called St. Paul's, and she can see what looks like a secret walled garden behind the building. It's the kind of place she knows her daughter would love to spend time in. Her little girl always liked old churches and graveyards, she liked a lot of things that gave Frankie the creeps. Daughters don't always take after their mothers.

Frankie's tummy rumbles rather loudly, reminding her that she hasn't eaten anything today. There is a cute looking café just down the road. Maybe she could leave the van here for a short while, some coffee would certainly help wake her up, and if she sits in the window she'll still be able to see the gallery. Hunger and tiredness persuade her to risk it.

She doesn't see the police car pull up farther down the street as she steps inside the café.

Frankie hasn't "dined out" for months. The place is cheap and cheerful but it feels surreal and extravagant. She finds a cozy table for one and starts reading the menu.

She doesn't see two policemen walk toward the gallery.

It is only a breakfast menu but there are so many options. People have far too many choices these days. Frankie decides to order two of the classic breakfasts—one to eat in, one to take away. She'll give it to the homeless person sitting on the street outside. She gives her order to the waitress, who makes excessive small talk about the weather in hope of a tip.

Frankie doesn't see a girl being put into a police car by the same detective who visited her boat this morning.

The food she orders arrives quickly, but her phone beeps inside her bag before she can take a bite, which means she doesn't see the police car drive past the window. Her phone hasn't made a sound for almost a year—unless it was an alarm she set herself—and the unexpected noise makes her jump. She checks the time on her

Mickey Mouse watch, and presumes it must be work getting in touch to see why she hasn't turned up today. But it isn't someone from the prison. It's her daughter. Almost exactly a year since she ran away.

The text message is short, just three words:

HELP ME MUM.

Clio

"You shouldn't have called the police," Clio says, following her brother as they climb the steps back up to the attic. She is relieved the detective left straightaway with the girl and didn't bother coming upstairs: it might have been awkward if DCI Chapman had discovered Clio *here*. Another police officer spoke to Clio and Jude after Patience had been driven away, but there are still so many other unanswered questions.

"Why shouldn't I have called them?" Jude asks, in the sulky tone he reserves just for her.

"Because if the girl does know where Mum is, she isn't going to tell us now."

Jude is out of breath already—he has always had a distant relationship with exercise—but the stairs are no rival for Clio. She marches on ahead, hoping to reach the attic before him, buy herself some time. She tries to think but her thoughts are scared of the facts. Maybe she has made a mistake.

"Mum didn't trust anyone—not even us—so why would she

trust some random girl she's only just met in a care home?" Clio says, thinking out loud. Jude doesn't reply. "Are you telling me the answer telepathically?" she asks but he still doesn't answer. Probably thinking about how to fix the problem instead of what caused the problem, as always. Clio wonders what the girl will tell the police.

"Explain it to me again," she says. "How this *teenager* started living here, and how she then got a job working at the care home where our mother was living? That seems like an awfully big co-incidence and you know I don't believe in those."

Jude shrugs, the same way he used to as a child when he didn't want to answer a question. He starts to fiddle with his cuff links, just visible on the crisp white shirt poking out from the sleeves of his tailored jacket. But then he surprises her when something sounding like the truth comes tumbling out of his mouth.

"The girl just showed up here about a year ago. She was a scrawny little bird of a thing with a rucksack on her back and a real attitude in her voice. She thought I was her long-lost dad, can you believe that?" He laughs, but Clio doesn't.

"Am I supposed to Columbo what you just said, or are you going to tell me what it means? Why on earth would she think that *you* were her father?" she asks, and it is clear they have reverted to the squabbling siblings they once were.

"Perhaps a simple case of wishful bloody thinking? If you stop gabbling and try *listening* for a change I'll tell you what happened. No wonder you can't get enough clients these days, they come to you for therapy and probably can't get a word in. As I was *trying* to say, I explained to the girl that I wasn't her father—having never slept with a woman it seemed fairly unlikely—and she started crying and . . . I felt sorry for her. She had clearly run away from someone or something and I wanted to help. If anything I think she reminded me of you, when you ran away. When we were still kids. So I said she could stay up here in the attic for a while."

Clio doesn't want to think about when *she* ran away from home, or why. That was a lifetime ago. "Did the girl pay rent?" she asks instead.

"No."

"But then . . . what was in it for you?"

"Darling sister, are you suggesting that I am incapable of charitable acts unless they benefit me in some way?"

"Yes."

"Rude."

"I think what we need to focus on now is finding Mum."

Jude rolls his eyes. "Good luck with that."

Clio looks around the tiny room and notices the papercut on the wall. It is of a black fox. "This looks familiar," she says, taking a closer look. "Didn't you send me one of these for Christmas?"

"Yes. I shouldn't have. They're proving to be quite popular in the gallery, I've sold—"

"Why *did* you send me a Christmas gift last year? We weren't even speaking at the time."

"I told you, the girl reminded me of you a bit."

"She looks nothing like me—"

"You're right, she's pretty. I mean her situation. I was still so young when you ran away as a teenager, but I remember it. I suppose I missed you back then because you were more of a mum to me than Mum ever was." Clio has never heard him say that before, she didn't even know if he remembered how often she put him to bed, took him to school, cooked him his dinner. Their mother was always at work. She told them she was a detective, that her job was *important*, but all she really did was catch the occasional shoplifter. Jude's face darkens again. "There's no need to get all sentimental. My judgment was clouded by a rare moment of nostalgia, that's all. Don't worry, it won't happen again. I don't know why I bothered to try to do something nice. I'm guessing you gave the papercut I sent you to charity?"

Clio doesn't correct him, or say how much she liked it—enough to hang it in the room where she spends most of her time.

"What now?" Clio asks, recognizing the expression her brother's face has always worn when he wins a bet or solves a puzzle.

"There was a woman," he says.

"That's a first. What woman?"

"A woman. Downstairs, with the framed papercut I gave *you* for Christmas. *Did* you dump it in a charity shop? I presumed that's where she found it."

Clio shakes her head. "No. A new client stole it from my house and climbed out the window with it yesterday." They stare at each other for a while. Their mutual hatred put to one side because they both know they can't fix this mess alone. "Did you pay the girl for her art?" Clio asks.

"I let her stay here rent free in exchange for the odd piece of work—"

"You mean you took advantage of her misfortune and exploited her talent."

"I was never anything but a good Samaritan. When that ghastly care home manager happened to mention how short staffed they were, I suggested the girl might be able to help out there. I put a roof over her head *and* got her a job. How was I supposed to know she was a con artist?"

It would have been like looking in a mirror, Clio thinks.

"You shouldn't speak ill of the dead, but I agree she was ghastly," she says.

"What? Who is dead?"

"The care home manager. You just said she was ghastly—"

"Are you saying Joy is dead?"

"I didn't know you were on first name terms, especially given you never visited the care home *or* our mother." Jude stares at her, his mouth opening and closing like a goldfish. "What? I did try to tell you earlier."

"When? How did she die?" he asks.

"She was found dead in the elevator with an out-of-order sign around her neck." Her brother's face does something unfamiliar, and Clio realizes this is what he looks like when shocked. "At least, that's what I *heard*. I obviously didn't see it with my own eyes," she backtracks.

"Bloody hell."

"Does it matter?" Clio says, wanting to change the subject. She notices that her brother's permanent tan has turned a little pale. "What *did* you think the police were arresting the girl for?"

"Stealing from Mum."

"I don't think they would have sent a detective, two cars, and two officers for some money disappearing from Mum's bank account, do you?"

"Why would someone murder Joy?" he asks.

"I imagine there was a queue of volunteers a mile long."

"Do *you* think the girl did it?"

"No," Clio says. "I'm almost certain she didn't."

Jude stares at her. "Do you think our mother did it?"

"Why would Mum kill the care home manager?"

"It would explain her disappearing act if she bumped Joy off and ran. But you're right, that's ridiculous." His face resets, and it's as though he has snapped out of a temporary trance and is back to being his awful self. "Well, we may as well put this money to good use, it was probably our mother's anyway," he says, starting to pick up the cash from the bed.

"The police said not to touch anything until they can send someone."

"What difference does it make if there are a few hundred pounds on the bed instead of a few thousand? It could take months to resolve Mum's will if and when this does go to court. Don't tell me you don't need the money too? There must be at least one month's mortgage sitting right there."

"You're acting as though Mum is *dead*. She's only missing. We might find her."

"You can't find something you're not looking for."

Clio tries to hide how his words make her feel.

"What about the girl's belongings?" she asks.

"That's what bins are for. I'll get rid of it all once the police have everything they need to charge her. Apart from the art—I can sell that downstairs."

"I think we should leave everything where it is for now," Clio says, but watches as Jude takes more of the money. Something about all of this is niggling her. Something doesn't feel quite right. A piece of the puzzle is still missing, she knows it.

"Mum had three visitors at the care home yesterday. That's what the police told me," she says, wondering whether it is a good idea to share this information with him.

"Popular! Who knew!"

"Me, a lawyer, and a woman pretending to be me."

"Why would *anyone* pretend to be you?"

"That's what I want to know. They signed the visitor book using my name—it was a shock to see it. I'm sure all of these things are linked."

"Well, I think the mystery is solved. The girl conned Mum, probably killed Joy, and now that she's been caught and arrested the new will won't be valid. Everything in here is rightfully ours as far as I'm concerned. Regardless of whether Mother dearest turns up."

Jude's floppy hair falls into his eyes just like it did when he was a kid. He has to sweep it away in a fashion that makes him look quite ridiculous at his age.

"What if you're wrong?" Clio asks. "What if the girl was telling the truth? What if she is innocent and our mother left everything to her simply because the girl was kind?"

"I think you're the one not being honest," Jude says, turning to face her.

Clio's chest tightens. "What is that supposed to mean?"

"We both know that the girl looks like someone else, and that's probably the real reason why Mum did what she did." His words feel like a punch but Clio nods. He does have a point. "Look, I know all of this has been . . . difficult," Jude continues. "But it will be over soon." It almost sounds as though her little brother is being kind for the first time in years and it causes her to feel off balance. Things weren't always like this between them. But by the time he finishes his speech, it's obvious that her brother is exactly who she thinks he is.

"When all of this is over . . ." he says, taking more of the cash from the bed and stuffing it into his pockets, "there's really no need for us to stay in touch. Once she's dead and buried, let's just go our separate ways. Okay?"

His words dismantle her.

Clio doesn't answer. Doesn't even look at him. Her mind is swirling with unwelcome thoughts and memories. She keeps thinking about the ladybug ring on the girl's finger and wondering what she will say to the police.

Patience

They have arrested me. I pretend things aren't as bad as they seem, tell myself that someone called *Patience Liddell* has been arrested and since that is not my real name, the real me is still free. But I don't *feel* free sitting in a square box of a room in a police station. Everything that has happened since I walked into Edith's room for the last time feels like something that is happening to someone else.

I sent a text message while in the back of the police car, nobody told me that I couldn't.

I received a text too, not long after:

If you keep quiet I will help you.

It was soon followed by another:

If you don't keep quiet you are on your own.

And another:

Don't say a word.

The driver pulled over when they heard my phone beeping. The officer in the passenger seat climbed out, opened my door, took my mobile, and then put a set of cuffs on my hands. The handcuffs were heavy and they hurt. I guess all the good cops were off duty today because I got two bad ones.

I do not like the police. Not just because of the cuffs or the way they have treated me, but because my mum didn't like the police either. Though I never really understood why. She taught me not to trust them, but then Mum taught me not to trust anyone. *People can't be trusted*, she would say with a little shake of her head and a tut. Perhaps I should have listened. I think I'm starting to understand why my mum spent her whole life running away, even if I still don't know why or what from.

I've never been inside a police station before. Since we arrived here, they have scanned my fingers and taken photos of my face. Various people—some in uniform, some not—kept talking at me, not to me. And I did *try* to answer their questions as best as I could. I told them the name I've been using for the last year and gave them my current address: "The Attic" in Covent Garden. They didn't believe that I didn't know the name of the street or the postcode. Having lived on a boat for most of my life, those aren't details I'm overly obsessed with.

After that, they left me in this grubby white room. There are two chairs and a table and little else. I haven't had anything to eat or drink today. I'm hungry and thirsty and I really need to go to the bathroom, but I am too afraid to ask. Too afraid to move. Too afraid to say or do anything. I've lost almost all of the money I spent the last year working so hard for, I can never go back to the attic now, which means I am homeless. I've lost my papercuts and all hope of going to art school. I've lost everything, and all because I tried to do the *right* thing.

When the door finally opens, it makes me jump, and I wonder if that makes me look guilty. It's very clear that they think that I am.

"Hello again, I'm DCI Charlotte Chapman. Sorry to have kept you waiting," says the woman I briefly saw before I was put in the police car. She closes the door behind her and sits down on the other side of the table. She's young, late twenties maybe, and has shoulder-length blond hair with a single pink highlight on one side. She's wearing a tweed trouser suit over a T-shirt, and has several silver rings on her fingers. She does not look like a detective.

"Can I get you anything? Tea, coffee, water?" she asks.

"No," I say, even though I am thirsty.

"You're sure? We're going to be here for a while."

I shake my head. "Thank you," I add. I was raised always to be polite, even to people I don't know or like.

"Suit yourself. For the record, you have stated that your name is Patience Liddell and that you are eighteen years of age. You reside at 'The Attic' above Kennedy's Gallery in Covent Garden. Is that correct?" My thoughts get a little tangled, and I can't seem to straighten them out fast enough to form a reply. So I nod instead. "Can you answer out loud please?" she asks, pointing at a little machine on the table. I notice that her fingernails are all painted different colors. My own are unpainted and bitten.

"Yes," I reply, self-conscious about my voice now that I know I am being recorded. I do not sound like myself.

"You have been arrested because of multiple accusations of theft from elderly residents at the Windsor Care Home. The adult children of one resident also claim that you coerced her to change her will." She raises her eyebrows at me then carries on reading. "That resident is named Mrs. Edith Elliot. Her bank card has been used at least once a week recently, even though by all accounts Mrs. Elliot hasn't left her room for several months. Someone matching your description has been captured on CCTV at the times when the card was used. The same bank card was found inside your purse earlier today, and Mrs. Elliot is missing." The detective looks up as though expecting me to say something. When I don't, she continues. "You were arrested in a flat above Mrs. Elliot's son's art gallery, where we later found a large amount of cash believed to have been taken from her account. And you were wearing the woman's jewelry, which you claim was a gift. Officers discovered other stolen items, and then there's the other matter to discuss . . . How would you describe your boss at the care home, Joy Bonetta?"

Rude, unreliable, incompetent, uncaring, untrustworthy, a bully, a liar, and a thief.

"She's okay," I say.

The detective stares at me hard. "I'm going to try to save us both some time and I'd appreciate it if you would do the same. Why did you kill her?"

It takes me a moment to process what she just said.

"I . . . didn't. I don't know anything about it. Is she really dead?"

DCI Chapman sighs. "I guess we're going to do this the hard way. Yes, she is dead. Very much so. The last time anyone saw her alive was when she was on her way upstairs to confront you about stealing things belonging to a . . ." she checks her notes "Mr. Henderson, who has been extremely helpful and gave a very thorough statement about you. Mr. Henderson's stolen war medals have since been found hidden under your bed in 'The Attic,' giving us no reason to doubt his version of events. Did Joy catch you in the act? Did she walk in and find you stealing the old man's things? Is that why you killed her?"

"I didn't—"

"Do you deny taking the war medals that we found under your bed?"

"I confess I took the medals but I was going to give them back. Joy did see me but—"

"But then you killed her."

"No!"

"Putting the body in a broken elevator meant nobody found her for a few hours, but we're still able to tell roughly when she died and it was around the time she came to find you. Nobody saw her after that. She died as a result of a blunt force trauma to the skull, we know that much, but what did you hit her with? And why did you drag her lifeless body to the elevator and put an out-of-order sign around her neck?" She pauses as though expecting me to speak but I have no words. I don't even react to what she just said because I don't know how to. "Where is the murder weapon?"

"I don't know," I say. It's the truth but she continues to stare at me. "I didn't murder anyone. Nobody said anything about *murder* when I was arrested."

"Sorry about that, strictly speaking I should have, but I was waiting for some tests to come back. It's amazing what the forensics team can do these days. The clues they can find at a scene that prove who did what. So that it really doesn't matter whether someone is or isn't a good liar: the evidence tells us everything we need to know. I think I've already wasted too much time on you. Any questions?"

"Don't I get a phone call?"

"That's a good question. Yes, you do. My turn to ask a question. Why did you do it?"

I remember the text telling me not to say a word and don't answer. She doesn't believe anything I say anyway. I'm tired of trying to defend myself and I've probably already said more than I should have. DCI Chapman nods as though she can read my mind and for a moment I am scared that maybe she can. She sighs and shakes her head.

"You're so young. You have your whole life ahead of you. If you tell me the truth about what happened, maybe you won't have to spend it all in jail." I still don't say anything but I do start to cry. "Okay, have it your way. Between us, you should ask about legal representation because you're going to need it. You haven't been formally charged yet, but you're going to be. I do have one last question for now: your name. It's not really your name is it? That's why it took a little while for us to process you, because there *isn't* anyone named Patience Liddell with your date of birth. We can check these things nowadays, you see. So, who are you? Really?"

I could confirm that Patience *isn't* my real name, and that I chose the surname Liddell because of Alice Liddell, the real Alice in Wonderland. It was my favorite book as a child—the one I asked my mother to read to me before I could read it for myself. But why should I help this woman who has already made up her mind about me?

I dry my tears. "I'd like to make that phone call."

Frankie

Frankie has texted her daughter back ten times already but there is no reply. According to her own phone, the messages haven't even been read. She must have dialed Nellie's number fifty times but it goes straight to voice mail. And it is just a generic recording, not her daughter's voice, a sound she misses so much. She keeps wondering if she imagined receiving the text but it's still there, every time she checks: HELP ME MUM.

Frankie has a pain in her chest and feels as though she can't breathe. She remembers this feeling. The first time her daughter disappeared—in a supermarket of all places—she was still so small. It doesn't matter that she is eighteen years old now; the sense of panic and the overwhelming fear feel exactly the same. Frankie's little girl needs her and she doesn't even know where to start looking. She puts some cash on the table for the breakfast she no longer has an appetite for, then leaves the café. She hurries back to the van—twenty-four steps—and sees a yellow parking ticket on the windscreen. She snatches it, stuffs it inside her bag, and looks up just in time to see them: the owner of the gallery *and* the woman from the pink house. Together. Standing in front of a narrow alleyway.

They walk toward the gallery and Frankie sees that the sign on the door still says *Closed*, even though it is now late morning. Jude Kennedy checks that the door is locked, then he walks away down the cobbled street toward Trafalgar Square. The woman in the pink house walks away in the opposite direction. They don't hug or say goodbye to each other. They look like strangers and the whole scene seems a little off, so Frankie decides to investigate the alley they just emerged from for herself.

Covent Garden is heaving with tourists and shoppers, but life has taught her that people are generally too preoccupied with themselves to notice what someone else is or isn't doing. There are forty-eight steps from the van to the alleyway. At first, it looks like there is nothing there—just some bins and cardboard boxes left out for recycling—but then she spots the door at the side of the building.

Picking locks is surprisingly easy. It's one of the first things an inmate at HMP Crossroads taught her to do. Lazy Jane—as she liked to be known—was genuinely shocked by how much Frankie once paid a locksmith when she lost her door keys. Jane—who was a workaholic on the outside and inside, not lazy at all—taught her enough so that she'd never need a man to unlock a door again. Modern locks are a little more tricky, but the basic kind, the variety you'll find on most doors, are simple to open when you know how. Frankie has a tool on her key ring and she's inside in less than thirty seconds.

The view that greets her is disappointing, just stairs. A lot of them. One hundred and twenty-three steps in total, she discovers when she reaches the top. Then there is another door, which means another lock to pick. She pushes the second door open and gasps. There is an unframed papercut of a fox on the wall, her daughter was here, she's sure of it. Frankie rushes to the bed and lifts the pillow to her face, it still smells of *her*. Nellie was probably in this room when Frankie was downstairs in the gallery earlier. The owner lied to her, not that she should be surprised. The Kennedys are a family full of liars.

She looks around slowly, as though scared of what else she might find. She recognizes some of the clothes on the rail and touches them to make sure they are real. There are other familiar items on the bed, including the Japanese tea tin Frankie used to keep their emergency money in. She checks inside but the tin is empty. The whole place has a strange feeling and it looks as though someone left in a hurry. Then she sees the art portfolio leaning against the wall. She unzips it and cries when she sees one papercut after another, her daughter made all of them, she is sure of it.

Frankie feels helpless as she stands in the middle of the abandoned attic. The love between a mother and daughter is like a contract signed with invisible ink, but the terms and conditions do vary. Everybody has a mother, but not everybody has a mother's love. Frankie will always love her daughter, no matter what. That's what she signed up to do. To have been this close to getting her back and to have somehow missed her is devastating. She doesn't know what to do now, or where to look, or how to find her.

But *they* know.

And Frankie knows how to find them.

She takes her daughter's art and runs back down the stairs—all one hundred and twenty-three of them—then hurries to the van. Frankie is going to pay the woman in the pink house another visit, and this time she isn't going to bother making an appointment.

Clio

Keeping busy keeps Clio safe from her own thoughts. Having too much time to think, to feel, to remember is dangerous. Normally there would be clients to see and to listen to, to try to help, but she canceled all of her appointments today. As a result, the house is too quiet and her own thoughts and fears are too loud. She needs the noise of someone else's anxieties to drown out the sound of her own. Clio wanders around the ground floor as though lost in the house she lives in, opening the doors as if expecting to find someone behind them. But there is nobody else here. Not anymore.

Reading people isn't just Clio's job, it's her superpower. But trying to understand herself has always proved difficult. And putting herself back together again simply wasn't possible after what happened, not that she really tried. She didn't think she deserved to be fixed.

Clio didn't always live alone in the pink house. It was just the three of them back then: Clio, her husband, and their baby girl. She had a happy family of her own once upon a time, though now it feels more like a dream. The edges of her memories a little torn and faded with time. Those were the best months, days, hours, and minutes of her life, but her happiness was stolen from her. She disappears inside herself, thinking about those three people who used to live here, people who had no clue that they were about to lose everything worth anything. That version of Clio no longer exists, and memories of that time make her feel as though she is being haunted by her own ghost. She wonders what she would have done differently if she'd been warned what might happen, and the answer is the same as always: everything.

Sure, she was tired all of the time looking after the baby, and maybe her marriage wasn't perfect—what marriage is?—but she had it all, and couldn't see it until it was all taken away. She should have enjoyed life more when there was so much to be happy about. Clio heads upstairs, past her bedroom, and along the landing until she reaches the room at the end of the hall. She used to be scared to open the door, but it looks different these days. This is now her *collecting room*. It's probably the nicest room in the house, with the best light and views, but Clio never used to spend too much time in here because of what this room *used* to be. Until she had a decorator paint over the pink walls with a sad shade of gray, replaced the carpet with a hard wooden floor, and paid a carpenter to line those gray walls from floor to ceiling with shelves. He thought he was building a library. It might have been a nice idea—to fill a room with stories that had happier endings than her own—but Clio doesn't collect books.

She loves and hates this house. She has consistently loved it and cared for it longer than any of the people in her life. Clio hates the house for not being the home it once was, but she can't ever sell it, could never leave for good, because she can't leave her pain behind. Doesn't deserve to. When the walls start closing in—the way they sometimes do if she doesn't keep busy—Clio allows herself to escape to the cemetery. It's a short walk, just one street away, and that seems only right and fair. She thinks she deserves the memories that haunt her day and night, and to be constantly reminded of everything that she had and everything that she lost. It is a form of self-harm that holds the remaining pieces of her together.

Today, like so many days before, the small cemetery at the end of the street is empty. The only thing that feels different to Clio is the strange sensation of being watched. The feeling gives her goose bumps, but when she turns around there is nobody there. Loneliness likes to play tricks on people. So does guilt. Clio finds the tiny headstone and kneels down in front of it, for once not caring if her clothes get dirty. She wonders where her mother would like to be buried, and it feels wrong that she doesn't know the answer.

Clio thinks that the girl who lived in the attic and worked in the care home probably knows. Maybe she knows all sorts of things about her mother that Clio doesn't. Strangers tend to see a different version of the people we love. And Clio does still love her mother, but she is committed to hating her too. She doubts that the girl in the attic knows about all the bad things her mother has done, if she did she wouldn't have been so keen to help. All anyone seems to see when they look at Edith Elliot now is a sweet old lady. Not everyone we meet in the present is the same person they were in the past.

Her elderly mother is missing but Clio doubts she is lost.

She thinks she knows where to find her but isn't ready to look.

And Clio is glad that the care home manager is dead.

The detective was right to suspect Clio of doing *something* wrong, but like her mother, Clio is very good at hiding her true self from the rest of the world. People are always too quick to judge other people based on their appearance, the way they speak, their job. A therapist is seen as someone kind, caring, and clever. Someone who people can be honest and open with. Someone they can trust. If people knew who she really was and what she was capable of they would never trust her again.

Clio kisses her fingers then touches the tiny headstone, knowing that there is nobody really there. She believes death is the end. She doesn't believe in God, but Clio sometimes wishes that she did believe in *something*. She feels jealous of people with faith, people who think there is something after we die. The loved ones Clio lost all those years ago are gone for good, and without them her life feels empty and pointless. Mother's Day this year stirred up some unhappy memories and caused her mind to incorrectly fill in the blanks. Hope pretends to be kind but is often cruel.

She hears something again, the sound of a twig snapping, but when she turns around she still sees nothing. She is alone in the cemetery and Clio doesn't believe in ghosts.

But she is haunted by her memories.

Sometimes she wishes she could run away, quit her life and start a new one. But she can't. Nobody can. Not really. The people we were always eventually catch up with the people we are. So Clio does something she hasn't done for years and lets herself cry.

Frankie

Frankie watches the woman in the pink house crouch down and sob in front of a tiny headstone, the variety that is only used when burying young children. She sees the way the woman's shoulders shake as she weeps, and the way she stumbles when she rises, as though grief has made it too difficult for her to stand. Frankie has a curious urge to comfort her—she doesn't like to see anyone in pain, even people who have hurt her—but she stays back, hiding behind a tree until she is sure the woman has gone.

Frankie followed her here and she's glad that she did. She thought she knew everything about the woman in the pink house, but she didn't know about this. She winds her way through moss covered graves, until she reaches the tiny headstone the woman was crying in front of. It still looks new. She reads the short inscription carved into the white marble:

ELEANOR KENNEDY
10 September 2002–30 March 2003
Forever loved

It is a child's grave for a baby girl, less than one year old. She sees that the child was born in September and can't help thinking about her own daughter. Frankie has so many happy memories of celebrating her daughter's birthday every spring, always at that glorious time of year when leaves start appearing on the trees after a long, dark winter and flowers begin to blossom. This poor woman didn't get to celebrate any birthdays with her daughter, not one. Knowing that the woman in the pink house has experienced the devastating pain of losing a child changes things. Frankie followed Clio, intending to confront her, but there is no longer any point. The woman does not know where Frankie's daughter is, Frankie is sure of that now.

She checks her mobile phone again but there are no new calls or messages. Just the last one:

HELP ME MUM.

Frankie wants to but she needs to find her daughter first.

She knows the police won't help her, but wonders if someone at the prison might be able to trace her daughter's phone. It's never a good idea to owe an inmate a favor but in this case it might be worth the risk. Yesterday, she didn't think she would ever go back to the prison or her job, but things are different now. She has hope and a purpose again; her daughter still needs her. If Frankie can find her and fix what got broken, keeping her job so she can support them both is crucial. She's several hours late for her shift, but she doubts anyone will notice if she gets there before today's group session. As head librarian Frankie is free to come and go as she pleases most of the time. It isn't as though she formally quit, she just wasn't planning to turn up for work again. Perhaps there is a way for everything to go back to how it was and pretend that none of this happened. Maybe they could still be who they were before.

It takes an hour to drive across London to HMP Crossroads,

and when she finally reaches the prison car park someone else has parked in her spot. Frankie doesn't own the parking space—obviously—and the car park is used by visitors as well as staff, but the space is where she *always* parks. This is not a good sign. She changes into her uniform in the van and hides her phone in her bra. Another risk, but one worth taking.

There should be seventy-three steps from the van to the prison gate, but because she couldn't park where she wanted, it takes eighty-two. Frankie feels discombobulated again. She hesitates, wondering if this is another sign, but then she sees the transfer van approaching in the distance. Staff and prisoners all have to be processed through the same gate. If she doesn't hurry there will be a queue and chaos, but chaos might be just what she needs. Frankie takes out her staff pass and heads inside.

She puts her bag in her locker, then silently counts the steps to the front desk. The guard on duty today is a small round man who is often off sick. It isn't anything any doctor can help with, the man suffers from incurable laziness. He is short of patience as well as in stature, and she can't help staring at his untamed curly white hair and matching eyebrows while he checks her security pass. He holds it too close to his face—as though he might need glasses—and he checks his screen twice, despite having worked with Frankie for almost ten years. He grunts and lets her through as though doing her a favor. The man reminds her of an unfriendly goat she and her daughter once saw at London Zoo.

There are twenty-eight steps from reception to the scanning room. Frankie puts her keys and anything metal on the conveyor belt as always, then walks through the body scanner, stopping when it beeps. She walks through a second time—as the rules state she must—and the machine beeps again, just as she knew it would. Frankie stands to the side with her legs slightly spread and her arms in the air, as is the protocol. She can already feel herself starting to sweat. The female member of staff now waving a metal detecting wand around her body is only borderline friendly. Even less so when the wand buzzes. Twice.

"Sorry, I think it might be my new bra. It's underwired," Frankie says.

"Got a hot date later, have you?"

"Lukewarm at best."

"Ha!"

They both turn when they hear the van-load of new arrivals walking into reception; this is one of the only female prisons in the country and it's about to get busy.

Frankie sighs. "Incoming."

"God help me," says her colleague. "I was just about to go for a smoke too. Go on through and good luck with the date!"

"Thank you," Frankie replies. She knows that if she had been caught smuggling a phone into the prison she wouldn't just have been fired, she would have been arrested. She gathers her things, checks her Mickey Mouse watch, and sees she needs to hurry. Frankie uses the biggest key attached to her belt to unlock the door, then crosses the courtyard, feeling watched. She uses another key to let herself inside block B. There are forty steps up to her floor, but she takes them two at a time today. Another key. Then twenty-two steps to the library. The last key and she is inside. The final fourteen steps take her to her desk, where she barely has time to sit down before someone knocks on the library door. It swings open before she can reach it.

"Oh, you're here! I heard you might be off sick," says Taylor. She is the most popular guard in the prison, well-liked by staff and inmates. Frankie doesn't understand why that is, or why she dislikes Taylor so much. Maybe it's her popularity, or the way her long ponytail swings when she walks, or how she is *always* inexplicably cheerful. Frankie doesn't trust people who are happy all of the time.

"Here I am!" Frankie says, trying to match the other woman's disturbingly cheerful tone. It sounds unnatural and her own smile tugs half-heartedly at the corners of her mouth.

"Great. Got four for you today."

"Four means death in Chinese," Frankie blurts out.

Taylor gives her an odd look. "Is that so?" Then she checks her watch as though she has somewhere more important to be, like the staff canteen. "Come on in, you lot. The books won't bite and I don't want to spend any longer with you losers than I have to." Taylor smiles as she insults the prisoners, and what is most bizarre is that *they* smile back. Frankie wonders if she should try the same approach, but she's never been good at insulting people. Or smiling at them.

Taylor hands over the list and Frankie takes it. There is a list for every activity in the prison, but luckily lists are something she is rather fond of. Inmates have to apply online for all activities, using a computer in their cell. When Frankie first started working here, she was surprised to learn that prisoners had computers, but they can only access the intranet. Supervisors for each session—like Frankie, who is in charge of all events and goings-on in the library—have to approve each application. Once approved, inmates get collected by a guard, then escorted to the activity, then signed off on a list just like the one Frankie is staring at now. Four people for an afternoon session is okay, about standard. Other activities are more popular—like hairdressing, and plumbing—but the best people choose books. That's what Frankie thinks. She checks the four women entering the room, ticking off each one, before thanking Taylor and closing the library door.

"Is the author visit still happening tomorrow, Miss Fletcher?" asks Liberty, one of the youngest prisoners at HMP Crossroads. Her parents' choice of name seems unfortunate given where the girl has ended up. Liberty is one of Frankie's favorites—well-read, always on time, always offering to help. She has a head of blond curls and ambition, and one of those thick cockney accents that sounds a smidgen put on to Frankie's ears, as though she has just walked off the set of *Mary Poppins*. Frankie can't remember what Liberty is in prison for, and there comes a point when it is rude to ask. Like when you've known someone for a long time but still don't really understand what they do for a living.

"Everything hunky-dory, Miss Fletcher? You don't seem like yourself," Liberty says, interrupting her thoughts, and Frankie realizes she has been staring at the girl. Probably because she is roughly the same age as her daughter.

"I'm sorry, miles away. What were you asking me?"

Liberty frowns, looking too much like a child to be in a place like this. "The author visit tomorrow. Is it still happening?"

Frankie had completely forgotten about it. "Yes, of course."

"Ace! She's someone I'd bite my right arm off to meet!" the girl replies. Frankie knows that means she is happy about it, and isn't actually going to bite off her own arm, or anyone else's.

"I know how much you all look forward to the monthly author visits," Frankie says, addressing the volunteers. "Which is why I thought we should spend our session this afternoon tidying the library, so that everything is spick and span for tomorrow." They all groan. "Or, I can call the guard to take you back to your cells if you'd prefer?" The library is as silent as it should be. "Good. Why don't you each take a corner, and start making sure the books are looking neat and tidy on the shelves. There are a pile of returns here that need processing and putting back too."

When they're all busy, or at least look like they're doing something vaguely useful, Frankie heads to her office and checks the schedule pinned above her desk. Each month she books an author to visit the prison, something which has proved popular with both inmates and staff. The inmates have to apply to take part and, once approved, they are given a copy of the author's latest book to read ahead of the event. The event normally consists of an author talk followed by an—often lively—Q&A. Frankie can't remember who she booked for tomorrow; she didn't think she'd still be here. But sees now it is a crime author—always popular in the prison.

Frankie checks to see that the volunteers are still busy, then retreats farther into her office before unbuttoning her shirt to retrieve the phone hidden inside her bra. There are no missed calls, no new messages, not even an alarm.

"Are you allowed to have a mobile phone in here, Miss Fletcher? I thought even staff had to leave them at reception and just use their walkie-talkies," a voice whispers behind her.

Frankie freezes, then slowly turns to see Liberty.

"I had a personal emergency," Frankie says. Half-truths are better than whole lies.

"That old chestnut. I've had a few of those too," Liberty replies, smiling. "Don't worry, Miss Fletcher. Your secret is safe with me."

It isn't a veiled threat, the look on the girl's face is one of genuine concern. Liberty respects Frankie too much to cause her any trouble. The perspective of youth is rarely level. Young people either look up to or down on their elders rather than viewing someone older as an equal. Frankie was just the same when she was young. The girl is about to go back to sorting a pile of books when Frankie remembers why she is in prison.

"Liberty?"

"Yes, Miss Fletcher?"

"It was hacking, wasn't it, the thing you are serving time for?"

"I don't like the expression 'serving time,' miss. I like to think that my time is my own, I'm just paying back what I owe. But yes, hacking is . . . what they caught me for."

"And, forgive my ignorance in these matters. But does that mean you might know a thing or two about tracing phones?"

Liberty shakes her head. "No it doesn't, but I do. I know a thing or two about plenty of things I shouldn't. You need some help, Miss Fletcher? Because if you do, I'm your girl."

Patience

So far, I've been arrested, charged, driven from a police station to a courthouse, and assigned a "duty lawyer" who spent more time checking his phone than listening to anything I had to say. I was made to stand in front of a judge who looked like he was going to fall asleep while my case was being read out, and I've been "put on remand," which apparently means I'm not going home any time soon. Not that I have a home to go to anymore. I'm now being driven to prison. Whenever I think things can't get worse, they do. The lawyer said I'll be in prison until my trial, but nobody can tell me when that will be.

The text said, Don't say a word, and I haven't, but maybe that was a mistake.

My one phone call was a complete waste of time too. It was the only number I knew by heart, but nobody answered. Now I am in a van with nine other women. They are all older than me, and while I don't wish to sound judgmental, they all look as though they probably did whatever they have been accused of. But maybe

I look guilty too? I must, because everyone seems to believe that I am. Nobody speaks and I try to avoid eye contact, because every time I get caught staring at someone, the way they glare back terrifies me.

The van parks and everyone else gets out as though this is a familiar routine for them. I follow but stop on the bus steps when I see where we are.

"HMP Crossroads?" I say.

"I'm sorry, did you think we were going to Disneyland?" the driver replies. She has gray hair and blue glasses, and looks like she should be driving a school bus instead. "Go on, hurry up and get off," she says. I do and the van door slams shut behind me.

This prison is where my mum works. Or at least it used to be where she worked the last time I spoke to her. I know she always liked to park in the same spot but I can't see her camper van. It's been nearly a year so I suppose she might have gotten a new job. She might have moved away. She might have changed her number. I take in the intimidating sight of the tall prison walls with barbed wire on top and try to hide my fear.

An angry-looking guard tells us to line up—like children—while we wait to go inside. There we are greeted—I use the term loosely—by a short fat man with curly white hair and matching eyebrows. He stares at us all, tuts, shakes his head as though very disappointed by what he sees. Then he grunts before reading our names off a list. I wait to be called to the front.

"Patience Liddell?"

"Yes," I say, stepping up to the desk.

"Face forward," he barks, and he reminds me a little of Dickens, barking and snapping at strangers. I wonder where Edith and Dickens are now, I hope they're okay. The guard growls in my direction again and I get a whiff of bad breath. "Place your right hand on the screen—"

"I already did this at the police station," I interrupt without thinking.

"Oh, I'm sorry. Are we taking up too much of your precious time? Are you in a desperate hurry to get to your cell for some urgent business that can't possibly wait?" he says and the rest of the new arrivals snicker. I shake my head. "Well, in that case I strongly suggest you just do as you're told while you're with us. And maybe keep your thoughts to yourself. Nobody is interested in you or anything you have to say, especially me. Got that? Right hand, then the left, then stare straight ahead at the camera."

I have met men like him before, so I do as I'm told.

Next we are all taken to a room full of scanners. There are three uniformed prison guards—one male, two female—and none of them look friendly. My pockets are empty—the police took everything I had, they said it was evidence—so when I remove my shoes and walk through the scanner it doesn't make a sound. One of the other women sets off the machine three times.

"Underwire bra?" one of the female guards asks. "They've been causing us problems today."

The woman triggering all the beeping is escorted behind a curtain where I hear her being asked to strip. Thankfully I am herded through another door and out into an open courtyard, where we wait an excruciatingly long time for the others to catch up. When they do, we are marched in a line toward another building, with one guard in front of us and one behind. The first guard is wearing a name badge that says Taylor.

I can see several large buildings, and they are all surrounded by extremely tall walls with barbed wire on top. Everything is gray: the ground, the buildings, the sky, the mood, the uniforms of everyone we pass. I follow the guard named Taylor to a large building with the letter *C* painted on the side of it. She pulls a key from her belt and, once inside, locks the door behind us. We walk up some stairs, then she takes another key to open another door, which opens to reveal a huge warehouse-type space, with cells on either side and a metal staircase in the middle.

I am not imagining it, everyone stops and stares at us. The guard stops walking abruptly outside a cell and I nearly walk into the back of her. Taylor tuts, then looks down to check the clipboard she is carrying.

"Patience Liddell?"

"Yes," I reply.

"This is your stop. You'll have your prison interview first thing tomorrow, and will be given your prison number and identity card then. Everything about this place and your time here will be explained during that meeting. For now, you'll find a prison uniform—which you are to change into straightaway—and clean bedding in your cell, along with a plastic cup, plate, and cutlery. There is also a wash kit, toothbrush, and a towel. You've missed the cutoff for dinner orders, but you should receive breakfast in the morning. Any issues, contact your case officer."

"Who is my case officer?" I ask.

"You'll be assigned one tomorrow."

I know the woman is speaking English, but she spoke so quickly that I don't understand half of what she just said.

"What if I have any issues tonight?" I ask.

"I suggest you don't." She holds the door open, stares at me as though I am causing an inconvenient delay, and I reluctantly step into the cell. "Besides, you'll have your cellmate for company. I'm sure she'll give you a warm welcome and make you feel right at home," she adds, before closing the door. I hear the already familiar jingle of keys as she locks me inside, and watch her walk away before I turn around to take in my surroundings.

The cell is tiny. There are two beds, one on either side of the cell, with a small table and an even smaller window between them. To the right of the door is a dirty-looking curtain barely hiding the stained toilet bowl and sink behind it. On the left is a desk, with what looks like a computer, which surprises me. One bed has a plain white sheet, with some bedding and clothes neatly piled at the end. The other bed has a She-Ra duvet and is covered with colorful cushions and cuddly toys. There is a young woman with curly blond hair sitting on that bed with an open book in her lap.

"Hello, I'm Liberty."

Edith

The sound of bells echoes through the old church and makes Edith jump. She only came back to St. Paul's to collect what she left here yesterday and wait for the rain to stop. Dickens sits next to the church pew, staring up at her and wagging his tail.

"I was just resting my eyes," Edith says.

The bell ringing comes to an end and she looks around to check that the place is still empty. She's pleased to see that it is, but also thinks it is such a waste. So many beautiful old churches are abandoned these days. Vacant castles of faith put out to pasture. Surely they could serve more of a purpose in the local community.

"Come on, Dickens. We've got lots to do," she says, sighing and hauling herself out of the ancient wooden pew. "Ladybug must be wondering where we are."

Edith gathers herself and her things and leaves the church. She dumps the magnifying glass statue in the first street bin she sees, so it will find its way to the nearest landfill. Then they walk across the cobbles back toward the alleyway. Edith finds the keys that the girl gave her, but there is no need to use them, the door is slightly ajar. There are so many steps to the attic, too many, so she uses the rail to help heave herself to the top, letting Dickens run up ahead. Falling over these days tends to result in a trip to the hospital, so Edith takes her time, watching her own feet so she doesn't trip over them.

"Oh dear," she says, seeing that the attic is empty. "This is an unwelcome conundrum."

All of the papercuts have been removed from the walls except for one. Ladybug is gone and so are her things. Edith checks under the bed and sees that her old pink leather suitcase is still there. She pulls it out, opens it, and is relieved to see that her belongings are inside. She opens a packet of custard creams and eats one.

"What are we going to do now, Dickens?" she asks, staring at the dog. "We can't go back to the care home and I don't want to die in jail. I'm too old for this malarkey. Too old and too tired." Dickens barks and Edith nods. "You're quite right, it's time to go home."

Clio

Clio double locked the front door as soon as she got home. Then she pulled all the curtains and blinds but still feels as though someone is watching her.

She sometimes hears them in the house.

Her daughter and her husband.

She tells herself that it is just her imagination.

It must be. He left her all alone in the world only six months after they lost their baby girl. She'll never forgive him.

Sometimes you have to fall down to remember how to pick yourself up. Her mother used to say that all the time and Clio used to agree. But fall too far, too hard, too fast and you forget how to climb out of the darkness. Forget to even want to. She needs to keep busy and take her mind off things, so she heads upstairs. Clio removed almost all of the mirrors in the house because she used to see their faces in them. There is one left at the top of the staircase—so that she can check her appearance before appointments with clients— but she avoids looking at herself at all other times. It's a journey her eyes don't want to make, scared of what they might see. She is what a life of regrets looks like.

Different people need different ways to cope with difficult issues, any therapist knows that. There isn't a one-size-fits-all approach to healing, and there are several brands of coping mechanisms, most of which prove unreliable in the long term. Fixing others has always been easier than fixing herself. Clio doesn't drink, or smoke, or take drugs—other than St. John's wort from the health food shop and the occasional aspirin—but she is addicted to something. Her collecting room is where she likes to lock herself away when life gets too loud. A sanctuary of sorts. Some people's secrets are written on their faces, but Clio keeps hers in boxes on bespoke wooden shelves, in a room that used to be a nursery.

She stands there now, admiring the neatness of it all—the stark contrast to the mess of her life. A room of her own where she can control things, keep them safe. This was supposed to be their forever home and in some ways it still is. She will stay here forever and her memories of them mean that they will too.

Nothing about becoming a mother was easy but it was all she ever wanted. It took them two years to get pregnant. She sometimes feared that it would never happen, then once it did, she sometimes wished it never had. She tries to forget the part before the baby arrived. It's little more than blurred recollections of exhaustion, sickness, anxiety, and an overwhelming fear that she was going to lose another child. Then her little girl was born. Then she lost her anyway.

She was perfect. They were a family. Until they weren't.

Clio gave her daughter life and all the love she was able to give. She insisted on giving Eleanor her surname too, a decision her husband pretended to be fine with. Clio kept Kennedy, her maiden name when she got married—giving up her name or any part of herself wasn't something she could comprehend or contemplate—and the baby was part of her. That's how it felt. Her daughter was a part of herself she had gained and lost at the same time.

This room was once her daughter's bedroom, but now it's where she keeps her collection. Clio has over five hundred pairs of trainers. They are all her size, but most of them have never been worn. Some are very rare: genuine collectors' items. It is a mix of nostalgia and a love of design that drives her passion for them. For a long time after she lost her daughter, opening a box of brand-new trainers was the only thing that brought her joy. A therapist would have a field day but, being one herself, she knows better than to ever talk to anyone about her bad habits.

Clio sits cross-legged like a child on the floor of her collecting room. She takes one of the shoeboxes from the shelf and slowly lifts the lid. Inside is a brand-new pair of Nike Air trainers from the 1980s, a collector's item worth several thousand pounds. She admires them, then carefully puts them back. If she were to sell just some of these boxes it would solve her financial issues, for a while at least, but she has already lost too many precious things because of her so-called family.

There wasn't any spare money for nice things when Clio was growing up. Sometimes her mother would make them choose between supper or having the heating on; they couldn't afford both. So Clio wore cheap plimsolls for PE at school, while all the other girls had fancy Nikes or Adidas or Reeboks. There have been so many things Clio wanted in life: a daughter, a husband, a loving family, a satisfying career—things that, even if she managed to briefly have, she soon lost again. But these boxes of sneakers are something she does have control over. Something she can keep safe, look after, hold whenever she wants to. Her collection is her dirty secret, one she feels deeply ashamed of. But it's not her only secret. And it isn't her biggest.

Clio wishes that there was someone she could call. She was always good at making friends but not so good at keeping them. When it happened, she avoided and ignored all of her friends until they stopped getting in touch. She suspects they were relieved; grief can be contagious. The initial outpouring of support when they lost their child—in the form of cards, flowers, phone calls, casseroles— all stopped in the end. People soon tire of trying to help when they realize that they can't.

Clio takes another shoebox from the shelf. This one does not contain trainers.

She carefully lifts out the small white photo album that she hid inside it many years ago. The photo on the first page is of Clio in a hospital bed holding her baby daughter. Clio is so young in this picture, so glowing with joy and health that it is almost like look- ing at a different person. She is smiling and it is the happiest she has ever seen her own face.

The next few pages are all filled with pictures of a baby. Her daughter was the most beautiful creature Clio had ever seen, they took photos of her everywhere. She smiles now at the tiny freckles on her daughter's tiny nose. Clio always liked to think of them as freckles even though the doctor said that was not what they were. He said they were tiny birthmarks. She didn't like the sound of that, or anything else that suggested there was something wrong with her perfect baby. Seeing her family reunited in the pages of a photo album reminds her of how happy they were until they weren't. Her smile fades when she finds the photo she is looking for: her mother, holding the baby for the first time. Clio's daughter is wrapped in a blanket covered in ladybugs, a gift from Edith, who is beaming at the camera. Clio's husband persuaded her to reconcile with her mother when their daughter was born. He thought family was important and insisted it was the right thing to do. He was wrong.

He never said that he blamed Clio for what happened, but he did. It wasn't her fault, but it took her a long time to believe that.

How could she have known that a trip to the supermarket would ruin their lives?

Patience

"Prison doesn't have to ruin your life. Stick with me and you'll be fine," Liberty says.

I don't believe her, but I am grateful for everything she has done for me. Liberty helped me to make my bed, offered me a can of Coke and some Doritos and spent the last couple of hours explaining everything about how the prison works. When Liberty's dinner arrived, she insisted on sharing half of everything, spooning more than half onto a red plastic plate using plastic cutlery. I had no dinner of my own because I'm not "on the system" yet. And now we're eating fish and chips and mushy peas, and things aren't as terrible as I thought they would be.

"How has your family coped with you being sent here?" Liberty asks.

I shrug. "I'm not sure they know where I am."

"You what? Didn't you tell 'em?"

"I tried to tell my mum, but it all happened so fast."

"That your family is it? Just you and your mum?" I try to hide my discomfort and she's intuitive enough to change the subject. "Well, in the future you should start getting your own meals delivered to the cell three times a day. You have to choose what you want for breakfast, lunch, and dinner on the computer. You can't do it yet because you don't have a prison number. Hopefully they'll give you one first thing tomorrow. We eat in the cells because otherwise there are fights over food. It's actually the thing people in here fight over the most. You wouldn't Adam and Eve it." I frown. "Adam and Eve it. Believe it. Whatever. Just so you know, the computer is also how you apply for activities, or accept visits, or arrange phone calls. Everything happens on the computer, but you need a password, and for that you need a prison number—"

"Which I can't get until tomorrow," I say.

"You got it! Everything in here takes donkey's years. Do you want a lollipop?" Liberty asks, holding out a bag of sweets. She's lying on the bed covered with the She-Ra duvet.

"No. Thank you. How come you have all this *stuff*?"

"Like what?"

"The kids' duvet, the toys, the sweets."

"My personal things you mean? Like I said, prison in real life isn't like it is in the movies. My mum brought these things in for me—she brings a cuddly toy almost every time she visits—and I'm allowed to keep them so long as I stick to the rules." When she speaks about the rules it makes me think about the care home. Edith was right: it was a bit like a prison. "My mum still thinks I'm a little girl, I bet yours does too. Mums who don't want their babies to grow up sometimes pretend that they haven't. I'm sure yours will bring you some of your stuff to make this feel a bit more like home when she comes to visit." My face gives me away again. "You sure I can't interest you in a lolly?" she asks. I shake my head. "Suit yourself." She peels the wrapper off a Chupa Chups then sticks it in her mouth. "So, here's the big question everyone will want to know the answer to. What. Did. You. Do?" She leans forward and looks like a child waiting for their favorite bedtime story.

"I didn't *do* anything," I tell her.

"Of course! None of us did!" Liberty crosses herself the way Catholics do, before pressing her hands into a prayer shape. "Everyone in here is a saint. Let me rephrase the question. What do they *say* you did? Allegedly and all that jazz?"

"It's a long list."

"Yeah, yeah, but you're only here on remand. We call people like you tourists. Just here on holiday for a couple of weeks before you travel back to the real world. You have to tell me what you're in for; if I'm sharing a cell with you then I've got a right to know whether it's safe for me to close my eyes at night. Them's the rules."

"Fine. I'm accused of theft, fraud . . . and murder."

Liberty takes out her lollipop and stares open mouthed. "*Murder*? You?"

The atmosphere changes instantly. "Like I said, I didn't do it. I think I've been set up."

She stares at me for a while. "I was taught never to judge a book by its cover, but it seems I mistook an Agatha Christie for a Jane Austen. I had you pegged as a shoplifter. I wouldn't have guessed *murder* in a month of Sundays."

"I'm *not* a murderer."

"Keep your knickers on, I believe you."

"Then you might be the only person who does." I try to compose myself. "Sorry, I'm just so tired and stressed, I feel like I'm losing my mind. Thank you for being so kind to me."

"Kindness is free. Besides, now I've done you a little favor, I know you'll do one for me when the time comes."

The lights go out and we are plunged into darkness. I blink several times, trying to adjust to the dark, but everything is black.

"What's happening?" I ask.

"It's okay, it's just lights-out," Liberty says, hearing the panic in my voice.

"At eight o'clock?"

"Yep. Same time, every night. They'll come back on at seven tomorrow morning. Try to get some sleep and try to be patient, Patience. Tomorrow will be a better day, you'll see. You said you think someone set you up. Who?"

"Someone I met in a care home and was foolish enough to trust."

Edith

Edith is lost. She got the number seventy-two bus and rang the bell when she passed the pub, but something is wrong. Her old house, her *home*, should be right here. But it's gone. So is her neighbor's house, and the one two doors down. This is the correct road—she's checked twice—but a fancy block of flats appears to have been built where her home used to be.

She's cold and confused and a little frightened, gripping her pink suitcase in one hand, and the dog's lead in her other, sitting at a bus stop but without anywhere left to go. What used to be a safe neighborhood doesn't feel like one anymore. It's dark now, and it's getting late. But Edith is all out of options. She doesn't know what to do.

"I don't understand," she whispers to Dickens. "I hoped if I knocked on the door, explained to whoever was living there now that it was really *my* home, I suppose I thought maybe they'd do the right thing: leave immediately and let me have it back." Her words make her sound like a fool and she knows that is what she has been. "The lawyer said he was confident he could help get my home back, but it's already gone. It's *all* gone."

Once upon a time, this street was just a handful of terraced houses opposite fields and a beautiful park where she and Dickens used to go for walks. Now everything that was here has been buried under concrete. The place is completely unrecognizable except for a single old-fashioned streetlight, dimly glowing in the dark. The world has moved on without her as though she was already dead. The light flickers and Edith wishes her coat was warmer. She feels the cold far more than she used to. Dickens shivers too. Edith hears footsteps approaching the bus stop and spins around.

"Who's there?" she asks, but everything beyond the streetlight is cloaked in shadows.

"Hello, Mum," says a voice in the darkness, then Clio appears like a ghoul.

"What do *you* want? What have you done to my house, my home?"

"I'm sorry you found out this way. I'm sorry you found out at all. We had to sell it," says Clio. "I didn't have a choice."

"Codswallop. People *always* have a choice. You just chose the easy option, the one that was best for you. Like always." She stares up at the star-speckled sky. "What did I do to deserve such selfish children?"

"You raised us to be like you. I'm sorry, I really am, but I'm too damn tired to do this dance again. It's late and it's cold. Shall I take you home?"

"I'm not going back to that place."

"I mean *my* home. For now."

"I don't want to go there either. I won't go where I'm not welcome."

"It's never stopped you before," Clio mutters.

"What did you say to me?"

"Nothing. Please can we get going? I have a taxi waiting and these things aren't free."

"Well, you should have some spare cash from selling my home behind my back."

"You signed the paperwork."

"If I did then I was tricked into doing it."

"Not by me. We needed the money to pay for your care."

"Who is *we* and what *care*? Those people didn't care about me and you couldn't care less."

"How can you say that after everything I've done for you?" Clio asks.

"The only person who cares about me is Ladybug."

"If you mean the girl in the care home, she only did the things she did for you because she was paid to."

"Liar. You don't know what you're talking about."

"*Paid* to take care of you in the home. *Paid* to give Jude little updates. *Paid* to get you out of there, by me. And now you've changed your will to leave almost everything to her. Why would you do that? If you think she's your long-lost granddaughter then you're even more deluded than I thought. Nothing you think you know about her is real. She didn't even tell you her real name."

Edith frowns. "You're wrong about her, about all of it."

"Fine. You're right, I'm wrong. So where is she now?" Clio asks, but Edith doesn't answer. "Come on, let's not do this. You're shivering, Dickens is too, and I bet you're both hungry. Why don't we talk about everything at home?"

Edith glares at her. "I'm not going anywhere with you."

"I'm fully aware that I'm your 'biggest regret' but I'm all you've got."

"What do you mean?"

"I read your notebook."

"How dare you go through my private things!"

"I've always known you didn't want me, didn't like me, didn't love me. You didn't hide it well. Didn't hide it at all. You constantly made me feel as though I were a mistake, and I've viewed my whole life through your lens. As though everyone I meet is someone I shouldn't have met, everything I see is something I shouldn't have seen, everything I do is something that should never have happened, because *you* made me feel like I shouldn't be here at all. And maybe that's why I lost my little girl. Maybe she wasn't supposed to be here either: because I wasn't. Because *you* never really wanted me. When I was a child and you got cross with me—which you so often did—you always said the same thing. *I wish you would disappear.* Maybe it's time your wish came true."

"Go on then. Good riddance," Edith replies as Clio starts to walk away. "Tell me one thing before you go. Have the police been to see you yet?"

Clio stops. She turns on her heel, checks over her shoulder, and marches back toward her mother. "About what?"

"Me."

"What about you?"

"Well, I'm missing, aren't I?"

"Hundreds of people go missing every day. The police have got bigger things to worry about than you."

"Like the murdered care home manager, you mean?" Edith says.

Clio is unable to read the expression on her mother's face. It can be dangerous to ask a question you might not want to know the answer to, so she doesn't. "Mum, I really think—"

Edith shakes her head and interrupts her. "I was there when she died, and I think maybe it's about time someone in this family did the right thing."

Frankie

Frankie sits in the van for a while, watching her boat to make sure someone else isn't watching it. Or waiting for her to come home. Having seen firsthand what happens to criminals who get caught, she doesn't plan on letting that happen to her. This is all Frankie's fault, but even if she could go back in time, do things differently, she wouldn't. The happiness her mistakes have given her still outweigh the sorrow. If she can just find her daughter then maybe everything will be okay, but everywhere she searches proves to be a dead end.

She is still freaked out that the police were here on *The Black Sheep* this morning. Frankie should have left already, but what if her little girl comes back and the boat is gone? Going to the prison this afternoon feels like a mistake too in hindsight. Liberty said she would "ask a friend" to trace the phone—all she needed was the number—but she didn't sound hopeful. Even if Frankie could figure out where her daughter was when she sent the text asking for help, the chances of her still being there now seem small.

She gets out of the van and walks along the riverbank, checking over her shoulder twice before heading inside the boat. As soon as she has locked and bolted the door, Frankie goes straight to her daughter's bedroom, wishing that she will magically be there. But she isn't. Everything is still exactly as it was when she ran away a year ago. There was a reason why Frankie couldn't show her daughter her birth certificate or tell her who her dad was. A very good reason. And even though she tried so hard to do the right thing, she still lost the one person who mattered most to her in the world.

The lack of sleep is making it impossible to think clearly, but how can she rest when her daughter is out there alone and in trouble? Frankie has already called all of the hospitals but nobody with her daughter's name has been admitted in the last twenty-four hours. She thinks a drink might help—even though it rarely does—so pours some red wine into her favorite mug. She lights the stove to take the chill out of the air, then sits in her favorite armchair in her cozy reading nook. Except it doesn't feel cozy tonight and she is too upset to read. Frankie sits and stares at the flames, mesmerized for several minutes before she notices the flashing light on her answering machine. She never bothers to check it these days because nobody ever calls. The only person who used to call the landline—the only person who had the number—was her daughter.

Frankie hits play.

The robotic voice speaks first. "You have one new message. Left today at two forty-three p.m." Frankie looks down at her Mickey Mouse watch, and sees that the message was left several hours ago.

"Mum, it's me. I don't know where to start. I'm in trouble and I'm sorry. I'm at the police station in Covent Garden. There is a detective called Chapman and she thinks I did something. Something bad." Her daughter starts to cry and the sound breaks Frankie's heart. "I'm scared, Mum. Please help me."

Frankie stares at the machine as though it is a ghost.

Chapman. The same detective who came to the boat earlier.

She sinks down to the floor, getting as close to the machine as she can, almost hugging it, then plays the message again.

As soon as it stops, she picks up the keys to the van, grabs her coat and bag, and heads for the door. The traffic won't be so bad at this time of night, she should be able to get to Covent Garden in less than an hour. She hesitates when she reaches the riverbank. If she is going to walk into a police station voluntarily after all these years, she needs to be sure that she is doing the right thing. She doesn't hesitate again. Frankie knows it is time to confess to what she did.

Clio

"I don't take dogs," says the taxi driver.

Dickens barks as though he understands and Clio glares at him.

"I'll pay you extra," she offers. "I need to get my elderly mother home."

"It's not about the money," he replies and Clio pulls a face. In her experience almost everything is about money in the end. "I have *allergies*," he adds.

Allergic to doing the right thing, she thinks.

"Why don't we just get the bus?" Edith suggests.

"Fine. Thanks for nothing," Clio says to the driver before he speeds away.

"There's no need to be rude to people, Clio," says the rudest women on the planet. "And there's no need to sulk. I know all the bus routes and it's free for me with my pass. Here's the number seventy-two now."

"Whatever you want. Let's get the bus and get out of here."

"Then I'm going to the police station."

"We can talk about that when we get home."

They board the red double-decker and head toward the back. It's not too crowded, but Clio would rather they weren't overheard, anxious about what her mother might say next. She needn't have worried, Dickens sits on Edith's lap staring out of the window and they spend the first five minutes of the journey in silence.

"Do you want a custard cream?" Edith asks, shouting above the sound of the bus. She reaches inside her pocket and takes out a half-eaten packet. "Or a cookie perhaps? They're chocolate chip!" Edith says, taking another packet from another pocket. Clio shakes her head. "Why not? There's no meat in them."

"I'm vegan."

"I *know*. It's why you look so ill. Do vegans not eat cookies? Are you worried about cookie welfare?"

Two people up ahead turn around in their seats to stare at them and Clio wishes she was invisible.

"Being vegan is a little more complicated than being vegetarian," she whispers.

"Everything with you is complicated and you've always been cranky when you're hungry, but suit yourself," Edith says, holding a custard cream and taking a bite. The bus windows have steamed up with condensation, and Edith uses her finger to draw a ladybug on the glass. "Everyone knows that ladybugs are lucky, but did you know that their black spots represent joy and sorrow?" she asks, with a mouth full of crumbs. "We all experience joy and sorrow in our lives. No life lived is perfect, we have to learn to balance the good times with the bad. Forgive each other for mistakes, because everyone makes them." Edith looks at her, but Clio continues to stare out of the window so she helps herself to another custard cream. "Ladybugs are *so* prolific, so determined to ensure their future and protect their legacy, that they sometimes give birth to pregnant ladybugs. Their daughters are born ready to have more daughters. Generation after generation, repeating and reliving the same lives as the last, never changing their spots. I never wanted you to turn into me. I wish—"

"I think we're here," Clio says, ringing the bell on the bus.

They get off at Notting Hill station and walk the rest of the journey, slowly winding their way down Portobello Road until they reach the quiet mews and the pink house.

"Never thought I'd be here again," Edith says, staring up at the place.

Neither did I, Clio thinks as she unlocks the door. She watches her mother—and the dog—walk inside her perfect house without even wiping their feet on the doormat. She tells herself to let it go. It's only for one night.

Clio forces her face to smile. "Welcome."

Edith raises an eyebrow. "Are we?"

"Of course. My only request is that you keep the dog—"

"Dickens."

"*Dickens* off the furniture. And I don't want him going upstairs."

"I don't know why you hate dogs so much, they're wonderful company. Especially for someone like you, living alone."

Clio bites her tongue. "Would you like some tea?"

Edith nods, removing her coat and already making herself at home. "Yes please. Milky and two sugars."

"I know how you take it."

"And maybe a cookie. If you have any. Something *normal*, none of that vegan crap."

And so it begins, Clio thinks as she retreats to the kitchen.

It was exactly like this the last time Edith was here. Her mother criticized everything and acted as if Clio's home was a hotel. One she didn't particularly like. It was as though she were doing her daughter some kind of favor by staying.

Just one night, Clio reminds herself while she waits for the kettle to boil.

She walks into her lounge carrying a tray with a cup of tea, a glass of water, and a plate of raisin and cinnamon oat snacks. But Edith is not there. Dickens is sitting on Clio's couch, staring up at her and wagging his tail.

"Get *down*," she says, but the dog just stretches and makes himself more comfortable. She puts the tray on the table and lifts the dog onto the floor, holding him at arm's length. "There are rules in this house. No sitting on the furniture, no chewing, no biting, no barking." The dog tilts his head sideways. "No going upstairs—"

"And no fun," Edith interrupts, walking back into the room. "This place looks more like a museum than a home."

"Thank you," Clio replies. "I like it."

"Well, you always were a few sandwiches short of a picnic."

"The spare bedroom is all made up for you at the top of the stairs. It's been a very long day, I think I'm going to head up now."

"You don't think we should talk?" Edith asks. She takes the cup of tea from the tray, then she picks up one of the oat snacks and sniffs it. "What are these?"

"Cookies."

Edith takes a tiny bite then pulls a face. "Balderdash. This is not a cookie."

"I'm really tired, Mum. Can we talk some more in the morning?"

"I don't think it can wait until then."

"What can't?"

"The dead care home manager. What if the police arrest the wrong person? I don't want that on my conscience at my age."

"They *have* arrested someone."

"Who?" Edith asks, eyes wide with worry.

Clio doesn't think it is a good idea to upset her again and wishes she hadn't said anything. "A detective decided to question me—"

"You?"

"Yes, but only because I happened to be visiting the care home around the time it happened. DCI Chapman was convinced there were three suspects, and said that *I* was one of them—"

"Who did she arrest?" Edith repeats, glaring at her daughter.

Clio sighs. "Patience."

"What? They arrested Ladybug?"

"Arrested and charged I believe."

"Why didn't you tell me sooner?" Edith shrieks. "This is all my fault. We have to go to the police right now."

Frankie

Frankie parks the camper van opposite the police station in Covent Garden. She could be fined for leaving the van here—she already got a ticket today—but right now that's the least of her worries. It takes thirty-three hurried steps to reach the main entrance. Thirty-three is a good number. It's unique and some people think it symbolizes bravery. What Frankie is doing now isn't brave, it's just the right thing to do.

The police station is old, with exposed brick walls and wooden fixtures and fittings. Her footsteps echo on the tiled floor. There is a desk behind a plastic screen in reception, with a police officer sitting at it reading a newspaper. His hair is receding, and his stomach is overflowing his belt. There is a shadow of stubble on his chin along with a dollop of mustard. He looks like an old man trapped in a slightly younger man's body.

"I want to see DCI Chapman," Frankie says, and is flabbergasted when the officer doesn't even look up. "About a missing girl," she adds. When he still doesn't acknowledge her existence, she tries something else to get his attention. "A missing girl *and* a murder."

"Sounds like a novel," he says, raising an eyebrow but continuing to read.

"I have something I need to confess."

"Have you tried talking to your priest?"

"This is serious."

"So am I. Do you know what time it is? The only people who come in here wanting to confess to something at this time of night are either high or crazy. Which one are you?" he asks, finally putting down the newspaper. He leaves it open as though planning to return to the page he was reading as soon as possible.

"I'm not sure how the time is relevant. Or do the police only solve crimes during office hours these days?" Frankie replies. She can only tolerate rudeness from strangers if she doesn't believe them to be dim-witted or lazy, and he is clearly both.

"DCI Chapman isn't here. Would you like to leave a message?" he asks, glancing down at the open newspaper again.

Frankie stares at the man, unable to process his words or his lack of urgency.

"This cannot wait. You have arrested an innocent person," she tries to explain.

"I haven't arrested anyone. I've been on desk duty since January."

"Which is why I need to speak to the detective or someone in charge."

He sighs and stares at the computer on his desk. "Name?"

"My name, the person who was murdered, or the person who was wrongly arrested?"

"What a lucky dip. Let's try the person who you think has been arrested first, shall we?" he says. His thin long fingers hover over the keyboard.

"Nellie Fletcher," Frankie says. She watches while he types each individual letter of her daughter's name with his pale stubby index finger.

He shakes his head. "Nope."

"No, what?"

"Nobody by that name has been arrested here today."

"Are you sure you spelled her name correctly?"

"Do I look stupid?" he asks, and she thinks it best not to answer the question.

"This really is quite urgent. Is there no way I can speak to DCI Chapman?"

"Of course you can. Come back tomorrow," he replies, then returns to his newspaper. Frankie wonders why so many men have the attention span of a gnat. If she is going to tell the truth about what happened, she isn't going to waste her confession on a man-child.

She mutters to herself all the way back to the van and is about to drive away when something catches her eye.

Someone else is walking up the steps to the police station at this late hour.

Somebody she recognizes.

The last person she would have expected to see here.

The End

Mother's Day, twenty years earlier

A male police officer and a female detective offer to give me a lift from the supermarket to the pink house. It was really an order disguised as an offer. I can tell that they suspect me of something. Accusations don't have to be made with words, looks are equally good at pointing fingers. A child has been taken but they keep wasting time asking *me* questions instead of looking for her. Sometimes the same questions they have already asked. I know what they're thinking. Liars tend to be good at spotting other liars.

I watch while they collapse the empty buggy and put it in the trunk of the police car, before opening one of the doors so I can climb into the back seat. I give them the address again. Even though it is already written in their notebooks, along with whatever else it is that they have been scribbling about me, about us, about her. This is what it must feel like to be arrested. To be taken away from the life that you knew, knowing that nothing will ever be the same again. But they are not arresting me. Yet.

I'm too numb to cry now. I can't *feel* anything. Other than guilt.

I wished my daughter would disappear and now someone has taken the baby.

Time bends out of shape during the journey. It feels too fast and too slow simultaneously. I can't keep my thoughts in order, and I worry about what my face might be doing. The walrus of a policeman who is driving keeps looking at me in the rearview mirror. Whenever our eyes meet, I look away. Partly because he disgusts me, partly because I am afraid of what he might be able to see.

"Nice house," he gabbles when we pull up on the cobbled street outside the Notting Hill mews. It is a ridiculous thing to say. A criticism disguised as a compliment. He exchanges a glance with the detective in the front of the car, and another unspoken conversation takes place between them. They might as well have said it out loud. First they didn't like me because they thought I was lying, now they don't like me because they think I am rich. They are only right on one count.

I try to open the car door, let myself out, but it is locked.

"I'd like to go inside alone," I say.

The walrus shakes his head and a new dusting of dandruff falls on the shoulders of his black uniform. "I don't think we—"

"Of course," the female detective says, interrupting him. She introduced herself at the supermarket but I can't remember her name. Something Chapman, perhaps. "But we will need to come inside when you're ready," she adds.

"I understand. I just need a moment to tell—"

"Take your time. We'll be right here."

Here. When they should be out there. Looking for the baby.

I let myself inside the pink house and close the door behind me, wishing that I could lock the rest of the world out forever. The curtains and blinds are still drawn even though it is early afternoon. I'm not sure how many days it has been since they were last opened.

Postpartum depression they call it nowadays.

It used to be called the baby blues.

I switch on the lights in the hallway, then the lounge, then the kitchen. All of the rooms—which used to be so tidy and perfect, like something from a magazine—are a mess. Like me. Like her. Upstairs is no different. The landing is littered with dirty cups and plates, and I can see the growing stack of unopened mail and unpaid bills. The nursery floor is covered with piles of laundry—it is unclear what is clean and what is not—and when I reach the master bedroom I am almost too afraid to open the door.

The baby's father is away on business.

The baby's mother is in bed.

She has not been well since the baby was born and I've been doing my best to help.

I offered to tidy the place up days ago. She pulled a face as though I had slapped her, so I left things as they were. Some people have a way of making you feel as though your good deeds are bad ones. With that in mind, I think better of opening the curtains in Clio's bedroom. Her behavior recently reminds me of when she was a teenager in more ways than one. All she seems to want to do is sleep, but she can't, that's why I have been looking after the baby for a few days. Now I'm exhausted too. The only reason Clio finally trusted me to take care of my only grandchild was because she was desperate. And because she didn't want her husband to know how bad things really are.

We don't have the best mother-daughter relationship.

There have been times throughout her life when I have resented my own child and loathed the woman she grew up to be. I thought when my daughter had children of her own it would bring us closer together, and it has, but only out of necessity. Clio only asked for my help as a last resort, because she doesn't have anyone else. For my part, I wanted to be a good grandmother. I suppose I hoped it might make up for my failings as a mum. But children are hard work, and babies are impossible, demanding creatures. I didn't enjoy looking after my own babies the first time around. I thought it would be different, *feel* different with Ladybug, but the child *never* stopped crying. Until now.

Of course the baby is almost always perfectly behaved in public. That is something Clio and I do agree on. It's as though at six months of age, little Ladybug is devious enough to save all of her tantrums for behind closed doors. That's why I took her to the supermarket today, to get the things I knew Clio needed—baby formula, nappies, coffee—then I was going to bring the baby home. Here. Because even though Clio clearly *hates* the baby, she misses her when she is gone too long. Wants to know she is close by at all times, even when she cannot stand to look at the child.

Clio didn't want my help when the baby was born and has been disinterested and ungrateful for my opinion ever since. I tried my best but she wouldn't *listen*. Always convinced that what she read in a book or on *the internet* was more valid than advice from her own mother. She behaved as though my experience and knowledge was all out of date. I'm only sixty, I haven't even retired yet, and she talks down to me as though I am old or senile, like someone who belongs in a care home. God forbid I ever end up in one of those. Clio always thinks she knows best, but look at the state of her and her precious pink house now. Having a baby is easy, taking care of one not so much. She needs *help*. Professional help. Given her occupation I would have thought she would recognize the signs. But she won't see a doctor. Won't talk to anyone about it. And no matter how much I have tried to help, my daughter doesn't trust me.

Turns out she was right not to.

I know the police won't wait outside forever and I know I need to tell Clio what has happened. But I don't know how. I sometimes wondered how things would turn out if my daughter disappeared. If I could raise my grandchild myself, my way. She would be my second chance and I would get it right this time. I was always too busy when Clio and Jude were little, working all the hours I could just to make ends meet. I didn't have the time or the energy to be the mother I could have been. I'm sure all children fantasize about what their life might have been like if they had different parents. I wonder what my life would have been like if I'd had different children. Or none at all. I hate myself for thinking unthinkable thoughts, even now as I watch my daughter sleeping. But my life really would have been very different if she had never been born.

I wished my daughter would disappear and now someone has taken the baby.

How does a mother tell her daughter that she has lost her child?

"Clio." I say her name quietly from the doorway. As though if she doesn't hear me, I don't have to tell her the truth. But she does wake up, and it is as though some motherly instinct—one I'm sure I never had—has informed her that something is wrong.

"Where is the baby?" Clio asks, her hair wild, her eyes already frantic. She's been a mess since the baby was born. It doesn't surprise me that her husband runs away for work so often these days, it's as though she can't see who she has become. But I can. She's turned into me, and that is not what I wanted for my daughter. Being home alone all day every day with a baby has taken its toll. She still has dark circles beneath her eyes, even though I'm the one who has been looking after the child for three days and three nights. Her clothes are dirty, she hasn't worn makeup for weeks, she smells as though she hasn't had a wash for a while either. She looks like she might be drunk, but she isn't. This is what real exhaustion looks like.

I choose my words carefully but none of the options feel like a good fit.

"I'm so sorry," I whisper.

Clio is up and out of the bed and rushing toward me.

"Sorry for what? Where is the baby?"

"I . . ."

How can I tell her that her baby is gone when she is already broken?

Just say it.

"She's gone," I blurt out. "Someone has taken the baby. I'm so sorry."

Clio stares at me, then pushes me out of the way and starts to search the house. As though the child is a missing key that will turn up if she just looks long and hard enough. I follow my daughter through the darkened rooms. "Please, wait. She's not here. We were at the supermarket. I turned my back just for a minute." *Maybe two.* "And then she was gone."

Clio stops, turns, and stares at me as though I am speaking a foreign language. Tears are already streaming down her face. I find a tissue tucked in the sleeve of my cardigan and try to wipe her tears away, like I did when she was a child, but she takes a step back.

"The police. We need to call—"

"They already know," I tell her. "They're outside. They want to speak to you."

She nods. Then she rushes to the bathroom, where she is violently sick.

I hold her unwashed hair away from her face until she is finished. Then I flush the toilet and offer her the tissue again. She refuses by shaking her head, and uses the back of her hand to wipe her mouth. Even now, she does not want my help. She's on her knees, so I offer my hand to pull her up but she ignores it. Ignores me. Just like she has for years.

"Is this real?" Clio asks. And suddenly my thirty-four-year-old daughter is my little girl again, the one who looked up to me, the one who needed me. I nod and she starts to sob. She closes her eyes, curls into a ball on the bathroom floor, and wails like a wounded animal. I am crying too, because I can see that I have broken what was left of her. Time stretches again. She cries like that for so long, too long. The sound of her excruciating pain hurts my soul.

"Yes, this is real. I'm so very sorry," I say, because I truly am. I try to hold her but she pushes me away. My little girl is gone again, replaced by the woman she grew up to be.

"Send them in," she says, wiping her eyes.

"The police?"

"Yes, of course. Then get out."

"Clio, I—"

"Get. Out. I don't ever want to see you again."

Edith

Edith lies awake in the spare room at her daughter's house. She remembers being here for three days and three nights when Ladybug was kidnapped, and then not being invited back for years. She lived here very briefly last year—before Clio stuck her in a home—but she has never really been welcome in the pink house. And she and her daughter have never been good at being in each other's company for too long.

Clio has promised that they will go to the police station first thing in the morning but Edith doesn't believe her. She only seems to make promises in order to break them. Dickens interrupts her thoughts by whining; he doesn't like sleeping on the floor.

"Shh. You'll get us both in trouble," Edith whispers. "You can only come up if you promise to keep quiet." Dickens wags his tail and jumps onto the bed, turning in a circle three times before sitting down on the pillow beside her with a satisfied sigh. "There's something I have to do, old friend," she whispers, stroking the dog. "You're not going to like it, but I have thought long and hard on the subject and it is the right thing to do. The *only* thing to do."

Ten minutes later, when Dickens is lying upside down and dreaming, and the rest of the house is quiet, Edith gets up, gets dressed, and creeps out of the room, gently closing the door behind her. There is another door at the end of the hallway, to a room which was once a nursery. Its door is open, and Edith can't stop herself peering inside. Moonlight floods the room and she takes in the sight of all the wooden shelves and shoeboxes. She has always found her daughter's obsession with shoes designed for exercise strange—especially given Clio hasn't set foot inside a gymnasium since she was at school—too scared of other people's sweat—but this is bonkers. One of the boxes is open and sitting out of place on the expensive-looking rug. There are no trainers inside this box, just newspaper articles from the looks of it. Some of which are still unfolded on the floor.

Her daughter has spent a lifetime hiding her feelings in boxes.

Edith picks up one of the newspaper clippings her daughter has kept all these years. It has yellowed with age, but she doesn't need to be reminded of the date at the top of the page. Edith can't remember what she had for breakfast, but she can remember everything about that Mother's Day twenty years ago. She sits down on the floor, partly because it feels like she might fall, and begins to read.

Heartbreak for Mother of Missing Baby

Police are still searching desperately for the six-month-old baby stolen from the Tesco supermarket in Notting Hill, West London. Eleanor Kennedy was taken from her buggy on Monday morning.

"It was terrible, really terrible. This woman just started screaming 'Where is the baby?'

Over and over again. I rushed to help, a lot of people did. The supermarket doors were locked almost immediately, but whoever had taken the child must have already got away. I've got two kids of my own. I can't imagine what that family are going through," said one eyewitness.

The baby's mother, Clio Kennedy, 34, from Notting Hill, spoke briefly at a police press conference yesterday. Clearly in a state of distress, her only words were: "Please bring her back. Please."

CCTV captured the moment baby Eleanor was taken. Despite showing the kidnapper removing the child from her pushchair and leaving the supermarket, the images were not clear enough to identify the assailant.

"We're unable to speculate on the age or sex of the kidnapper. It's impossible to be sure from the images we have so far," said a police spokesperson. They are appealing to members of the public who might have noticed anything suspicious that day to come forward.

Edith picks up the next newspaper article, dated one month later.

Still No News on Missing Baby Eleanor

Police say they won't stop looking until baby Eleanor is found, despite it being a month since she was taken. The child's parents have offered a reward of £10,000 for any information leading to them being reunited with their daughter. New images of the abducted child, who had distinctive freckles on her nose, have been released.

Edith takes out another article from the box. The stories always got shorter, the more time that passed.

Where Is Baby Eleanor?

One year on since the kidnapping of six-month-old baby Eleanor, and the police say they won't close the case until she is found. Despite a special task force and thousands of police hours, they are no closer to uncovering the mystery of what happened to the missing child.

The last one has a picture of Clio, her husband, and their baby girl. The child has curly blond hair like her father, big green eyes like her mother, and freckles on her nose. The freckles were the reason Edith called her Ladybug. The reason she gave Patience the same name.

When you lose a child you see them everywhere forever.

Edith is even more certain than she was before, she *must* speak to the police now, this can't wait until morning. She has an impossible choice to make, but if she can fix this maybe it will help fix what got broken all those years ago and history won't keep repeating itself.

Patience

"You okay?" asks Liberty.

"No."

"You will be, promise. Do you need anything else before I turn in for the night?" She switches on a torch and holds it beneath her chin like a child.

"I thought it was lights out?"

"It is. But I've got to take my makeup off—bad for my complexion if I don't, innit—and I like to read a book beneath the covers for a while before I go to sleep. Helps me unwind. The guards don't mind, so long as I'm not doing anything bad."

I wonder what bad things a person could possibly do when locked in a cell.

I watch as Liberty ties back her curly blond hair before cleaning her skin with a face wipe.

"You have freckles on your nose, like me," I say.

"Yes, we are freckle twins. But I like to hide mine with tinted moisturizer. You must be knackered; you should try to get some rest, the first night in here is always the hardest. Wake me up if you can't sleep. I'm off to Bedfordshire."

She disappears under her duvet with a novel. Invisible were it not for the dim glow of her torch, silent except for the occasional sound of a page turning. A short while later, the light goes out and the cell is pitch-black again.

I don't understand how anyone can sleep in prison. There are constant noises, some of which I can identify while others remain a mystery. I am afraid of all of them, and I have never known terror like the one I feel now. I am scared of the dark, of things I cannot see. I think everything that has happened is finally sinking in. Liberty was a welcome distraction and I'm tempted to wake her, this place is too loud without her to drown it out. My fear seems to rush around my body just like my thoughts collide inside my mind, until I can't think straight. Can't seem to see a way out of this or even understand how I got here.

In the last twenty-four hours I have lost my dog, my only friend, my job, my home, and now I have lost my freedom too. It's hard to comprehend how things went so wrong. Forty-eight hours ago I was okay. I didn't know it at the time, but my life was actually all right. I was safe, I had a roof over my head, I could afford to eat rather than accept the charity of sharing someone else's dinner. Maybe people don't know they have a good life until life turns bad.

I hear another sound my ears can't interpret. Metal against metal. A key in a lock perhaps? My eyes dart to the cell door but there is nothing there, only darkness. I close my eyes and try to sleep again but I can't. I hide inside memories of happier times, anything to distract myself from the present. It will be my birthday soon and I wonder if I'll still be in here.

My mum loved birthdays. She would decorate the narrow boat with paper chains and balloons, and buy far too many presents. She always gave me a gift for each year of my life, so last year there were eighteen parcels wrapped in pretty paper and tied with ribbons. It must have taken her ages and so much thought went into each gift—some big, some small, all perfect. Nobody knows me like my mum. Each gift was labeled with a number, which indicated the order they were to be opened in, but with a slight twist. When I was four years old, there were four gifts but they were labeled one, two, three, and five. There was no gift number four, because Mum worried that it was bad luck.

"You might think I'm crazy . . ." she would often say, and I confess I sometimes did. "But the whole of China agrees with me. The number four is bad luck. It means death. That's why there is never an option for a fourth floor in Chinese elevators."

I have never been to China, neither has Mum, but she takes numbers very seriously.

When I unwrapped my eighteen gifts, I was careful not to tear the paper, but keen to see what was inside. There were books, clothes, a new papercutting knife, a beautiful pair of earrings, but the one thing I wanted most was not there.

"You promised," I said. Promises were like contracts in our family of two.

Mum nodded and looked sad. I can still picture her face now, and I remember feeling grateful that she didn't pretend not to know what I was talking about. She had promised to show me my birth certificate when I was eighteen, I'd already been waiting years to find out the truth about my father.

"I'm sorry," she said. "I can't."

The rage I felt was all-consuming. Because she had no intention of showing me my birth certificate and had clearly lied to me. I remember what we said next, word for word. I expect Mum does too, because it was the last time we ever spoke to one another.

"I don't care *who* my dad was. I don't even think I want to meet him—he obviously didn't care enough about me to stick around or show any interest. I just want to know his name. To know where

I came from. How can you not understand that? You *promised* to show me my birth certificate."

"I know. I'm sorry," Mum said, staring at me with tears in her eyes. "I just can't."

"You mean *won't*."

"Please, let's not ruin today. Can't we just celebrate your birthday and talk about this tomorrow?"

"No, because you never want to talk about it. I joined an ancestry database online. I couldn't find anything about *us* on there at all. It's as though we don't exist—"

"You did what?"

"So then I went to the library, and asked for help to get a copy of my birth certificate for a passport. The librarian sat me down at a computer and showed me how. And guess what, I don't exist there either. There is no birth certificate in the UK for someone my age named Nellie Fletcher. Who am I? Are you even my mum?" She was crying hard then. All of the terrible things I'd been thinking for days tumbled out of my mouth and I couldn't stop them. "It isn't as though we look alike. Or think alike. We have nothing in common."

"Yes we do," she whispered. "We have the same green eyes, everyone says so." She sounded defeated and started pacing, walking up and down the narrow boat, and I knew that she was counting her steps, trying to keep herself calm. Her fingers were gripping and twisting around her wrists as though she needed to hold her own hands.

"Who am I, really?" I asked, terrified of the answer. "Why did we move to different places all the time when I was little? I'm not a child anymore, you can tell me the truth."

"I can explain . . ."

"Go on then."

"Please try to be patient."

"*Patient* is all I've ever been. That should be my name: *Patience*."

"As you know, I was very young when I became a mum. I was only eighteen, the same age you are now—"

"Where was I born? Which hospital?" I interrupted, and when my mother didn't answer, the fear that had been filling my mind for months resurfaced. "Are you really my mum? You didn't answer earlier."

"Of course *I'm* your mum. I don't see anyone else here cooking your dinners or making your bed or buying you presents on your birthday—"

"If this really is my birthday." The look on Mum's face made me feel sick. She took a step toward me, and I took a step back. "Oh my god. This isn't even my real birthday is it? What is happening? I don't understand!"

"Please calm down."

"Did you give birth to me?"

I have never seen her look so afraid. All of her was trembling. "Can we please just—"

"Did. You. Give. Birth. To. Me?" I shouted.

We stared at each other for a long time before she answered. "No."

I felt my legs giving way. "Who am I?" I whispered.

"You're my daughter," she said, tears streaming down her face.

"But I'm not, am I? Who am I?"

But Mum didn't answer. She just cried and then she went to her room.

So I went to mine and packed a few things in a backpack. Then I took the black and gold Japanese tea tin and the money inside it from the place where she had hidden it in the kitchen. If Mum heard me taking the tin she didn't say anything, didn't come out of her room. If she heard me leave the boat, she didn't try to stop me. I cried as I walked to the train station, secretly hoping that she would come after me, but she didn't do that either.

I haven't seen or spoken to her since.

She called and texted at least once a week but I never replied.

Until she was willing to tell me the truth about my real parents I didn't want anything to do with her. I've never stopped missing her, but now I need her. I need her to be my mum again, even if she isn't. I don't have anyone else.

I blink into the darkness, looking around the gloomy prison cell and seeing nothing but shadows. I close my eyes again, desperate for sleep to find me but it doesn't. Tears come instead. I think about Mum, then I think about Edith, then I think about Edith's daughter. Clio Kennedy acted as though we had never met in the attic above the art gallery, but she knows who I am. Then she sent a text telling me to keep quiet, so I have. I didn't tell the police about Clio because it's my word against hers and they'll never believe me. Why would they? They already know I'm a liar, and the detective was furious when I refused to tell her my real name.

She didn't seem to understand that I couldn't, because I don't know what it is.

Edith

Edith is crying as she prepares to leave her daughter's house in Notting Hill for the last time. Not because of what she has to do, but because of what she must leave behind. She made herself a cup of tea and some toast before leaving—her daughter's vegan bread and "plant-based" butter *almost* tasted like the real thing—and nobody should confess to anything on an empty stomach. She tries to close the front door as quietly as she can so as not to wake anyone. Edith continues to cry on the night bus and only stops when she walks up to the entrance of the police station at Covent Garden. Partly to concentrate on the steps in the dark, but mostly because it is best to compose yourself before speaking to officers of the law; she learned that lesson a long time ago. When she looks down at the steps she sees that she is still wearing her slippers. Now they will definitely think she is a crazy old lady. Perhaps she is. Maybe that's what life turned her into.

"I want to see Detective Chapman," she says to the man slouching behind the desk.

"Blimey, she's popular this evening," he says, checking his watch. "Are you aware it's almost midnight?"

"There is always time for truth," Edith replies. "It's rather an urgent matter."

"Is that so?"

"Well, I think so. And I would hope, given your profession, that you would agree. There has been a serious miscarriage of justice."

He nods at the pink leather suitcase in her hand. "You off somewhere, are you?"

Edith shrugs. "Prison, I suspect."

He peers over the desk and stares down at her slippers. "Are you sure you should be out at this time of night on your own?"

"Are you sure you're in the right job? Did you hear what I said, young man?"

"Why do all the nutters pay a visit on *my* shifts?" he mumbles.

"What did you say?"

He turns to the computer on his desk. "I said why don't we start with your name?"

"Edith Elliot. And the dead woman is called Joy, despite being rather miserable."

"Death can have that effect on a person. A bit like working here."

"The innocent girl is called Patience."

"I need that myself tonight."

Edith notices that the police officer has stopped typing. He stares at her with a look of pity she has become accustomed to. As though being old and being helpless are the same thing. But she won't be silent this time. She will do the right thing. People have always underestimated and overestimated her. Sometimes to her advantage, but more often than not to her detriment. The only person who knows what she is really capable of is her.

And a frightened young girl from all those years ago.

Edith's mind starts to wander and she forgets where she is for a moment.

"Is there someone I can call?" the officer asks gently and Edith snaps out of her trance.

"Yes. Detective Chapman. Or frankly anyone less cloth-eared than you."

"Now, listen here—"

"No, you listen, you silly little man. There's been a murder—at the Windsor Care Home—and you incompetent fools have arrested an innocent person."

He leans back in his chair and folds his arms. "And how do you know that they're innocent?" he asks.

"I know who did what because I was there."

Frankie

Frankie recognized the elderly woman walking into the police station—she'll never forget that face—but she doesn't understand what *she* is doing here or how the pieces of the puzzle slot together. She tried to speak to Edith Elliot in the care home yesterday, to tell her exactly what she thought of her—thinking it would be her final chance—but the ghastly care home manager ruined her plans.

"Who are you?" Joy asked, blocking her path in the hallway.

"I'm here for Mother's Day. To visit someone," Frankie replied.

"Then you'll know that all visitors are required to sign the visitor book," Joy said, handing it to her along with a pen. Frankie hesitated, then scribbled some details before giving it back. She could feel her cheeks burning red while Joy's beady eyes scanned the page. The woman smirked and it made her grim face even less attractive.

"Clio Kennedy?" she asked.

"Yes," Frankie replied.

"You are not Clio Kennedy. I'm the manager of this care home and I've just been talking in my office with Clio Kennedy, room thirteen's daughter. Her *only* daughter. I've also been informed by one of the residents that a strange woman is going around asking strange questions. I'm guessing that's you. So who are you really?" Frankie didn't answer. "We take security very seriously at the Windsor Care Home." Joy's eyes narrowed into slits. "If this is an inspection, you know you have to give us at least forty-eight hours' notice. If it *isn't* then get out or I will be forced to call the police."

Frankie had had her fill of people speaking to her as though she were a piece of shit on their shoe. Something inside her snapped.

"Why don't you drop dead," she said before leaving.

A short while later, when Frankie returned, the woman was.

Frankie had pressed the call button for the elevator several times before it finally started to descend from the fourth floor. When it eventually arrived, Joy's lifeless body was slumped in the elevator with an out-of-order sign around her neck. No wonder the Chinese don't have fourth floors, the number four really *does* mean death. Frankie closed the elevator doors and fled before anyone saw, and before getting her chance to confront Edith.

They say revenge is sweet and a dish best served cold, but she would rather take hers when hot and savor the moment. Frankie has waited too long for Edith and Clio and Jude to get what they deserve. And now it seems the *whole family* are somehow involved in her daughter's disappearance. Frankie was wrong to discount the woman in the pink house, and she is furious with herself for having lost more time. The benefit of the doubt is rarely of real benefit to anyone. She made a bad choice, that's the truth of the matter. But choosing between right and wrong isn't always as black and white as some people think.

Frankie counts the cars she passes on the road to Notting Hill and it helps keep her nerves under control. There are a surprising number given the late hour. She sees a young couple kissing near the closed tube station, and too many homeless people sleeping beneath cardboard boxes in shop doorways. The way some lives continue to happily unfold while others implode has always fascinated her. Is it luck? Fate? Destiny? Is it really just about being the right person in the right place at the right time? She often feels like the wrong person in the wrong place, maybe that's why things rarely seem to go right for her. Some kind of self-fulfilling prophecy. One thing she has learned is that moments of happiness should always be celebrated. Joy is only ever on loan and can be taken away just as fast as life gives it; best to appreciate the good times before they turn bad.

She parks at the end of the street, as far away from the pink house as possible where she can still see the building. Then Frankie sits and stares at the house, collating all the hateful thoughts she has gathered over the years about the woman who lives there. She looks around the van to see what she might have that she can use as a weapon. Just as she is about to get out, Frankie spots something crossing the street. At first she thinks it is a dog, but it isn't. It's a fox. A black one with a white-tipped tail. Frankie has never seen a black fox before, but she has read about them and knows that seeing one is considered to be a warning. It's the variety of bad luck she takes very seriously.

Then she sees something else.

The door to the pink house is slightly ajar.

Frankie stares up at the building and sees that the whole house is in darkness, except for what looks like the beam of a flashlight in one room upstairs. She notices the shadowy form of someone moving behind the curtains. The woman in the pink house lives alone. Frankie knows this, along with all sorts of other things about the woman. Frankie knows far more about the woman in the pink house than Clio knows about her. She gets out of the van, crosses the street as quietly as possible, then stands outside the open front door and listens.

Frankie was right to be upset about seeing the black fox. It *was* a warning.

She hears the sound of something smashing inside the house.

Followed by a high-pitched scream.

Clio

Clio is woken by the sound of a vehicle outside in the middle of night. It is normally quiet in the secluded little mews where she lives, but she has worn earplugs when sleeping for years. Since her daughter disappeared. She kept imagining the sound of a baby crying in the night without them. Maybe it's the stress of the previous day putting her on edge, or perhaps she just can't sleep under the same roof as her mother, but the earplugs aren't doing their job tonight. Life is too loud.

Something draws her to the window and she sees that she wasn't imagining the sound she heard. A pair of headlights are glowing at the end of the road. Clio ducks behind the curtain when she sees something move beside what looks like a camper van. But it isn't a person, it's a fox. A black one with a white tail. She stares transfixed as the fox creeps along the street and stops right outside her front door. Illuminated by the streetlight, it appears to look up in her direction.

Is she dreaming?

She hears something else then. A noise downstairs. The black fox seems to hear it too, and darts across the street before running inside the communal gardens, disappearing through the black bars of the gate as though it was never there. Clio hears the noise again, it's impossible to identify what it is from up here—something like muffled footsteps down below—so she leaves the bedroom to investigate.

The house is in complete darkness, so she feels for the switch on the wall to turn on the landing light. When nothing happens she flicks it again, but the lights aren't working. She tries to turn on the metal table lamp on the dresser in the hallway, but that doesn't work either. Clio wonders if there has been a power cut, but then she hears another noise downstairs and her imagination provides other possibilities. Bad ones. Clio has always had a rational mind and her fear soon passes. It's bound to be her mother down there, making a nuisance of herself just like always.

Edith has probably tried to make some toast with the dodgy toaster in the middle of the night and tripped the fuse board. It wouldn't be the first time; the wiring in this old house is as fragile as Clio's nerves. She uses the torch on her phone, then slowly, quietly, takes another step toward the stairs. She strains to hear any more unfamiliar sounds but all she can hear is her own heartbeat. She gently pushes open her mother's bedroom door and sees the shape of someone sleeping in the bed. So it *isn't* Edith downstairs.

Clio's fear returns. She often leaves the key in the kitchen door at the back of the house, even though she knows it is a security risk. She always seems to lose the key when she doesn't, and now she can't remember whether she did or didn't put it in the drawer last night. She hears the sound of something smashing down below then, and her fear turns to rage. With her torch in one hand and the metal lamp from the dresser in the other—the best makeshift weapon she can think of to grab—she hurries down the stairs. Every one of them is disloyal, creaking loudly to let the intruder know she is coming, but Clio doesn't care. Her fury outweighs her fear and makes her brave—how dare someone break into *her* home—they'll soon wish that they hadn't.

When she reaches the ground floor she sees that the front door is open. Clio would never have left it like that; she always puts the chain on before going to bed.

She hears another sound, close enough to pinpoint now.

Someone is in her consulting room.

Her hands are trembling as she creeps toward it. A seesaw of bravery and fear steering her toward the room then away from it. Anger trumps them both.

She bursts through the door and sees that her imagination was not playing tricks on her.

Someone is there. Sitting in her chair.

On seeing who it is, Clio doesn't hesitate. She screams and runs toward them.

Edith

Edith thinks the detective looks awfully young with her pink bits of hair and pierced ears.

"Are you sure you're a detective?" she asks.

"I get that a lot," the young woman replies. She sits down in the chair opposite Edith and takes a sip from a ridiculously large takeaway coffee. She made "proper tea" for Edith, as requested. "I am indeed DCI Charlotte Chapman and I'm older than I look. There weren't any custard creams, sorry about that."

"Is this the room where Ladybug would have been?" Edith asks, staring at the white walls, thinking how much jollier the place would look with some art on them.

"If you mean Patience Liddell, then yes."

"She's innocent."

"So I hear. The sergeant said you were quite certain of that when he called and woke me. Seeing as I've come to work in the middle of the night at your insistence, I'm hoping there might be a few things you can help clear up."

"I'd be happy to," Edith replies.

"How do you know that the care home manager was murdered?"

"Were you trying to keep it a secret? The woman was found dead in an elevator with an out-of-order sign around her neck. News like that travels fast."

"Why did you leave the care home?"

"Have you ever stayed in one? If you had, you would know why I left."

"Okay, why did you leave on the same day as the care home manager died?"

"Do you believe in coincidence?"

"No."

"Very wise. You'll make a good detective one day."

"I *am* a detective—"

"But not a good one. Not yet. You'll hate me for saying this, but there are some things only experience can teach a person. I might have been a mere store detective, but I learned how to watch people and see who they really are beneath the disguises we all wear. My daughter said you thought there were three suspects in this case, including her."

"That's right."

"That's poppycock and piffle. But probably due to a lack of experience and common sense. We all make mistakes, that's how we learn. Don't be too hard on yourself when you realize how wrong you've been."

"Thanks, I'll try not to be. Are you talking about the daughter you hadn't seen or spoken to for months until yesterday? She thought you were missing. Sounds as though you've been reunited."

"We often ignore each other for months at a time."

The detective nods, takes another sip from her vat of coffee. "Mother and daughter relationships can be complicated—"

"I don't see what's complicated about it. We just don't like each other."

"I see, silly me. So . . . why was your daughter at the care home yesterday?"

Edith shrugs. "It was Mother's Day. I suspect it was a mix of guilt and anger. It's always been difficult for her."

"Mother's Day?"

"That's what I said. Are you hard of hearing?"

DCI Chapman puffs out her cheeks before loudly blowing air from her lips. She pinches the bridge of her nose between her thumb and her index finger. Edith notices that her nails are all painted in different colors. "Why is Mother's Day a difficult day for your daughter?" the detective asks.

"That's a much better question, there's hope for you yet. Mother's Day is how all of these events are connected. Because that's when the other one took the baby."

"What baby?"

"And then *you* arrested the baby for something she didn't do. Are you really allowed to have pink hair and work here? They wouldn't have put up with those sorts of shenanigans in my day." The detective leans her elbows on the table and holds her head in her hands. "The problem with your generation . . ." Edith continues. "One of the many problems, in my opinion, is that you've forgotten the art of listening. You know how to use your eyes, staring at your screens all day long, but you don't use your ears. It was my fault."

"What was?"

"All of it."

DCI Chapman steeples her fingers. She laces them together except for her index fingers so that her hands look like a gun. "Are you telling me that the murder in the care home was your fault?"

"No! But everything else was. A few months after the baby was taken Clio's husband suggested they arrange a service at the local church, even though neither of them was religious. He said they needed some form of closure in order to move on—as though Clio ever could—then he left my daughter soon afterward. So I suppose it did help *him* to move on with his life—he moved far away and started a new one. That day, at the church, we all watched while they buried a tiny, empty white coffin, but the baby wasn't dead."

The detective stares at her as though she is speaking a foreign language.

"Mrs. Elliot, I think it might be best if we take you back to the Windsor—"

"Fiddlesticks. I'm not going back there!" Edith stands up so fast her chair topples to the floor. "I do not belong in a home!"

"Then we'll have to call your daughter."

"Fat lot of use she'll be. Might as well call the tooth fairy. Talking to you really is like talking to a brick wall but less interesting. Tell me, are you fluent in gobbledygook or do you only speak gibberish? Why can't you see what is right under your nose? There were a queue of people with a motive to kill Joy Bonetta. The most obvious solution is rarely the right one."

"With all due respect, I disagree."

"With all due disrespect, I don't give a fig what you think. People literally get away with murder because of incompetent twits like you. I had a friend at the care home named May and she was murdered, and nobody did a damn thing about it."

The detective leans forward. "Go on."

"May was admittedly a few sandwiches short of a picnic—she would sometimes get confused and tell people she was looking for her corgis—but she had a beautiful mind. She could not be beaten at Cluedo or gin rummy and we were friends."

"Fascinating stuff, but what does that have to do with this?"

"If you stop interrupting, I'll tell you. May was a detective—like you, but older and wiser and better—and had this theory that *someone* at the care home was making deals with relatives of residents to bump them off. Either when the bills were too steep or they needed the inheritance in a hurry. She said there was a pattern, and she was going to tell her granddaughter about it next time she visited, but then a few days later May was dead. She didn't get the chance to tell anyone what she knew. Maybe whoever killed Joy had a good reason for doing so."

DCI Chapman stares at her for a long time. "Do you know who May's granddaughter was?" she asks. Edith shakes her head. "Do you know May's surname?"

"No, I'm not sure I ever did. Everyone just called her Aunty May."

Detective Chapman tries to take another sip of coffee but the enormous cup is empty. "It's an interesting theory but there's no proof—"

"But what if there *was* proof? What if Joy *was* responsible for the premature deaths of residents at the care home and finally got what she deserved? Isn't justice supposed to be about protecting good people from bad ones?"

"Please sit down. You really shouldn't worry yourself like this—"

"I saw what happened and Ladybug didn't kill Joy!"

"Then tell me who did."

Frankie

Frankie stops dithering and steps inside the pink house. She didn't imagine the sound of someone screaming, it was real, and it came from the consultation room she was in yesterday. The room she took the papercut from. What kind of person would Frankie be if she walked away when she knew someone was in trouble? Even someone she hates.

"You shouldn't be in here!" the woman in the pink house shouts behind the closed door, and Frankie feels compelled to help her. The hallway is in complete darkness so she has to feel her way.

"I've got a weapon and I'm not afraid to use it," Frankie says, bursting into the shadowy room.

Clio spins around and shines the flashlight from her phone in Frankie's face.

Frankie stares back, taking in the scene.

There is a dog sitting in the turquoise armchair. Clio is holding a metal lamp in her other hand and staring at what Frankie is holding in hers.

"Are you planning to polish me to death?" Clio asks, still staring at the can of Mr. Sheen. "Right, well, that's it. The final straw. I literally can't deal with any more shit from anyone about anything. I'm calling the police."

"No! Please don't," Frankie says, dropping the polish and holding her hands up as though afraid Clio might shoot her. "Your door was open, I heard you scream and—"

"And what? You thought you'd invite yourself in? It's the middle of the night, what are you even doing here? If you've come back to steal some more art from the house, I don't have any. I've had clients develop stalking tendencies before, but rarely after one *incomplete* session. Who *are* you?" Clio asks. "Because I didn't believe anything you said yesterday. Why are you watching my house in the middle of the night and who are you? Really?"

Frankie feels as though she can't breathe.

Four walls, three windows, two chairs, one woman in the pink house.

She looks at Clio, then at the dog sitting on the turquoise chair. He tilts his head to one side and stares back. There were eighteen steps from the front door to this room. If she turned and ran now she could be in the van in less than two minutes. But Frankie came here in the middle of the night to find her daughter, nothing else matters.

"I need to talk to you," Frankie says.

"Then book an appointment. Or better still, find another therapist."

"It has to be you."

"Why? Why does it have to be me?"

"Because I have to tell you something."

"Whatever it is, I don't want to know."

"I think you do and even if you don't, I still need to tell you."

"So say whatever it is you want to say then get out of my house."

Frankie stares at Clio then closes her eyes and starts to count.

Four walls, three windows, two chairs, one dog, one woman in the pink house.

"I took your baby."

Clio

Clio stares at Frankie. "What did you just say?"

"I stole your baby from a supermarket twenty years ago," the woman whispers, then stares down at the floor. It's hard to see her face properly in the dark room as she shields her eyes from Clio's flashlight.

Clio wishes now that she could remember the woman's name, but she can only remember her as Case File 999. Her autopilot kicks in, out of habit and self-preservation. Clio does what she always does when a client says something shocking: she waits to see what they will say next. It helps her to determine whether the things they are telling her are true, imagined, or reimagined stories told in the hope of receiving attention.

"I'm not here to apologize," says Case File 999 with an air of defiance that is new. "I'm not sorry I took her and I never will be."

"Now I really am calling the police."

The woman snatches the phone from Clio's hand. "No, you're not. We're going to sit down and talk like we should have yesterday.

Like we should have all those years ago." Clio tries to leave the room but she blocks her path. "Ten minutes. That's all this will take. Then, if you still want me to leave, I will. You have my word."

Clio assesses the situation and Case File 999. Before she can decide what to do next, the power comes back on. It restores the light and her confidence. Clio studies the woman for a moment as though trying to solve a difficult sum, and thinks she sees her clearly now.

"You've obviously looked me up. You've probably read some old newspaper articles and, for reasons I don't care about, you've come here pretending to know something about my missing child. It's been a while, but do you have any idea how many people claimed to know something about her disappearance for *years* after she was taken? Hoping for a reward. Or just attention. Years of my life have been destroyed by disturbed, delusional liars like you."

"I'm not lying. Why don't you believe me?"

"What do you want, money? Because if you think I have any just because I live in this house in a posh part of town, you are sadly mistaken."

"I need your help or I wouldn't be here at all."

"Well, we agree on something. You do need help."

"I can tell you that she was wearing a pink onesie. I can tell you that your mother was looking after her that day and had taken her to the supermarket. I can tell you that the time was ten minutes past ten when I took the baby from the buggy and walked right out of the store with her."

"All of which you could have read in the newspapers. If you *are* telling the truth, then do you know that my husband left me six months after our little girl was stolen from us? He couldn't stand to be around someone as broken as I was, and he knew that there was no way to fix me. He was right. I lost my child and my husband and myself because of what happened. I lost everything. *There's* something you won't have read about."

"I'm sorry."

"Please leave."

"She looks like you, your little girl. You have the same eyes."

"Get out."

"Why won't you tell me where she is?"

Clio hesitates. "I don't know who or what you are talking about!"

Case File 999 fumbles with something inside her bag. Clio takes a step back, fearing she might have a weapon more dangerous than a can of polish.

"This is your daughter," the woman says, holding up a photo.

Clio stares at the picture. "That is not my daughter. That is Patience."

"Patience?"

"I *knew* she couldn't be trusted. What an elaborate con the pair of you have constructed. Well, she might have fooled my mother but she didn't fool me. What's the plan now? Blackmail? Good luck with that." Her phone starts to ring and she stares at it. "How handy, the police are calling me." Clio regrets taking the call as soon as she hears the detective's voice.

"I wasn't expecting you to answer given it's the middle of the night," says DCI Chapman. "Touch of insomnia is it? Worried about your missing mother?"

"I've found her—"

"And then lost her again it seems. She came here, to the police station in Covent Garden."

"What? Are you sure?"

"Unless she has a twin."

"I'm sorry. She's such a nuisance. I'll come and collect her as soon as I—"

"You can't. That's why I'm calling. She said she knew who killed the care home manager . . ." Clio's thoughts collide like clouds creating a violent storm inside her head. She only hears the last few words the detective says. ". . . And that's where she is now."

"Sorry, where is my mother now?" Clio asks.

"The hospital. Like I said, she got herself extremely worked up and was very upset. The paramedics said they thought it was a heart attack, she was unconscious when they put her in the ambulance. If you want to see her, I suggest you go right away."

Frankie

"I don't know how I let you talk me into this," Clio says, sitting in the passenger seat of the camper van and checking her seat belt for the tenth time. Frankie is equally surprised that the woman in the pink house accepted her offer of a lift.

She shrugs. "Well, it's hard to get a taxi at this time of night."

"I know the way to the hospital. So if you're planning to drive me down a back lane or a dark alley and—"

"I'm not trying to hurt you. I'm just trying to help," Frankie says.

"*Why?*"

"Because your mother is in the hospital."

They drive in silence for a while. It is too uncomfortable but Frankie can't think of anything appropriate to say.

"I like your red trainers," she blurts out eventually.

"What?"

"Your trainers, I think they're really cool."

Clio stares at her. "Do you have any inkling what a weird thing that is to say, given the circumstances?"

"I was just trying to be nice."

"Well, don't. If any taxi company had been able to send a car sooner, this would not be happening."

"You're welcome," Frankie says.

"Maybe we could just travel in silence?"

"Maybe you should learn to drive."

Frankie puts the radio on. Once again, this isn't playing out the way she imagined. All these years she thought she was a good person who did a bad thing. But now she's starting to doubt herself. Do bad people know that's what they are? Maybe all villains are the heroes of their own stories.

Clio reaches for the radio and switches it off. "Tell me about her."

"Who?"

"Your daughter."

Frankie hesitates, not sure if she wants to share the person she loves most with the person she hates the most.

"She's your daughter too," Frankie says, staring at the road ahead.

"Please don't start that again."

Frankie smiles. "*My* daughter is perfect. She's clever, she's kind, she's funny . . . and she's beautiful. Inside and out. It will be her birthday soon, she's almost nineteen—"

"Well, you didn't do your research as thoroughly as you should have. My daughter was born in September and would be—"

"A little older than that, yes. I didn't know her real birthday when I took her—how could I? So I made one up. And I wanted to pretend she was a little younger and delay her turning eighteen because . . . well, childhood goes too fast, don't you think?"

"I think my mother genuinely believed that this girl, *your* daughter, was her missing granddaughter. That's why she did what she did. It's quite the scam you people have going on."

"My daughter wouldn't scam anyone. She doesn't even know you exist."

Clio laughs. "Oh, yes she does."

"What does that mean?" Frankie asks, but Clio ignores her and turns the radio back on.

A minute later Frankie switches it off again. "I don't understand why you don't believe me?"

"Because I know that you're lying."

"How?"

"For starters, my little girl had a head of blond curls just like her father. I'm surprised you didn't pick up on that in the newspapers."

"Her hair was blond when I took her, but it darkened when she was a toddler. Have you never heard of blond babies growing up to have dark hair?"

"Please. Stop. Talking."

"I just want to understand why you won't believe what I am trying to—"

"Because my daughter is *dead*," Clio says matter-of-factly. "I feel it. I know it. Here," she says holding her hand over her heart. "The hospital is the next left. If you drop me off at A and E I'll be able to find my way from there."

They drive in silence for the final few minutes, until Frankie pulls over outside the main entrance. "Do you want me to wait?" she asks.

"What for?" the woman in the pink house says.

"I feel bad that you're alone, but maybe you prefer it that way. Take this, please," Frankie says. She reaches over, opens the glove compartment, and pulls out an envelope.

Clio stares at it as though it might contain poison. "What is it?" she asks.

"Proof."

Clio

Clio has been at the hospital for over an hour. She was directed to a large waiting room filled with sorry-looking people, and nobody has spoken to her since. She's phoned her brother, five times, but Jude didn't answer. So she is dealing with their mother all by herself, again. She doesn't sit down, even though there are plenty of chairs. They look grubby and the people sitting on them look less than appealing too. Clio has never been fond of dirt. Or people. She disinfects her consultation room every evening after the last client of the day has left. Their problems make her feel dirty. As do hospitals. The stench of death and despair is making it difficult to breathe. When she can't stand not knowing what is happening for a minute longer, she stops pacing and approaches the nurse behind the desk.

"I'm Edith Elliot's daughter," she says, noticing how the nurse's face softens instantly. Her eyes fill with sympathy Clio neither wants nor needs.

"A doctor will come out to talk to you about your mother as soon as they can."

Clio can't stand not knowing what is going on, not being in control. She hates the sympathetic nurse, she hates the doctors for keeping her waiting, and she hates her mother for causing her endless heartbreak. She hates everyone and everything in this moment and just wants it all to stop. Most of all, she hates herself for feeling and being this way. The maps inside our minds that lead to happiness and sadness are all self-made. We are not born with mapped-out lives, we are the cartographers of our own destiny. Children only know how to love until the world—or their mothers—teach them how to hate.

After what feels like a long time but might only have been a few minutes more, while other people all seem to come and go around her, a doctor finally appears in the doorway. He is too young, too thin, and too tall—as though life has stretched him—and she hopes this isn't the doctor she's been waiting for.

"Clio Kennedy?" he asks, as though her name is a question. As if she is a puzzle that nobody—including herself—quite knows how to solve. Clio doesn't answer straightaway. She feels so alone in this moment, but she couldn't think of a single person to call to be here with her. Grief is only ever yours, just like guilt; it isn't something you can share. Clio doesn't feel like herself. She is struggling to *feel* anything at all. But when the tall, thin doctor says her name a second time, she steps forward, finally leaving the aptly named waiting room.

The doctor looks weary. He speaks to her out in the corridor as though he is too busy to go anywhere more private. Doesn't have time to deliver this news in a more sensitive way. Clio is grateful for that. She doesn't want this to take any longer than it needs to either.

"I really am very sorry," he says at the end of his speech, and she wonders how often he says those words to strangers. Every shift? Every hour? "I read your mother's notes. She had been prescribed heart medication after a previous episode. Was she taking the pills?"

Clio doesn't like his tone or the way he is looking at her. "She knew she was supposed to but . . . I don't know."

"Sometimes patients don't take them on purpose. Try not to be too hard on yourself. It's not your fault." Clio hadn't thought that it was until now. "Do you want to see her?" he asks when she doesn't respond. Clio's words get stuck so she nods, and it is enough for him to understand and lead the way. "We did everything we could for her," the doctor says when they reach the quiet room the hospital reserves for moments like this. When people say they did everything that they could, it always sounds like they didn't. And it feels as though they are all accusing her of not doing enough: the care home staff, the police, the doctor.

She's been cast in the role of bad daughter one last time.

The too tall and thin doctor stoops to open the door, revealing a scene Clio would rather not see. Now that she's here she doesn't want to go inside. She doesn't want to be any closer than this, but her feet carry her forward. Clio cries when she sees her mother's face. She didn't think that she would feel like this, wasn't sure if she would feel anything at all. Anticipation and reality are rarely a perfect match.

Edith's skin has a grayish tint to it and her eyes are closed. There are tubes coming out of her nose, and wires connecting parts of her to a machine. Clio wants to stop crying—she feels embarrassed by her emotion—but she can't. The doctor gives her a well-practiced look of pity and offers some insincere words of comfort. He mistakes her tears of relief for tears of sorrow. That's what they really are: tears of relief and regret.

"I'll leave you alone with her," the doctor says, already backing out of the room. Clio almost begs him to stay.

"How long does she have?" she asks.

"Not long. It's hard to say exactly. If I had to guess, a few hours." Fresh tears fall from Clio's eyes without permission. "She's unconscious, but your mother might still be able to hear you. So if there's anything you want to say, it might not be too late," he tells her, and Clio wonders what he means by that. Maybe everyone has something they wish they had said to a parent while they still could.

Clio thanks the doctor, waits for him to leave, then wipes away her tears. The sun is starting to rise outside. A new day. Probably her mother's last. Clio takes out her phone and calls Jude again, her frustration increasing with every unanswered ring. She leaves a message this time. She won't call him again. Edith looks so old lying there in the bed. So small, so fragile, so helpless. Just a shadow of the strong, foreboding woman she used to be. Clio stands as near to the bed as she can without touching it. Then she leans down, close enough to whisper in her mother's ear, hoping that she can still hear her.

"What did you tell the police, you silly old fool?"

Patience

I open my eyes and sit up fast, staring at the unfamiliar surroundings before remembering where I am.

"Day's a-dawning. You okay over there?" asks Liberty from her bed. "Congratulations on surviving your first night in the clink!" I blink, adjusting to the bright light, and look around the cell. I was having a nightmare, and appear to have woken up in another. "They turn on the lights at seven every morning. I like to pretend it's the sun," Liberty says, sitting up and stretching. Her blond curls are a little flat on one side from being slept on, and the freckles on her nose are even more noticeable than last night. "Come on, no time to dillydally. Got to get up, get washed, get dressed. Breakfast will arrive soon. I'll be off to the library later, so you'll have to get by on your own for a bit."

"What did you say?" I ask.

"I said you'll have to get by on your own for—"

"No. The other bit. You're going to the library?"

"Yes."

"Can I come?"

"To the library? Not on your nelly. They won't let you out of your cell until you are in the system. If you're that desperate to read a book, you're welcome to borrow one from my shelf—"

"My mother works in the library and I have to see her," I blurt out. The look on Liberty's face immediately suggests I shouldn't have.

She shakes her head and her curls shake with it. "Frankie the librarian is your mum?" I nod and the residue of a frown lingers on Liberty's face. "Well, that's thrown a spanner in the works. Do you know how unpleasant things could get for her, and for you, if people in here knew that your mother is one of the staff?"

"I . . . didn't think of that. I really need to see her and I trust you."

Liberty's smile has vanished and the expression on her face is one I can't read. She takes a step toward me, then another.

"You might be pretty but you are also pretty stupid," she says, standing too close now. "What was the first rule I taught you about surviving in this place?"

I try to take another step back but I am against the wall. When I try to speak my voice comes out in a whisper.

"Never trust *anyone*."

Clio

Clio leaves her mother's bedside in search of coffee. She needs something to help her stay awake and get through this. It's still early, but the hospital has come to life since the sun came up. She can't help staring at all the people she passes and wondering why they are here. So many of their faces are painted with worry, fear, and pain. But some show signs of optimism or even joy. She feels jealous of the ones with hope in their eyes, it is such a precious thing to have.

Clio finds a small café on the ground floor and buys a black coffee and a vegan KitKat. Her mother taught her that breakfast was the most important meal of the day, so she has always refused to eat a healthy one. She sees the small envelope in her bag that Frankie gave her and decides to open it. Inside she finds a silver ring shaped like a ladybug. She slides the ring onto her finger, it fits, and Clio feels like she is falling. She hurries back through the maze of staircases and corridors to Edith's room, and it is a shock when she opens the door and sees that her mother is no longer alone.

"You got my messages, then?" Clio asks, quickly stepping inside.

"It would appear so," says Jude. "She's still alive, I see."

"Shh," Clio says, closing the door behind her. "The doctor said she might still be able to hear."

"I don't care."

"Never a truer word."

"How long did the doctor say?" he asks.

"Not long."

"Good, I've got things to do. This is all for the best, you'll see. The girl is out of the way, the changes Mum made to her will are bound to be reversed. You'll be able to pay your mortgage and I'll be able to keep the gallery. Everyone's a winner!" Jude says.

"How can you talk like this?"

"I open my mouth and the words come out."

"For god's sake."

"Speaking of the chap, I suppose Mother dearest will finally meet her maker."

"She didn't believe in God anymore."

"What?"

"She said they had a falling out. How do you not know *anything* about your own mother?"

"I know she made us go to church, and always put money in the basket at Sunday mass even when she couldn't afford to put food on the table."

"I sometimes wonder if she did all of that to get us into a good school—"

"Nonsense. On the rare occasions when she wasn't at work, she was running off to confession, desperate to hide in a wooden box and tell the priest her sins and secrets."

"I don't remember that," Clio says.

"Do you remember when you refused to be confirmed and how angry she was with you?"

Clio hasn't forgotten what happened then. It's hard being raised in a religious home when you can't believe in the things you are supposed to. And Clio couldn't. Her First Holy Communion was meant to be a good day, but eight-year-old Clio felt like a fraud. She wanted to make her mother happy and she wanted to believe in God, but both things proved to be too difficult. By the time she was a teenager, she was sick of her mother's rules and sick of God's too. Neither of them made sense to her, and she has felt that way ever since. The sky doesn't have rules, neither does the ocean. It is distinctly human to make up rules, and disappointingly human to follow them without question. Telling her mother that she didn't want to be Catholic when she was thirteen years old did not go well.

"Do you remember how she started buying you chocolate and sweets and putting them in your school lunch box, while I got nothing?" Clio asks.

"Punishing one of us by being kind to the other was pretty standard," says Jude.

"And that time when she said she couldn't afford to get me new school shoes, even though the ones I was wearing literally had holes in—"

"Then she bought me a brand-new pair of trainers. Expensive ones. What were they?"

"Nike Air," Clio replies instantly. She remembers them well. "I had asked for them for Christmas. She bought you a pair instead to make a point. You didn't need or want them."

Sometimes we want things just because other people have them. And Clio started wanting all sorts of things she'd never wanted before when she was a teenager: trainers, freedom, boys. Her mother punished her relentlessly for not believing in the same things as her, and for wanting things her mother thought she shouldn't want.

"It wasn't all bad though, was it?" Clio says, remembering

happier times. Halloween parties with homemade costumes for just the three of them, a trip to the seaside, a parents' evening when Edith was bursting with pride, the best Christmas when they all helped cook the roast dinner and Edith gave Clio a special watch wrapped in silver paper. Clio had seen it in a shop window weeks earlier and Edith remembered, saved up, and went back to get it for her. Their mother loved them sometimes. Just maybe not enough.

Jude shakes his head as though trying to dislodge his thoughts from it.

"No, it wasn't all bad, but it wasn't all good either. I won't forgive or forget what she did to me." He doesn't need to say any more than that. When Jude told their mother he was gay she treated him like a stranger. "And I haven't forgotten what she did to you," he says.

Clio feels herself shrink. "Well, that's all in the past now—"

"How so, when it is still ruining your life in the present? I was only eleven, but I remember when you ran away from home. And I remember why. I sometimes wish you'd never come back."

"Thanks—"

"Because I think your life would have turned out very differently if she didn't make you get rid of the baby when you were sixteen."

Clio doesn't want to talk about this. Can't. Won't. She's hidden all memories of her second child in shoeboxes, but the memories of her first are locked away in a much bigger box inside her head. One she never opens. She's always wondered if her second child was stolen from her that day in the supermarket because she got rid of her first. But she was *so* young. Too young to get pregnant and far too young to keep it. At least that's what her mother said, over and over again. Edith persuaded her that not keeping the baby was the right thing to do, but Clio has spent a lifetime regretting that decision.

Funny how her oh-so-religious mother was suddenly in favor of abortion.

There is a knock on the door and Clio is grateful to whoever has interrupted them.

Until she sees who it is.

"Knock, knock, sorry to intrude. It probably seems deeply inappropriate for me to turn up like this at the hospital, when you are trying to spend some quality time with your mother and say your goodbyes," says the detective. She's carrying a black-and-white cuddly bear.

"Who are you?" Jude asks, in the posh middle-class voice he reserves for strangers.

"DCI Charlotte Chapman."

Jude raises an eyebrow. "Well, from what I hear you have killed our mother."

"From what I hear that's what you wanted," the detective replies and everything stops.

He stands a little taller, trying to appear bigger than he is, like a puffer fish when it feels threatened. "What did you just say?"

"I think you heard me. You wanted your mother dead."

"How dare you. I don't know what you're talking about, but when this is over I'll be making a formal complaint."

"I collect complaints, formal and informal, all welcome. And if I've made a mistake I'll be the first to make an apology. Making mistakes is how we learn, don't you think?"

Jude stares at the detective as though she might be crazy. "Our mother is *dying*. Could you show some respect and leave us alone?"

The detective ignores him and steps farther into the room. "I'm normally pretty nifty at my job," she says, tucking a pink strand of hair behind her pierced ear. "I confess I *thought* this case was going to be relatively straightforward. There were three suspects, two murders, and one victim, and I was sure I knew who was who from the start."

"Do you know what she's talking about?" Jude asks Clio, but Clio is frozen to the spot and too afraid to speak. She knows she was a suspect. And she knows why.

"Let's start at the end, because the end is so often the beginning," the detective says. "The second murder victim was Joy Bonetta, manager at the Windsor Care Home, beloved by no one and found dead in an elevator with an out-of-order sign around her neck. Our three suspects were: a recently fired employee calling herself Patience; a woman named Frankie, who had no obvious reason to be there and who signed the visitor book *pretending* to be Clio; and . . ."—she turns to Clio—"the real Clio Kennedy. All *three* suspects were seen or heard arguing with Joy Bonetta shortly before she died, and all three of them lied about it. I'm a big fan of logic and logically it had to be one of them. But sometimes, in order to make things right in the present, we have to look back at the past. Victim number one was May Chapman a few months earlier. She was also a resident at the Windsor Care Home and my grandmother."

"Did you say *May Chapman*?" Clio asks. She thought the name was a coincidence until now.

Jude ignores her. "I don't see what any of this has to do with—"

"You'll learn more listening to others than you ever will listening to the sound of your own voice," the detective says with a smile. "We're all connected. That is true of life as well as this case. My grandmother, known fondly by all as Aunty May, was an incredibly kind and clever woman. None of us wanted to put her in a home, but she suffered from dementia and we had no choice toward the end. When May was younger she was a detective—"

"I hope she was a better one than you," Jude says.

"Oh yes, much better. But there was one case she could not solve and it haunted her for the rest of her life. A case about a six-month-old baby kidnapped from a supermarket on Mother's Day twenty years ago. Does that ring a bell?"

Jude is quiet for once. So is Clio. She thinks she is going to be sick.

"My grandmother was murdered in the care home. I was sure of it, they even found cotton fibers inside her mouth indicating that someone had held a pillow over her face. But I had no proof, no real evidence, and no motive. All of which tend to be a smidgen important in my line of work. But then there was a second murder—of Joy, the care home manager—and the pieces of the puzzle started to come together. Unfortunately they didn't quite slot into place straightaway, and I confess the case had me miffed for a while. I was right about the three suspects, two murders, and one victim."

"Why only one victim if there were two murders?" Jude asks.

"Because I think one of them deserved it. I wasn't wrong about that, but I was wrong about what some mothers will do for their children."

"I don't understand," Clio says.

"You will. Your mother used to be a detective too, is that right?" DCI Chapman asks, looking over at Edith.

"A *store* detective," Jude says.

"Well, she did a better job of solving all of this than I did." The detective opens the door and invites two police officers to join them. "Jude Kennedy, I am arresting you for conspiracy to murder. You do not have to say anything. But, it may harm your defense if you do not mention when questioned something which you later rely on in court. Anything you do say may be given in evidence."

"You think my brother killed the care home manager?" Clio says.

"No," DCI Chapman replies, putting a pair of cuffs on Jude. "But thanks to your mother, I know who did."

The End

Mother's Day, twenty years earlier

"We know this is very difficult," DCI May Chapman says to Clio. "I can't imagine what you must be feeling, but I need to ask you some questions. The first twenty-four hours really are crucial when a child goes missing."

"She isn't *missing*. I didn't *mislay* her. She was *taken* from a supermarket," Clio replies.

Her pink house is filled with police and people wearing forensic suits and it all feels like a bad dream, as though she is living inside her worst nightmare. Strangers are quietly crawling around the place, infesting every room, opening every cupboard and drawer, touching her precious things. Looking at her. Judging her. All thinking the same thing no doubt: *Bad mother*. They're not wrong. That is how Clio thinks of herself too.

Her own bad mother is still here. Perhaps it is hereditary. Maybe the maternal gene is missing from her DNA. Even though

Clio asked Edith to leave, she keeps making everyone tea and coffee, as though these people are guests in Clio's home. But they are not guests and they are not welcome and they should be out there, looking for her baby, not here asking her the same questions over and over again.

The four of them are sitting in the lounge now. Clio, Edith, a male police officer, and the female detective. May Chapman is old, early sixties perhaps, with a gray bob and matching gray eyes. She sounds kind but Clio doesn't trust her. Clio doesn't trust any of them.

"So your mother had been staying with you for a few days to help look after the baby? Is that right?" the detective asks.

"You know that already," Edith says, speaking up for the daughter she rarely speaks to.

The detective turns to her. "Perhaps you could show DS Tusk the baby's room again, Mrs. Elliot?" Edith leaves the room with the officer and Clio can't help noting that his surname is Tusk and he looks like a walrus.

"You did a better job of getting rid of her than I did," Clio says when they are gone.

"You and your mother don't get along?"

"Just normal mother-daughter stuff," Clio replies.

"But she was here helping with the baby?"

"My husband is away for work and I don't really have anyone else. I haven't been feeling well." The detective waits for her to say more and this is a trick Clio is familiar with; she uses it on her clients all the time. It's amazing the words that come out of people's mouths in desperation to fill an awkward silence. Something tells Clio not to mention having postpartum depression. Not everybody understands what it is, they sometimes hear *bad mother* instead.

"We have CCTV of the moment the baby was taken. Can I show you some images from it?" the detective asks. Clio nods, even though this is something she already knows she does not want to see. "This is your mother pushing the buggy inside the entrance to the supermarket. Your baby, Eleanor, is clearly visible." Clio looks at the image and starts to cry. "This next one is the aisle where it happened." Clio sees her mother with her back turned, talking to another woman slightly out of shot. The buggy is facing the camera and the baby is still visible in her pink onesie. "This is one minute later." The detective shows her another, almost identical image. But this time the buggy is empty.

"Are there no images of what happened during that minute?" Clio asks.

"Yes, but they don't identify who took her. It's a person of medium height wearing a hoodie with their back to the camera." She hesitates. "Is there anyone you can think of who had a reason to want to hurt you or the baby?"

"To hurt *her*? Who would want to hurt a baby?"

"Is there anyone you might have upset? Someone with a grudge?"

Clio shakes her head. "No." And she sounds so sure of herself at first. "Not that I can think of." The woman's stare makes her feel small and exposed. She worries that the detective can see inside her head. "The only person I ever seem to argue with is my mother."

"Can you think of anyone who *she* might have upset?" the detective asks.

"How long have you got? Look, I don't wish to sound rude, but shouldn't you be out there, looking for her? Doing something?"

"And you said that your husband is—"

"Away for work. He's been gone two weeks."

"Where?"

"Scotland. Edinburgh, I think. He's away a lot lately. I can't remember the name of the hotel, but I can give you his number. He's on his way back now. Obviously."

The detective scribbles something else in her notebook and Clio imagines it says *Marriage on the rocks*.

DCI May Chapman looks up. She rearranges her face into something resembling kind, then says something which is not. "The sad fact is that in the majority of cases of child abduction, child abuse, and child murder, it's someone the child knows. I'm sorry for the next question, but where were you between ten and twelve this morning?"

Clio stares at her. "You think I stole my own baby?"

"I'm just asking the questions that need to be asked."

Frankie

You can't trust *anyone*, Frankie knows this. *People* will always let you down in the end, life taught her that lesson when she was young. She waits in the hospital car park because she is exhausted and has nowhere else to go until her shift starts in a few hours. Frankie must have dozed off for a while because night has turned into day; a beautiful sunrise now stretches over the city. She is about to leave when she sees DCI Charlotte Chapman walking toward the main entrance. She wonders why the detective would come to the hospital, it doesn't make any sense, so Frankie heads inside to find out.

She starts to count her footsteps and it makes her think of her own mother. She is the reason Frankie needs to count things, just like she is the reason Frankie learned not to trust *people*. Rosamund Fletcher was a formidable character, one who knew her own mind and how to manipulate the adoption process. The care system wasn't as careful about who children were entrusted to back then. The woman who became her mother was sometimes a monster. She had an inhospitable heart, one where love refused to live no matter how many times it had been invited.

Rosamund loved Frankie in her own very quiet way. The variety of love that isn't spoken out loud or displayed—in public *or* in private—but a love that was demonstrated by the things a person *doesn't* do. When she loved her daughter she didn't scream and shout at her. When she loved her daughter she didn't lash out. Sometimes her mother just wanted to be alone. The older Frankie got, the more she understood. Her mother didn't just crave solitude, she needed it.

"You run and hide, count to one hundred, and I'll come and find you."

That's what her mother used to say when Frankie was little, but it was often a lie. Sometimes Frankie would count to two hundred before she realized that nobody was coming. Her mother frequently didn't try to find her at all.

The worst time, when Frankie was seven years old, she knew that her mother must have seen her run and hide inside the cupboard hole below deck on the narrow boat. Because Frankie heard her creep up to it and lock her in. She wasn't afraid of the dark until that day. And that night. And the day after. The hiding place was damp. It had a musty smell Frankie will never forget, and was so small she could barely turn around in it, even though she was still little herself. For almost two days Frankie was trapped in a tiny dark hole, with nothing to eat and nothing to drink, and only a keyhole to peek out of. All she could do was count.

Her mother never explained, never apologized for locking her away. She never told her where she went or why it took such a long time to come back. Counting her fingers and toes as the minutes and hours passed, in the dark with her eyes squeezed closed, was the only thing that made Frankie feel safe. When Rosamund finally did let her out, she saw the dark circles beneath her mother's eyes, and the bruises on her neck, arms, and legs. Frankie knew better than to ask where she had been.

Sometimes her mother had visitors to the narrow boat late at night. The visits often happened when the fridge was empty or they were running out of gas. Rosamund's bedroom was right at the other end of the boat, but Frankie could still hear the visitors and the noises they made. She would cover her ears and count until the visitors went away. Storms always pass if you wait long enough; so do people. Counting helps Frankie to make sense of a world that has never made sense.

When Rosamund died, the news came as a shock. It was not long after Frankie had found out that she was adopted—a revelation that had put a strain on their already strained relationship. Frankie inherited the narrow boat, along with her mother's desire for solitude. She wasn't sure whether either were good for her, but *The Black Sheep* was the only place that had ever really been home. When her own daughter came along a little later, it felt like a chance to make it a happy one. She had missed the freedom of living on rivers she knew so well, having grown up navigating them. The boat didn't just offer her a place to live, it offered her a place to hide.

Frankie sees a small café just inside the hospital and decides to get herself a coffee. She sits for a while—watching other people come and go, listening to their conversations—and when her first coffee is finished she buys herself another, along with a cinnamon swirl. She decided to loiter in the café because two uniformed police officers have now entered the hospital, and she doesn't want to miss whatever is going to happen next. Ten minutes later, her curiosity and patience are rewarded when she sees Jude Kennedy being escorted from the building in handcuffs. Now Frankie *has* to know what is going on. She thinks of something sad to make herself cry—a trick her mother taught her, which has come in handy often over the years—then walks up to the reception desk.

"Can I help you?" asks the woman sitting behind it.

"I'm looking for Edith Elliot. She was brought here in an ambulance . . ."

The woman sees her tears, checks the screen, then tells Frankie where Edith was taken. Frankie is watchful as she heads in that direction. The last thing she needs is for the detective to catch her here as well as at the care home. There were things Frankie wanted to say to Edith the other day, but the dead care home manager meant she had to leave before she got the chance. Maybe she can say all the things she wanted to say now. She follows the signs down one corridor and along another, then takes the stairs toward the ward she is looking for. A few more corridors—and ninety-nine steps later—she is almost there when her phone makes an unfamiliar noise. The sound of a missed call.

Frankie thinks it is her daughter—who else could it be—and her hands are trembling as she dials her voice mail. But it isn't her little girl.

"Miss Fletcher, it's Liberty. I know I shouldn't really be calling you, but I thought it best to tell you as soon as possible. I know where your daughter is."

Clio

"I don't understand," Clio says as two uniformed officers lead her brother out of her mother's hospital room. "Who is he supposed to have conspired to murder?" she asks DCI Chapman.

"Your mother," the detective replies.

"Jude tried to kill Mum?"

"Nothing that hands-on. Joy Bonetta offered to do it, in exchange for some of his inheritance once she got the job done, and Jude said yes. They exchanged a series of texts that were highly incriminating and not too cryptic. But Bonetta didn't get the job done—a dishonest, incompetent, and unreliable character by all accounts—and someone killed *her* instead. You'll be pleased to know you are no longer a suspect. Your mother told us what happened."

"She did?" Clio says.

"Yes. Nice trainers, by the way." Clio stares down at her red sneakers. It's the second unwelcome compliment her footwear has received today. "And then there's the bear." The detective holds up the black-and-white bear she has been carrying. "I believe this was a gift you sent to your mother?" Clio can't find the right words, so nods. "Can you tell me what made you purchase an expensive spy camera disguised as a toy bear for an eighty-year-old woman?"

Clio looks over at Edith, lying so still and small in the hospital bed.

"I was worried about her. She wouldn't let me visit anymore and I never really liked the Windsor Care Home. I had a bad feeling about the place from the start. My brother chose it, not that we had a lot of choices, it was almost impossible to find residential care for Mum when we really needed it. Whenever I came to visit, the staff seemed so disorganized, disinterested, and incompetent. Nobody I met at the care home really seemed to *care*, and a lot of residents were dying. I know it is somewhere people go to die, but they seemed to be having far more deaths than the national average for a home of that size. I wanted to keep an eye on Mum without anyone knowing. Make sure she was safe."

"If you were so worried about her, and if money was tight, can I ask why didn't she live with you?"

Clio shrugs. "Would you want to live with someone who had ruined your life?"

DCI Chapman stares down at the red trainers then back up at Clio. "After your mother came to the police station last night, we conducted another search of the bedrooms at the care home. Especially hers. That's when we found this cuddly bear and discovered the footage from the camera inside. I'm the only one who has seen it. The footage corroborates a lot of Edith's story. It shows Joy Bonetta creeping into your mother's room then holding a pillow over her face, just like I'm sure she did to Aunty May a few months earlier. Unfortunately it would seem the camera got knocked over by a dog and the rest of the footage is harder to interpret." Clio doesn't say anything. "Either way, what it does or doesn't show after that is less significant now."

"Why?"

"Because your mother confessed to killing Joy."

Patience

"I didn't do it," I tell Liberty for the tenth time.

"It doesn't matter to me what you did or didn't do," Liberty says. "I can't help you get to the prison library—this place has rules *about* the rules—all I can do is pass a message on to Miss Fletcher. If she really is your mum then she can decide what to do."

"What if I went in your place, pretended to be you?"

"The prison officers have lists of who is approved to go where and when. Look, Patience, you're going to have to start living up to that name of yours, because this is a long game. You might be here for more than a minute so you've got to learn to think quick and play smart. Do you understand what I'm telling you?"

Not really.

I nod.

"I don't believe in much, but I do believe that what's meant to be will be," Liberty says. "If Miss Fletcher really is your mum, I'm sure she will come up with a plan to help you. That's what mums do, right? They love us and protect us and the best ones would do anything for their children." Liberty frowns. "You want to share whatever thoughts inside your head are making your face look so sad and ugly?"

"I'm not really her child," I say quietly.

"I thought you said Miss Fletcher was your mum?"

"I think I might have been adopted."

Liberty stares at me. "Did she love you?"

"Yes."

"Did she protect you?"

"Yes."

"Do you think she would do anything for you?" I nod. "Sounds like you've got a great mum to me. You don't have to give birth to a child to be their mother. I know plenty of people who *do* know their real mums and wish they didn't. You should maybe think about that. Not everyone is fortunate enough to be loved, it's like winning the lottery. If you get those lucky numbers in life it doesn't matter where you bought the ticket."

Clio

"You can keep this, we don't need it anymore," DCI Chapman says, giving the spy camera bear to Clio. She leaves the hospital room, closing the door behind her, so that Clio is alone with her mother again. She returns to Edith's bedside, feeling like she needs to sit down. As soon as she does, Edith's eyes open and Clio leaps back out of the chair.

"Jesus Christ!"

"I thought you didn't believe in him," Edith says in a quiet, croaky voice. "Is the detective definitely gone?"

Clio rushes to the door. "I'll get the doctor."

"No, no more doctors. Just sit with me for a while."

Clio hesitates. "I really think that I should—"

"Please. I want us to talk. Before it's too late."

It's already too late, Clio thinks, but she sits back down in the chair next to her mother's bed. If they are going to talk, then there are things Clio wants to know.

"Why did you tell the police that you killed the care home manager?" she asks.

"I'm dying, Clio. I don't want to waste whatever time I have left talking about her."

"I'm sorry."

"That I'm dying, or sorry for asking the question? Death is a mystery, isn't it? We're all dying from the moment we are born, it is only a question of when. Did you know that two people die every second in the world? Over one hundred people die every minute. Over six thousand every hour, one hundred and fifty thousand every day, five million every month, sixty million deaths every year. And that's only humans. That's a lot of death and dying."

"You're not dying."

"I think we both know that I am," Edith says. "I'm sorry you're having to go through this alone—like so many other things— but you're strong. You're the strongest, bravest person I've ever known, Clio. And I'm proud of you for that and for so many other things. I know I didn't say it very often, even when I should have, but I do love you. I hope you know that."

Clio wonders what drugs her mother is on because she doesn't sound at all like herself.

"If you love me, then why did you change your will?" Clio asks.

"So that you'd find her."

"Who?"

"Ladybug. Your daughter."

"I knew it. She's not my daughter, she's just a con artist. They both are."

"What do you mean *both*?"

The machine Edith is hooked up to starts to beep a little faster.

"It doesn't matter," Clio says. "Take it easy, Mum. Maybe just rest—"

"She *is* your daughter."

If her mother is going to insist on talking about this again, there is something Clio would like to know. "Do you remember this?" she asks, showing Edith the silver ladybug ring Frankie gave her.

"Of course. I had three of them made when your daughter was born. One for you, one for me, and one for her, which I put on a little chain until she would be old enough to wear it. I didn't know you kept yours."

"I didn't. But I've seen two of them today."

"Two? Where?"

"A woman gave this one to me earlier. It looks so much like the original."

"I think it *is* the original. I had them made especially, there *were* only three. I'm so sorry Clio. I have so many regrets and—"

"And I'm top of the list. I know, you wrote it in your notebook and I found it, remember?"

Edith shakes her head. "My biggest regret isn't *you*, it's about you. That's what that line in my notebook meant. My biggest regret of my life is that I wasn't a better mother to you. I wish I had known how to love you the way you deserved to be loved, and how to fix what got broken because of me. My biggest regret is letting *you* down." Clio doesn't know what to say, but when Edith reaches for her hand she holds it. "Don't make the same mistakes as me and don't leave it too late to learn how to be happy. It's not who we are, it's who we think we are that holds us back in life and stops us from being who we could be."

The machine beeps again. Clio stares at it but Edith only looks at her.

Clio starts to stand. "I really think I should find a doctor—"

"I'm dying, Clio. There is nothing any doctor can do for me now, and I don't want to spend my final moments with a stranger. I got almost everything wrong with you, at least let me do a good job of saying goodbye."

Clio starts to cry, she feels like a little girl again. "Mum, I don't know what to do."

"Yes you do. In here," Edith says, placing her hand over her heart. She wipes away Clio's tears, just like she did when she was a child, then holds her daughter's hand once more.

"We are all made from stars, the result of explosions millions of years ago. You, me, everyone we meet, we're all stardust and stories. Try to remember that," Edith says. She closes her eyes and is very still. Her grip on Clio's hand loosens. The machine makes a different noise and a doctor comes rushing into the room.

When it is over, and the doctor has confirmed that her mother is dead, Clio feels a wave of emotion she did not expect. It washes over her and drags her under until she feels as though she can't breathe. Clio starts to walk away, then she runs.

Frankie

Frankie listens to the voice mail twice. When she is sure that she has understood correctly—that Liberty knows where her daughter is—she rushes out of the hospital and to the camper van. The journey from West London to the prison takes longer than it should in the morning traffic; there are too many cars being driven by too many *people*. Frankie counts the number of seconds it takes for a red light to change to green. When it doesn't change fast enough she drives through anyway, ignoring a cacophony of car horns bleating their annoyance.

She eventually pulls into the prison car park and sees that her favorite spot is available. This is a good sign. It's still early, the car park is empty, so she changes into her prison uniform in the front seat. Frankie lived in this van once upon a time, before she inherited the narrow boat. This van was her home when she was a bookseller in St. Ives. There isn't much she hasn't done in it: travel, eat, drink, sleep, take care of a baby girl she stole from a supermarket. You can do almost anything in a van like this.

Frankie notices that the belt on her uniform now needs to be fastened on a tighter notch—she's lost weight. She looks in the mirror and sees that the shadows beneath her eyes are a shade darker than they were before too. Frankie doesn't wear makeup; her mask is skin-deep. But she doesn't look or feel like herself today.

She climbs out into the cold morning sunshine and is about to lock the camper van, when the side door suddenly slides open, revealing someone crouching behind it. Someone who must have been hiding back there for well over an hour while Frankie drove, and undressed, and counted the number of seconds it takes for red lights to turn green.

"Hello," says Clio.

Clio

"So this is where you work, is it?" Clio asks, taking in Frankie's uniform, before staring up at the imposing prison walls behind her. Frankie doesn't speak—she appears to be in a state of shock—so Clio continues. "I saw your van when I came out of the hospital. It's hard to miss. I didn't expect the doors to be unlocked, but when they were I decided to take a look inside. It's probably the most spontaneous thing I've ever done, but I'm not exactly feeling *myself*. I did just watch my mother die."

"Edith is dead?"

"How do you know my mother?" Frankie doesn't answer. "Never mind. I heard you coming back to the van and I panicked. Then I hid and now here we are, outside a prison. Which seems appropriate because I'm starting to believe that you did steal my baby."

"Please don't call the police."

"Is the girl in the photo you showed me really my daughter?"

"Yes," Frankie whispers.

Clio stares at her, as though looking for clues on her face. "If that *is* true—"

"It is."

"Then *why*? Why did you take her? Because that is the question I have asked myself over and over again since the day it happened."

Frankie thinks very carefully before she answers. "Because all children deserve to be loved."

"You think I didn't love my daughter?"

Frankie stares at the ground. "I know you didn't."

Clio waits for her to make eye contact again but she doesn't. "Why did you give me this?" Clio asks, holding up the silver ladybug ring.

"I told you. Proof. It was on a little chain tied to the baby's buggy the day I took her. I thought if you saw it, you would know that I was telling you the truth. I'm fairly sure the ring was never mentioned in the newspapers," Frankie says. "I'm sorry but I have to go. She is all I care about, and someone in there knows where she is."

"Wait," Clio says as Frankie turns to leave. "You stole the papercut from my house because you thought your daughter made it?" Frankie nods. "But why did you leave an old ten-pound note, one that isn't even in circulation anymore, in its place?"

"Because that's how much your mother paid me."

"What?"

Frankie checks the time. "I really do have to go."

Clio stares at the Mickey Mouse watch on Frankie's wrist. "Where did you get that?"

Frankie yanks down her sleeve, hiding both the watch and the *Shh* tattoo. "Stay, go, call the police if you want. I don't care about you anymore." She starts to walk away.

"Please, wait."

"I can't."

"Then I will," Clio says. "I'll wait here until you come back out."

Frankie shrugs. "Suit yourself."

Frankie

Frankie walks fast, she needs to talk to Liberty as soon as possible and find out what she does and doesn't know about her daughter. Once again, the conversation with the woman in the pink house did not go according to plan. She realizes that she left the keys in the van but doubts she needs to worry. Frankie doesn't think Clio would steal a camper van; the woman is always getting taxis, she probably can't even drive. She whispers the number of steps left before she reaches the main prison entrance.

Twenty. Nineteen. Eighteen. Seventeen.

Once Frankie is inside the main door, the overheated air hits her. She nods a silent hello to the guard on the desk and tries to smile, to *act normal*, but it isn't easy. There are twelve short steps to her locker, where she leaves her bag and phone, since she can't chance setting off the scanner two days in a row. Frankie heads to the front desk and signs in, then she walks through the double doors to the scan and search room. Nobody stops her today. When she gets to the door leading to the courtyard, Frankie reaches for the biggest key in the set attached to the belt on her uniform. She unlocks the door and breathes deeply, gulping down the cool air as she steps outside.

There are fifty-eight steps across the courtyard, then the big key again as she allows herself inside prison block B. She feels herself relax a little as she locks the door behind her. There are five steps to the bottom of the stone staircase, then forty steps up. She is a little out of breath by the time she reaches the top.

Ten. Nine. Eight. Seven.

She counts down the final steps to the library door, reaching for the smallest key on her belt in preparation. Then she lets herself inside, her trembling fingers making it tricky to slot the key in the lock. As soon as she is in, she closes the door firmly behind her. The sight and smell of all the books on the shelves makes her feel instantly calmer.

A bell rings in the distance, just like the bells that used to ring when Frankie was at school. She checks her Mickey Mouse watch and sees that she only just made it in time. There is a knock on the library door before she even reaches her desk. Frankie heads back the way she came, opens the door, and is met by one of the guards on duty today. The short, stocky woman looks unfamiliar, which means she must be new.

"Delivering your library volunteers," she says gruffly, handing Frankie a clipboard with a list. Frankie thanks her and takes it, staring at the names printed on the sheet of paper. She ticks the inmates off one by one, relieved when she sees Liberty's name. Frankie needs to talk to her alone.

"You all know the drill," she says to the rest of the inmates. "Tidy the shelves, put up the posters, and arrange the chairs so we're ready for the author visit today. Liberty, can I have a word?"

Liberty follows her to the office but neither of them speaks until the door is firmly closed.

"I got your message," Frankie says.

"Sorry about that, Miss Fletcher. I didn't know what to do."

"You said you know where my daughter is."

Liberty nods. "Yes. She's here."

Frankie stares at the girl, wondering if she has misheard. "You traced my daughter's phone to the prison?"

Liberty shakes her head and her blond curls shake with it. "There was no need to trace the number in the end. Your daughter shared my cell last night."

Frankie takes a second to process the information then heads straight for the door. "I have to go to her—"

"No, miss. That's the thing. She was here, but now she isn't."

"What do you mean?"

"They released her."

"What? When?"

"Just now."

Patience

I didn't believe them at first when they said they were going to release me. It turns out leaving a prison is almost as complicated as arriving at one. There were a lot of forms—most of which I didn't understand but signed anyway because the guard said I had to—and a lot of "security checks" but eventually I was taken from the prison block to the main building. My clothes and my belongings were returned to me, including Edith's silver ladybug ring, which I slipped on my finger straightaway.

Being walked out of the prison was the strangest part of it all. I'm not sure I'll ever get over having my freedom stolen from me, or take freedom for granted again. Everything seems more special than before; even looking up at the sky and hearing the sound of birds. All the things most people get to enjoy every day without realizing how lucky they are. I'm hoping that this nightmare is finally going to end.

My optimism turns into fear when we reach the outside gate. What if this is a mistake and they aren't really going to release me?

Even if they do, I don't have anywhere to live now and I don't have a job. I've lost everything that I worked so hard for, everything and everyone that mattered. But then the guard opens the gate and I see my mother's blue and white camper van in the prison car park.

She's here.

My fear turns into joy and everything changes in a heartbeat. I'm going to be okay. Mum will take me home and I will be safe and this will be over. I'm walking, then I'm running toward the van. More than anything I just want to see her face again. We haven't spoken for almost a year, not since she confessed that she wasn't my real mum. But none of that matters now. She is the only person in the world who I trust. And *Mum* is the only name I will call her, because that's who and what she is, regardless of whether she gave birth to me.

I see her silhouette in the driver's seat and am overcome with love and happiness.

I knock on the window and am filled with confusion.

Because it isn't my mum, it's Edith's daughter. The woman who begged me to trust her then let the police arrest me. I take two steps back, almost tripping over my own feet.

"Wait," she says, opening the van door and rushing toward me. "We need to talk."

"I have *nothing* to say to you."

"I have everything to say to you. But first, I just want to say that I'm sorry."

"What for?" I ask.

"All of it."

Frankie

Frankie is out of the library, down the stairs, and across the courtyard in less than a minute. Once inside the main building she heads straight for the security office.

"Did an inmate just leave?" she asks, still a little out of breath.

"They did indeed. Checked in yesterday, checked out today," replies an elderly officer called Robjant. He has long white hair, Harry Potter glasses, and a habit of repeating himself. "Cops dropped the charges," the old man adds.

"*Shit*," Frankie says.

"Everything okay? They might not have gone through the main gate yet?" He reaches for the phone on his desk. "I can call the hut, get them to hold on to her—"

"No, it's fine. I'll try to catch up," Frankie replies, already heading in that direction.

"Did someone forget to return a library book?" Robjant shouts.

She turns back, forces her face to smile. "Yes, that's right. They're all thieves in here, even the bookish ones."

The thirty-two steps to the outside gate seem to take longer than ever before. Frankie walks at a normal pace, resisting the urge to run, desperate to avoid doing anything that might look suspicious. When the outside gate is within touching distance she can hear her heartbeat thudding in her ears. She tries to hide her impatience while waiting for the guard on duty to open the gate. When he finally lets her through she looks around, expecting to see her daughter for the first time in almost a year. Longing to hold her in her arms and never let her go.

But Frankie doesn't see her daughter.

The car park is empty.

And her camper van is gone.

Clio

Clio has never driven a van before. She doesn't even own a car, and hasn't driven anything that wasn't automatic for years. She grinds the gearbox more than once.

"Why do you have my mother's van?" the girl sitting next to her asks again. "You said you'd explain on the way."

"I told you already, your mum asked me to take you home," Clio lies.

"But how do you know my mum and why didn't she pick me up herself?"

"It's complicated."

"Which part?"

"All of it," Clio says. "I know you don't trust me, but please let me help you."

"I don't need your help and I'll never trust you again."

Clio wishes she could study the girl's face instead of having to concentrate on the road ahead. She wants to look at her, talk to her, find out everything about her. Everything that she has missed.

"You have the same ring," the girl says. Clio glances over and sees that she is wearing a silver ladybug ring, exactly like the one on her own finger.

Clio stops at a red light. "There's something I need to tell you."

"Unless it's where my mum is, I'm not interested," the girl replies. "We had a deal. You said to keep quiet and I kept quiet. You also said that if I got Edith out of the home that you would—"

"Well, I'm here, aren't I? And you're out of prison, aren't you? I'll get you the money."

"Keep it. I don't want it."

"Don't be a fool. I said I'd pay you and I will. I don't want to get off on the wrong foot."

"Ha! Is that a joke?" the girl says, staring out of the passenger window.

"I don't want to lie to you. Can we hit the reset button? Start again?" Clio says.

"Thank you for the lift home, but after that I don't ever want to see you again."

The words wound Clio more than she would have thought possible. They drive in silence after that, so when the girl finally speaks it makes Clio jump.

"Take the next exit," the girl says, and they turn off the main road before navigating a seemingly endless network of narrow country lanes. It feels a million miles from the city. The girl winds down the window and the fresh air tastes good. They drive through pretty villages passing old churches and quaint pubs. There are rows of tiny terraced old houses and Clio can see smoke rising from some of the chimneys. She notices pretty gardens and fields of lush green grass, an old stone bridge, a river . . .

"What river is this?" Clio asks.

"The Thames."

"It doesn't look like the Thames."

"Rivers are like people. They change, they go where they have to. Sometimes they don't look like themselves but they're still who they are."

"Who told you that? Your mum?"

The girl glares at her. "Yes."

"You love her, don't you? Your mum."

"She's the best person I know," the girl says without hesitation.

Clio thinks on those words for a while, wondering what to do with them. She feels jealous and grateful and happy and sad, all at once.

"This is it," the girl says abruptly. Clio said she'd take her home—it felt like the least she could do, and she just wanted to spend some time alone with her—but all Clio can see is a country lane and the river. She pulls over anyway. "You said you needed to tell me something," the girl says, already reaching for the door.

Clio turns off the engine. "Is there somewhere we can go?" The girl shakes her head and Clio fears she will open the door and run. "Here is fine. Can I ask you one question first?"

"One."

"I don't know what to call you. What's your real name? I know it isn't Patience."

The girl hesitates. "Nellie."

Clio beams, struggles not to cry. "Nellie! Short for Eleanor. That's a very pretty name."

The girl really *is* baby Eleanor. The name is too much of a co-incidence for it not to be true. Her eyes, her smile, her scowl, Clio suddenly recognizes them all. She wants to touch her so badly but knows that she can't. She finally found her baby girl and her heart is breaking all over again.

"One more question," Clio says, but Nellie reaches for the door handle. "Last one, I promise. Did you have a happy childhood?"

Nellie doesn't think for very long before answering. "The happiest."

Clio nods, smiles, wipes away a tear with the back of her hand.

"That's good. Right, a promise is a promise. There is something I need to say to you and it isn't easy, but I do think you have a right to know. My mum, Edith, she died today. It was peaceful. She wasn't in any pain. But . . . she's gone."

Clio wasn't sure what to expect but Nellie's face is one of pure devastation.

"I trusted you when you said you wanted to help Edith," Nellie says. "You said she would be safest out of the care home and I believed you. I did what I did because of you. Now she's dead? Your mother was right, you are a terrible daughter."

Clio feels as though she has been stabbed in the chest.

Nellie grabs her bag and runs from the van without looking back. Clio watches as she crosses the road before disappearing down some steps to the towpath.

And then she is gone.

Clio lost her baby girl, then she found her without knowing she had.

Now she wonders whether she'll ever see her daughter again.

Frankie

Frankie has searched everywhere for her daughter. She called for a taxi to pick her up from the prison and went straight to the pink house in Notting Hill first, but Nellie wasn't there. Neither was Clio, or Frankie's camper van. She went to the attic in Covent Garden next, but that was a dead end too. So Frankie got a taxi home because she couldn't think of anywhere else to go.

Frankie has lost everything. Everything that ever counted for anything. She wonders whether she will lose her job now too—having walked out today with no explanation and leaving prisoners unsupervised—then realizes that she doesn't care. Things she thought were important to her, aren't. Things she thought mattered, don't. And the worst part about all of this, is that it feels as though everything bad that has happened is her own fault.

She walks along the towpath to where *The Black Sheep* is moored, then Frankie steps onto the deck, opens the door, and locks it behind her. She stares at the door to her daughter's bedroom. She's checked it every time she came home for over a year, but it seems pointless now. She is all out of hope but something makes her do it anyway. Perhaps just her need for routine, like her need to count things.

Four steps to her daughter's bedroom door.

It is slightly open. Frankie thought she had closed it.

Three steps.

Frankie is sure that she must be seeing things.

Two.

Or dreaming.

One.

Because Nellie is sitting on the bed.

"Hi, Mum," she says.

Frankie stares at her as though she might be a ghost. Nellie's hair is longer than it was before, and she looks older, thinner, and tired. But it really is her little girl. Frankie rushes over, pulling her into a hug, needing to feel her to know that this isn't a dream. But her daughter is real and she is safe and she is home.

"Are you okay?" Frankie asks, holding Nellie's face in her hands, examining every inch of her for damage. They are both crying.

"Yes."

"Are you sure? I didn't know you were at the prison until it was too late. By the time I found out, they had already released you and you were gone."

"I thought you were outside waiting for me. But a woman called Clio Kennedy was in your van. She drove me home, said that she knew you—"

Frankie feels sick. "What else did she say?"

Nellie stares at her. "How *do* you know her, Mum?"

Hearing Nellie call her that makes her heart ache.

Frankie holds her daughter's hand, scared to let her go. "There's something I need to tell you."

"That's what she said."

"I'm surprised she didn't."

"Didn't what?" Nellie asks.

"There's no easy way to say this—"

"Then say it the hard way. I don't want us to have secrets from each other anymore. And I don't care whether you're my birth mum, I love you. I just want to know the truth."

"I might not have given birth to you, but you are my daughter. That's the truth."

"I'll always be your daughter."

Frankie's eyes fill with tears again. "And I'll always be your mum. I've looked after you and loved you since you were a baby. But you're right, I'm not your birth mother, and you do deserve to know the truth. Even though you might not like it, or me, when you do."

They sit down next to each other on the bed, just like they did when Nellie was little and Frankie used to read her bedtime stories. Frankie tells her another story now. One about a supermarket, and a store detective, and a woman in a pink house. A story about a stolen baby called Eleanor. A baby who grew up to be a girl called Nellie, living on a narrow boat with a woman who was not her real mother.

It's a lot to take in.

Nellie turns and pulls away, hugging her knees to her chest.

Frankie knows it must be impossibly difficult to process the enormity of what she has just been told. She watches her daughter, waiting for a reaction, checking to see if she has understood. When Nellie finally opens her mouth to speak, Frankie is terrified of what she will say. She can't bear to lose her little girl all over again. Her daughter's words sound strange and distorted, but Nellie is looking at her for confirmation.

"That's right," Frankie says. "I'm your sister."

Clio

Clio parks the van at the end of the mews outside the pink house. Inside her home nothing feels the same as before. Her little girl isn't dead but isn't her little girl anymore either. The child she once loved more than anything else in the world is a complete stranger. Clio is exhausted, too tired to do anything but sleep. So she heads upstairs and walks along the landing toward her bedroom. She stops outside the room where her mother was sleeping last night and the memory comes as a shock. Her daughter is alive but her mother is dead.

Clio feels as though she is trespassing in her own home when she steps inside the spare bedroom. The shape she saw earlier of someone sleeping is just the pillows made to look that way beneath the sheets. Her mother's things—her clothes, her custard creams, her pots of moisturizer—are all still there, and the room smells of Edith's perfume. Clio finds a letter addressed to her on the dresser. She doesn't want to read it, but can't seem to stop herself.

Dear Clio,

I fear we might not get to have this conversation face-to-face. That's my fault—like so many other things—I've been putting it off for years. There is something I need to tell you, something I should have told you a long time ago. I only hope that you can find it in your heart to forgive me.

I was wrong when I told you not to keep the baby when you got pregnant at sixteen. And when you decided to ignore me and have it anyway, I was wrong not to support you. When you struggled with being a mum at such a young age, just like I did with you, I should have done more to help. I thought you giving up the baby for adoption was the right thing to do, because I wanted you to have a better life than I did. I wanted you to be free. Children are such a heavy burden, you must know that is true, but I see now that it was a burden you wanted to carry.

When you got pregnant again all those years later, this time married with a home and a husband, it felt like a second chance. Not just for you, but for me too. I thought it might bring us closer together. But, like the first time, you struggled. I hope you don't mind me saying that. I honestly thought I was doing the right thing when I turned her away.

It was when I was staying with you for a few days to help with baby Eleanor. It was the first—and sadly only—time you trusted me to help. You were upstairs, finally sleeping, so was she. I was cross when I heard the knock on the door, I didn't want anyone to wake you or the baby. When I opened it and saw the girl standing there, I presumed she was selling something. I still remember everything she said.

"I'm looking for Clio Kennedy."

"I'm her mother, how can I help?"

She stared at me for a few seconds before she spoke. "I'm her daughter."

I don't know what my face did, but I knew instantly that she was telling the truth. My mind did the math and confirmed she was the right age, that she could have been a baby when I persuaded you to give yours away. She looked like you did at that age, such a pretty, sweet young girl, with big green eyes full of hope. I didn't invite her in, didn't even fully open the door, so she babbled away on the doorstep about how her mum had revealed she was adopted on her eighteenth birthday. It had clearly come as a shock to her and—wanting to know who her real mother was—she had tracked you down. She had struggled to find you—I was surprised to learn you had ticked the "no contact" box on the adoption paperwork two decades earlier. All she knew was that your name was Clio. But then she saw a picture of you at Kennedy's Gallery in the *Evening Standard*—one of Jude's exhibitions with warm white wine—and was so sure that you were her mother, she visited the gallery the next day. She met your brother and tried to find out more about you. She asked him if you'd had a baby who would be eighteen years old now, and Jude did what has always come naturally to him—he lied—but, as you know, he's never been very good at it. She used him to find you, but then found me instead when I opened your front door.

I told her it wasn't a good time and closed the door in her face.

I can imagine the pain you might be feeling while reading this, but put yourself in my shoes in that moment if you can. You were *depressed*. I don't remember the fancy terms for the baby blues these days, but you had them in a big way. I was worried you were going to harm yourself or the baby. I didn't think you could cope with any more stress or emotional upset.

She knocked on the door again. When I didn't answer

she started yelling through the letter box, said she needed to know who you were in order to know who she was. I told her to go away, but she kept knocking and this time she woke the baby. I answered the door a second time, holding baby Eleanor in my arms. I needed the girl to know she wasn't welcome. I was trying to protect you.

"This is my granddaughter," I said. "Clio has a new baby now and they are a proper family. You should be grateful that she went through with an unwanted pregnancy. Surely you're old enough to understand that mistakes happen. That's all you were to her, a mistake. There's nothing for you here." The girl looked as though I had struck her. "Come now, you must have known you were adopted for a reason? My daughter didn't give you away by accident. Why are you really here? What do you want, money?"

The girl shook her head but I took out my purse anyway, balancing the baby on my hip. Eleanor started to howl again and I was terrified you would wake up and come downstairs.

"Sorry, I only have this." I gave her an old ten-pound note, made her take it.

"The baby is crying," she said, frowning at the screaming child.

"I know, I'm not deaf. She does that a lot. So did you when you were born."

"Is that why?" she asked, still hovering on the doorstep like an unwelcome salesman.

"Why what?" I snapped.

She looked like she was going to start crying too. "Why my mother gave me away?"

"If it's more money you want, I don't have any. My daughter isn't well. I have to protect her and my grandchild. Why don't you leave some contact details, and maybe, if there is a better time in the future, we will get in touch with you then."

"The baby is still crying," she said, as though it was my fault when really it was hers.

"Yes, she is. How much will it cost to make you disappear and take her with you?"

I didn't mean it. Of course I didn't. I was tired too.

She walked away without another word. But I know she followed me to the supermarket the next day, Mother's Day. Your daughter stole your baby. I knew that she had taken the child, but I didn't know how to find her. I didn't even know the girl's name.

She came to see me at the care home a few months ago. She found me again, all these years later. But this time she was looking for her daughter, not her mother. I could have helped her but I didn't—why should I after all the pain she caused you—but now I think I might have been wrong again. Which is why I have to make things right.

I'm going to the police station now. It's the only thing I can think of to protect you all. I've been a bad mum all my life, let me be good just this once. I didn't kill Joy Bonetta—I wish I had—but the detective seems to think it was one of you. I can't let Ladybug take the blame so I will say I did it. Confess to a sin I'm not guilty of to atone for all the ones I did commit. Besides, I doubt I have long left anyway. People presume that there will always be a tomorrow. The existence of cemeteries and common sense should dictate that one day they will be wrong about that. I would give almost anything to rewrite the story of you and me and us. There is still time for you to change the ending of your story. Do whatever you have to do to love and be loved and don't let history repeat itself.

Your mum.

X

Clio is crying by the time she finishes reading the letter. She remembers the day her first baby was taken away from her to be adopted. She put her Mickey Mouse watch in the crib at the last minute, wanting to give the child *something*, even though at sixteen she had very little to give. The same watch she saw Frankie wearing a few hours ago.

Clio goes to her room and empties her bag. The black-and-white teddy bear that the detective gave her falls onto the bed. She doesn't know whether she wants to see the footage it recorded, but forces herself to watch it anyway. It's all there on the tape: Joy coming into her mother's room, holding a pillow over Edith's face. Shortly afterward the camera gets knocked over, so that the angle of the shot is of the floor. It does show someone else rushing into the room, but it only reveals what they were wearing on their feet: a pair of red trainers.

There is a noise on the stairs and Clio freezes. But they are not heavy footsteps. A face appears in the doorway, one she had forgotten about until now.

"I said you are not allowed upstairs."

Dickens lies down, his head between his front paws, his big eyes staring up at her.

Clio wonders if he somehow knows that Edith has died.

"Fine, come on then," she says, patting the bed.

He jumps up beside her and makes himself comfortable on her lap.

"You need a bath. You stink of dog," Clio says, stroking his fur. "Then what am I going to do with you?" Dickens looks up at her then licks her face. Clio is strangely glad of the company. The dog stares at her as though he understands everything that has gone on. "You're right," she says. "I should be kinder to you. After all, you're one of the only witnesses to what really happened that day at the care home. You and this bear."

Patience

Mother's Day, two days earlier

"You're fired, obviously, and don't bother asking me for a reference," says Joy, standing with her arms folded, and glaring at me from the doorway of Mr. Henderson's room.

I know it looks bad. I did have Mr. Henderson's money and his things in the pocket of my uniform, but I was putting it all back. I'm clearly not cut out to be a thief: my conscience won't let me commit a crime. I try to tell my side of the story, but Joy won't listen so I start to panic. Work is hard to come by without any ID, or a bank account, or a real name. "Please, I can explain," I say. Her face is a stop sign but I carry on anyway. "I can't lose this job."

"And I can't employ a thief. Get your things and get out. Leave your keys and your badge in my office, you can return the uniform once you've washed it. I don't have time to listen to your lies. Thanks to you I have even more work to do."

She points at the door and I walk toward it.

My bag is still in Edith's room.

So is Dickens.

I can't leave without him but Joy has followed me to the landing. She is leaning against the rickety top floor banister, watching me as I walk toward the stairs. I don't have many options and there is no time to decide what to do. Right and wrong are so hard to tell apart sometimes.

"And don't bother trying to get another job in a care home in this city. I'm going to make sure *everyone* knows not to employ a girl called Patience."

"Go ahead," I say, and mean it.

I start to walk down the stairs—the elevator is broken again thanks to me jamming the buttons earlier. When I'm halfway I glance up and see that Joy is still standing there on the top floor, looking down on me in more ways than one. Once out of sight I head to the staff room and get my coat, grateful that there is nobody to see me. Visiting time is over. God's waiting room has been restored to its sedate self, and the rest of the staff and residents are out of sight and earshot in the dining room. If someone wanted to do something bad here and get away with it, this would be the time to do it. I go into Joy's office. I leave my name badge on her desk but keep my set of keys. Then I force open the petty cash tin, and fill my pockets with its contents. It's no more than she owes me for days I have already worked. When I've taken what I see as mine, I head for the front door and make a point of slamming it closed, knowing that Joy might still be watching.

As soon as I am out of view I creep around the back of the care home and start to climb up the fire escape. I'm sure Joy will have retreated to her office downstairs by now—she rarely leaves it to do any real work—and I don't plan to stay long once I've let myself in through the emergency exit on the top floor. All I want to do is get Dickens, say goodbye to Edith, and get out of here. For good this time. I creep along the landing and see that Edith's bedroom door is slightly open. When I step inside the room it all happens so fast.

Edith is lying in the bed.

Joy is holding a pillow over her face.

Another woman rushes up behind her.

What I'm seeing doesn't seem real. Can't be. Dickens bursts through the bathroom door. He crashes into the chest of drawers so hard that a stuffed bear and a metal statue tumble off it. Joy turns and sees the other woman and they start to fight. Edith doesn't move, her eyes are closed and she looks lifeless on the bed. Joy knocks the other woman to the floor and turns back to finish what she started. The dog growls and launches himself at Joy. She grabs him by the scruff of his neck, he whimpers, and she hurls him across the room. Something inside me snaps. I rush at Joy but she knocks me down on the floor too, then turns back to Edith. The other woman gets up, clutches at Joy from behind, and hooks her arm around Joy's neck. I don't know if the woman can hold her. I see the metal object that fell from the dresser—a bronze statue of a magnifying glass—I grab it and whack Joy on the head. There is a horrible cracking sound when I do.

Joy crashes to the ground and doesn't get up.

The other woman stares at me in shock but doesn't say a word.

I rush over to Edith.

"Is she alive?" the woman asks.

"I don't know. Who are you?"

"I'm Clio, Edith's daughter. Is she alive?"

"Yes," I say.

"Good. I don't think *she* is," Clio replies, looking at Joy, who is still on the floor. Joy's eyes are wide open. She isn't moving.

I feel as though I'm going to be sick. "Should we call an ambulance?"

Edith sits up in the bed, gasping for air and taking in the scene. Dickens jumps up beside her and licks her face and I am so relieved they are both okay. "What happened?" Edith asks, staring at us both. "Oh dear," she adds when she sees Joy.

Clio kneels down next to Joy and checks for a pulse, then shakes her head. "I walked in and she was holding a pillow over your face," she says.

Edith frowns as though trying to remember. "So you *killed* her?"

"I didn't do anything. This girl hit her over the head with your retirement statue."

"Sounds like she saved my life. My friend May was right. She knew Joy was up to no good, that's why Joy killed her. Thank you, Ladybug."

"We both saved you, it wasn't just me," I say.

Clio turns to me. "Now hang on. All I did was restrain her, *you* bludgeoned her to death."

"If you weren't holding her I wouldn't have been able to. If she's dead you're as much to blame as I am."

Clio shakes her head. "We should call the police."

"They'll send me to jail," I tell Edith frantically. "We'd just argued, and . . . I was coming back to get Dickens and say goodbye after Joy fired me."

"She fired you, Ladybug?"

"Why are you calling her that?" Clio asks Edith, staring at me.

"Because this is Ladybug."

"No, Mum. It isn't."

"I sort of deserved to get fired," I say.

Edith shakes her head. "I doubt that, but you're right, it makes a bad situation look even worse. Well, then. No police."

"A *bad* situation?" Clio says. "Mum, this strange girl whacked her on the head. And I argued with Joy earlier too. We have to call the police and let them sort it out."

"Oh, like they sorted out your problems last time? This isn't a strange girl, she's very important to me. Both of you saved me and now I have to protect you both."

"I won't go along with it," Clio says, but her voice is distant. She is gazing at my face with a strange intensity.

"Do you want your picture in the papers all over again? And this time you'll lose everything you had left: your reputation, your clients, your precious pink house. How many people heard you arguing with the care home manager earlier? It doesn't matter what you did or didn't do, what people believe you did is all that counts. The police will call this murder and you'll both be suspects," Edith says. "So will I if they find her in my room."

Clio starts pacing and she reminds me of my mother. "This can't be happening to me. I'm a *good* person."

"Are you? Really? Are any of us? I'm living proof that only the good die young," Edith says. "Sometimes bad things happen to good people, so good people have to do bad things. There will be a way to fix this, I just need to think—"

"We could put her in the elevator," I say. "Nobody will look in there again until the repair guy turns up."

Clio shakes her head. "The elevator? Really?"

"Do you have a better idea?" Edith asks. "We each need an alibi. Patience, can you go straight home and make sure someone sees you there?"

If I go back to the flat Jude will no doubt come up to find me. "Yes."

"I've got an appointment with a new client in less than an hour," says Clio.

Edith starts clambering out of the bed. "Good, they will be your alibi. If we all keep quiet we should all be okay."

"What about you?" Clio says.

"I haven't figured that out yet, but I'm not staying here."

Clio and I carry Joy's body to the broken elevator while Edith packs some things. I can tell Clio doesn't trust me. To be fair, I don't trust her either.

"I knew my mother wasn't safe in this place," Clio says beneath her breath.

"If you *knew* then why did you put her in here, and why did you make her stay?"

"I'll pay you," she says, ignoring the question. "If you could look after my mum for a couple of days, then bring her to my home, I'll have figured out what to do by then—"

"Why can't you take her home with you now?"

"Because that's the first place they'll look when they discover she's missing."

She's not wrong. "Okay, but I don't want your money."

"I'll pay you anyway. If you keep her safe and keep quiet about all of this. Five thousand pounds. Does that sound fair?" That amount of cash could literally change my life. I can leave the attic and find somewhere better to live *and* apply for art school.

"It's a deal," I say holding out my hand for her to shake. "By the way, my name is—"

"I don't want to know," Clio replies. She doesn't shake my hand either. She stares at me intently again, then shakes her head and looks away. "My mother has always been good at putting bad ideas in my head. The less we know about each other the better. I'll give you my address so you know where to bring Mum, but other than that let's pretend we're strangers, that we've never met."

I put the out-of-order sign around Joy's neck before pulling the elevator door closed.

"Is that a good idea?" Clio asks.

Before I can answer the elevator lights up, rumbles to life, and starts to slowly rattle its way down toward the ground floor.

"I thought you said it was *broken*!" Clio whispers.

"I thought it was." I hear the sound of the elevator opening downstairs, but I'm surprised when I don't hear anything else. No cry for help. No sound of screaming. As though someone just discovered Joy's body in the elevator and left it there. "We need to hurry up and get out of here."

"Wait," Clio says before we go back into Edith's room. "How do I know I can trust you?"

I tell her something Edith has told me many times.

"You don't, but you can. Strangers are less likely to let you down than people you know."

The Beginning

Mother's Day, one year later

"Thank you," Mum says, when she opens the papercut card I have made for her.

It's been six months since she quit her job at the prison, and she looks so different. Younger, happier, carefree. She's started wearing more colorful clothes now that her work doesn't require a uniform, and today's outfit is a carefully chosen floral dress. Her newly highlighted hair has been shaped into a neat bob that frames her face, and she smiles more these days too.

"Thank you very much," she says, reading the card.

I kiss her on the cheek. "You're welcome."

"They'll be here soon, we should finish getting everything ready."

I can see Mum's lips move as she silently counts the steps from the small galley kitchen on our boat to the main door. I know she's nervous about today, we both are. I follow her out onto the deck, before stepping up onto the riverbank. The narrow boat looks completely transformed, and not just because of our new surroundings on this quieter stretch of the River Thames. It's still called *The Black Sheep* but has been painted turquoise. Life is different now too, mostly for the better.

Inside, the boat is spotless. Mum was up before the birds today, cleaning and tidying every inch of it so that now the whole place smells of Mr. Sheen. But it is a beautiful sunny Sunday afternoon, so we have set up a table on the grassy riverbank, along with some bunting and festoon lights for when it gets dark. The table is set for four: us and our two guests. Mum has used her "best plates" and her favorite—mismatching—colored glasses and pretty napkins. There is a cake stand soon to be filled with delicious treats for an afternoon tea by the river, and there are champagne flutes on the table too, because today is a celebration.

Mum has a new job. She's the manager of a new independent bookstore in London.

We head back inside and she wipes down the kitchen one last time. There is a postcard from Liberty on the fridge. She got out six months ago and is now backpacking around South America, and Mum said she might give her a job when she gets back. She is busy putting some flowers in a vase when we hear the taxi pull up.

"Is it them?" she asks.

"I can't see from here. Relax. Everything looks great."

A moment later there is a knock on the door and we stare at each other.

"I'll get it," I say when she doesn't move.

Clio is a changed woman too, it's as though she has softened around the edges. And Dickens looks like a different dog. He has regular trips to the groomers since he started spending time at the pink house—Clio looks after him whenever I can't—and he looks rather dapper today in a black velvet collar and matching bow tie. He wags his tail as soon as I open the door.

"Come in, lovely to see you both," I say.

Clio and Mum do not hug, but they do smile when they say hello. It's still awkward but I hope it won't always be this way. Like it or not, we are family—an unusual one—and I want both of these women in my life.

"I brought some champagne," Clio says, taking a bottle of something expensive-looking from her bag. "We have so much to celebrate."

It's true. We do.

All charges against me were dropped. Jude Kennedy went to prison for conspiracy to murder. With Edith's third of the gallery along with her own, Clio became the majority shareholder. In her brother's long-term—probably permanent—absence, she decided to turn it into a bookshop. She asked mum to run it and, so far, business at Black Sheep Books is booming. The walls are lined with beautiful turquoise bookcases and the tables are piled high with books. The steps on the wooden spiral staircase leading up to the mezzanine are decorated in quirky book wallpaper, and there are fairy lights draped around the banisters. There is a free coffee machine in the corner, the floor is covered in rugs, and the beanbags and cozy armchairs are always filled with visiting book lovers.

I kept the rest of what Edith left behind and Clio did not contest the will. Then I split it three ways among Clio, Mum, and me. I like to think that is what Edith would have wanted if she'd known how things would turn out. The end of her story was the beginning of ours. Clio sold her pink town house in Notting Hill and bought a similar—but significantly cheaper—house in the countryside. She did not sell any of her trainers.

I give Clio a papercut Mother's Day card and she gets a bit teary: it's the first one she has ever received despite having two grown-up daughters. I see Mum flinch but she doesn't say anything. There is often a gap between what we think and what we say: it's where what we feel lives. We sit down at the table outside, even Dickens has his own chair and a bowl filled with gravy bones. Then Clio opens the champagne and I'm glad, I think we might need a little something to help us relax.

"I'd like to make a toast," I say, when the glasses have been poured. "Here's to the women in my life. I'm very grateful for you both, happy Mother's Day."

"And congratulations on getting into art school, Nellie!" says Clio, smiling at me.

I use the name Mum gave me again now. I'm happy to be myself and I like who that is.

"Thank you. I'm excited but terrified at the same time."

"Don't be nervous," Mum says, taking a sip of champagne. "What if I told you that I had already seen the future, and that your life was going to be happy, healthy, and successful? Then there really would be no need to be anxious, would there? Being nervous about something you already knew was going to be wonderful would make no sense at all." A ladybug lands on the table and we stare at it. I know we're all thinking of Edith now.

"The police never did solve the mystery of who really killed the care home manager, did they?" Mum says. Clio and I share a quick glance but don't say a word. I've never told Mum what really happened that day. Mother knows best but sometimes it's best Mother doesn't know.

I look around at my strange but happy little family of three and smile. Some family trees need to be cut down. Some just need a few branches removed in order to grow. I like to think that we are good people who did something bad, something anyone might have done if they found themselves in a similar situation. I often find myself thinking about DCI Charlotte Chapman, wondering if she felt the same way. She was so determined to find the truth in the beginning, but she let me go, dismissed Edith's confession, and Mum and Clio never heard from her again. Despite all the detective's talk of three suspects, two murders, and one victim, she let us all walk away. Maybe some mysteries are not meant to be solved. I think Edith was right. Sometimes bad things happen to good people, so good people have to do bad things.

Acknowledgments

When I started writing this novel, I had no idea of the heartbreak that was waiting just around the corner in my personal life. I have always hidden inside stories when the real world gets too loud, but for weeks I was unable to write a word. I have never felt more broken or lost. Thank you to Jonny, Kari, Viola, and Christine for helping me find my way back to the story I had been trying to tell.

Forever thank you, as always, to Jonny Geller and Kari Stuart for being the best agents and two of my most favorite people. I am so grateful to know them. Thank you to Kate Cooper, Nadia Mokdad, and Sam Loader for all the translations of my novels. Seeing my books out in the world will never be anything less than magic. Thank you to Josie Freedman, Luke Speed, and Anna Weguelin for the screen adaptations of my stories. And thank you to everyone else at Curtis Brown and CAA who do so much for me and my books, especially Viola Hayden and Ciara Finan.

Huge thanks to my kind, patient, and exceedingly clever editor, Christine Kopprasch, who sometimes whispers in my ear when I am writing even though she is in New York and I am in Devon. I could not have finished this book without this wonderful woman. Thank you also to the rest of the amazing team at Flatiron—they are all the best—with special thanks to Bob Miller, Megan Lynch, Malati Chavali, Nancy Trypuc, Katherine Turro, Marlena Bittner, Claire McLaughlin, Maxine Charles, Frances Sayers, Donna Noetzel, Rhys Davies, Sam Glatt, and Amber Cortes.

Huge thanks to my editor in the UK, the one and only Wayne Brookes, and the rest of the brilliant team at Pan Macmillan, with special thanks to Lucy Hale, Josie Turner, Becky Lushey, and Kate Bullows. And thank you to all my foreign publishers who take such good care of my novels.

Thank you to everyone who helped with the research for this book, with special thanks to the prison librarians who took time to give me tours and answered all my questions. Thanks also to Farncombe Boat House for helping with *The Black Sheep*. Many years ago I worked as a care assistant in a residential home for the elderly. I'm pleased to say it was nothing like the Windsor Care Home, but that experience and my memories of that time were invaluable when I wrote this book. The people who care for our loved ones are heroes.

Thank you to the librarians, booksellers, journalists, and book reviewers who have been so kind about my books. And thank you to all the book bloggers and bookstagrammers: I love seeing your beautiful pictures from all around the world. Thank you to my Daniel, my first reader, my best friend, and my favorite human. My final and biggest thank-you is to my readers: I really wouldn't still be here without you. This story takes place on Mother's Day and this book is for all the daughters.

About the Author

Alice Feeney is the *New York Times* bestselling author of *Daisy Darker*, *Rock Paper Scissors*, *His & Hers*, *I Know Who You Are*, and *Sometimes I Lie*. Her novels have been translated into more than thirty languages and have been optioned for major screen adaptations. Alice was a BBC journalist for fifteen years and now lives in the Devon countryside with her family. *Good Bad Girl* is her sixth novel.

BEAUTIFUL UGLY

*Look out for the brand-new thriller
from the queen of twists . . .*

COMING SPRING 2025